**Two brand-new stories in every volume...
twice a month!**

Duets Vol. #41

Bestselling Harlequin author Kate Hoffmann kicks off
with a special Christmas Double Duets this month.
This writer never fails to "thrill us with light-hearted
humor, endearing characters and piquant situations,"
says *Romantic Times Magazine*.

Duets Vol. #42

Talented Jill Shalvis also presents her own fun-filled
Double Duets this holiday season. "Get ready for
laughs, passion and toe-curling romance, because
Jill...delivers the goods," says reviewer Kathee Card.

Be sure to pick up both Duets volumes today!

"About that kiss, Katie—" Bryan said.

"I kissed Matt, not you," Katie insisted. "In the Santa costume."

"No. You kissed me. In the Santa costume. And I think you already know it."

"In your dreams."

"Really? Then why are you always staring at me?"

"I am not always staring at you!"

When Bryan only waited patiently, she blew out a frustrated breath. "Much," she muttered.

"I'm flattered," he said.

"Don't be! I did *not* kiss you!"

"I could prove it to you, if you like."

He could prove it to her. Oh, Lord. Katie's palms were clammy, her heart raced. The flu, she decided. But that didn't explain why the thought of him "proving it" to her had her nipples hard and achy. "How could you prove something that never happened?" she asked with remarkable— totally false—calm.

"By kissing you again..."

For more, turn to page 9

Hug Me, Holly!

"Can I help you?" Riley asked.

Holly gave him the once-over, her gaze lingering on his badge. "Is this town actually *big* enough for a sheriff?" she questioned.

Her voice was smooth and cultured, and everything about her screamed "city girl." "We're big enough to court trouble," he said lightly. "Can I help you find something?" *Like the highway?*

"Is this really the Café...Nirvana?" She tilted back her head and studied the stark blue sky, then the wide open landscape. Finally she shook her head. "It's some sort of joke, right?"

She leveled those light blue eyes on him with what could only be described as hope. He slowly shook his head. "Nope. No joke."

Briefly she closed her eyes. "Cosmic justice," Riley heard her mutter.

Then she was walking away from him, but not out of his life. No, she went into the café, her look of determination as strong as her stride.

For more, turn to page 197

HARLEQUIN DUETS

ISBN 0-373-44108-8

KISS ME, KATIE!
Copyright © 2000 by Jill Shalvis

HUG ME, HOLLY!
Copyright © 2000 by Jill Shalvis

This edition published by arrangement with Harlequin Books S.A.

® and TM are trademarks of the publisher. Trademarks indicated with
® are registered in the United States Patent and Trademark Office, the
Canadian Trade Marks Office and in other countries.

Visit us at www.eHarlequin.com

Printed in U.S.A.

Kiss Me, Katie!

JILL SHALVIS

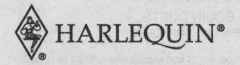

HARLEQUIN®

TORONTO • NEW YORK • LONDON
AMSTERDAM • PARIS • SYDNEY • HAMBURG
STOCKHOLM • ATHENS • TOKYO • MILAN • MADRID
PRAGUE • WARSAW • BUDAPEST • AUCKLAND

Dear Reader,

Ever kiss that perfect guy? In *Kiss Me, Katie!* my heroine
thinks she has. Only problem, she laid her lips on the
wrong guy, and now that wrong guy—the baddest,
sexiest man in town, thank you very much—wants
another kiss! And who can resist Bryan Morgan?
Because once the daredevil rebel has his mind set on
something, he gets it, and he most definitely has his
mind set on Katie.

In *Hug Me, Holly!* my heroine doesn't care about kisses.
All this sophisticated city girl wants is to get the heck
out of Nowhere Town, U.S.A. After all, the place doesn't
even have a dry cleaner! But Sheriff Riley McMann is
gorgeous as sin and kisses like heaven. What is she
supposed to do with a man like that, a man who can
see right through her tough, bite-me veneer and still,
still love her? Hopefully, keep him forever.

Happy holidays,

Jill Shalvis

Books by Jill Shalvis

HARLEQUIN TEMPTATION
742—WHO'S THE BOSS?
771—THE BACHELOR'S BED

HARLEQUIN DUETS
28—NEW AND...IMPROVED?

Don't miss any of our special offers. Write to us at the
following address for information on our newest releases.

Harlequin Reader Service
U.S.: 3010 Walden Ave., P.O. Box 1325, Buffalo, NY 14269
Canadian: P.O. Box 609, Fort Erie, Ont. L2A 5X3

1

SHE WAS REALLY going to do it, she was going to seduce Santa Claus. It wasn't that she had a thing for guys in a white beard and red suit, although she did have to admit, she liked the belly laugh.

But what Katie Wilkins really wanted was the man beneath the costume. Mr. Perfect from the executive offices down the hall. He was everything she wanted in a man: mature, polished...safe. So safe that she'd known him all year and he hadn't once made a move on her.

She hoped to change that tonight.

The holiday party was in full swing around her, even though Christmas was still three weeks away. Christmas carols blared out of speakers hanging from the rafters of the hangar, and everyone from the airplane mechanics to Mr. Riggs, the director of Wells Aircraft—the small, private airport where they all worked—was ready to party with the proper festive spirit.

The spiked punch helped.

Or that's what Katie figured when she saw Mrs. Giddeon, their usually prim receptionist, with an empty glass in one hand and Mr. Riggs in the other, a decisively naughty gleam in her eye as she dragged him toward the mistletoe hanging from the nose of a jet parked in the far corner.

Then there were Dale, Jake and Evan, the linemen, and usually the most polite of young men, cheering and egging on Julie, Cassandra and Eloise, three of the women in her office, who were at the moment exhibiting go-go dancing skills to the tune of "Jingle Bell Rock."

Katie shook her head in amazement. She hadn't imagined this when she'd volunteered to decorate. She'd known everyone had been working hard, trying to keep up with the expansion plans that had them putting in long hours and stressful times with new clients. But to totally let loose? Was she the only grown-up here?

It felt like it.

And yet, from deep inside her came a yearning to join them, to brush off years of restraint, down a glass of spiked punch and toss caution to the wind.

Which brought her back to jumping Santa's bones.

Katie glanced across the huge hangar, wildly

decorated with gold and silver streamers, red and green ornaments, and of course the pathetic four-foot Christmas tree. Pathetic because, this being Southern California, and a drought year at that, the poor tree looked as though it were on its last legs.

Next to the straining tree stood Santa. Tall, smiling and charismatic. Because she knew who was under the suit, Matt Osborne, a.k.a. Mr. Perfect, her heart sighed.

Go for it, a little voice whispered in her head. *Do it. Kiss him.*

As a rule, Katie didn't feel the holiday spirit. She wasn't exactly Scrooge, but the truth was, she'd been Christmas cursed. It had all started when she was six. Her neighbor, Holly Stone, got the Barbie vacation house and Katie didn't. Then, when they were twelve, and still neighbors, Holly cheated at her holiday party spin-the-bottle game in order to kiss the boy Katie had a crush on. The topper had come three years ago, when they'd been twenty-one—no longer neighbors, but in the small town of San Limo there was no escaping anyone—and Holly had stolen Katie's fiancé.

Her own fault really. Katie knew she was too careful, too methodical…too much like an accountant, darn it. Yes, she was happy enough, financially stable, yadda yadda.

But she was also dateless.

This was the year that would change. No more bad luck. She was going to see to it herself. She was going to make a Christmas wish, a really good one, and make sure it came true.

What she would wish for would be different from anything she'd ever wished for before. Not a new adding machine, not a new pair of slippers, not a new set of I.R.S. regulations. No, this year she wanted a knockout kiss from Matt Osborne; sophisticated, handsome, intelligent, and all-around perfect guy.

"You're not going to chicken out, are you?"

Katie rolled her eyes, then because that was an irrationally childish gesture, she carefully schooled her features into indifference before turning to face Holly, aforementioned arch rival, and unfortunate co-worker. Holly was decked out in a sexy little silver-sequined number that blared self-confidence, and a perfect size-six frame, to the world.

"I never chicken out," Katie said.

Holly laughed deeply. "We don't have time to go down that road."

"I don't see *you* kissing anyone."

"I'm not the one with a boring sex life."

Nonexistent was more like it, Katie thought.

"Besides..." Holly examined her perfect manicure, which was neon red and topped with ten different, and very wicked, appliqués of Santa in compromising situations. "If *I* wanted to kiss Matt, I'd just go right up to him, grab him and plant one on him. I'm not shy."

No kidding. Katie had plenty of incidents to prove that one, years' and years' worth, but time was passing and she had a mission—getting Santa beneath the mistletoe, mistletoe she'd purposely planted in several spots with grand hopes for the evening ahead.

In light of that, Katie squinted across the action-filled hangar, past the confetti-covered Cessnas and Learjets and overdressed office staff, to the man in the red suit. "You sure Matt is the one in there?"

They both studied Santa. He had a red festive hat, a white beard and mustache. He also wore the required stuffed belly and red suit. He looked... jolly. But that could have been caused by the very spiked punch. Truthfully, other than being the correct height, which was approximately six feet tall, there was absolutely no way to be certain *who* was under there.

"It's him," Holly said decisively.

Katie definitely knew better than to trust her, but what could go wrong this time? Everyone knew

Matt was going to be Santa, it'd been in the weekly office memo.

The office memo never lied.

"Okay." She handed her still full flute to Holly. "Wish me luck."

"Merry Kissing and Happy Fondling," Holly said, lifting her drink in a toast.

Katie smoothed her dress in a useless attempt to scoot the thing farther down on her thighs. Purchasing the bold, red, stretchy number had been a huge departure for her, not to mention a bit of a strain on her checkbook. She could only hope Santa liked it, since she'd spent nearly her entire month's budget on it.

That was okay. If it worked, it'd be well worth having to eat macaroni and cheese from a box for the next month.

She stopped tugging at the hem and straightened, which emphasized the provocative bodice. *Good*. She, secret chicken of the world, needed all the help she could get. With a hard swallow, she let her high heels lead the way.

To Santa.

To the perfect man beneath the costume.

To a good, hot Christmas kiss.

He saw her coming, she watched as he focused

in on her. To be sure he got the full effect, she took a deep breath.

In response, Santa…choked on his drink. The woman standing next to him, Edwina, who ran the small coffee shop in the lobby, starting pounding on his back, which brought on a fresh attack of coughing.

Grabbing his glass, Edwina set it aside and lifted his arms over his head—or that's what she tried to do, but as Santa was tall and Edwina was…well, not, the only thing she managed to accomplish was to flail his arms near the region of his chest as she bounced up and down in front of him.

From a distance, this seemed like some sort of comical dance, and since Edwina wore a short green cocktail dress, now flapping wildly as she leaped around in front of him, she looked like an elf to Matt's Santa.

Finally, he waved a hand to indicate he was fine, and when he managed to convince Edwina of this, she left him alone.

"I think it's the costume," she whispered as she passed Katie. "It's really such a trial to wear it successfully. That poor man should be nominated for sainthood."

"I agree," Katie murmured, because now that she was close, she could see how right Edwina was. The suit had to weigh a ton, what with the heavy red material and white faux fur, not to mention the added belly and big black boots.

Could she even press close enough past all that tummy to kiss him?

Yes, she decided. Yes, she could. Besides, she couldn't back out now, not with Holly's gaze burning a mocking, laughing hole in her back.

The mistletoe she'd decided on was only about five feet behind Matt, around the corner, out of view from the rest of the party. Smiling sweetly, heart thundering, she stepped closer. She really didn't know what she expected...maybe for him to make things easy, to back up, possibly right beneath the hanging plant?

He didn't. Instead, he held his ground, watching her from beneath the silliest pair of glasses she'd ever seen. The outside of the lenses were tinted in a design of Santa's bright, laughing eyes, so that she couldn't see Matt's own blue gaze.

She assumed he was smiling, too. Hard to tell with the beard, but hoping for the best, she took another step, silently willing him to help her out.

Why wasn't he backing up?

Instead he tilted his head, as if asking her what she was doing.

She thought that should be rather obvious!

"I don't know if you realize this," she said. "But right behind you and around the corner, there's some mistletoe...just sort of hanging there."

Nothing.

"I helped decorate. It's waiting for some couple to get themselves beneath it. So they can kiss," she added helpfully.

Still no response!

Okay, she could admit she didn't know Matt well, but she did know he wasn't an idiot. He was vice president, for God's sake. Yes, he was sedate, he was mature and focused, but she was offering to kiss him!

What was wrong with him? According to *Cosmopolitan* magazine, there wasn't a red-blooded man alive who would turn down a kiss! The editors had promised!

But Matt didn't budge and her nerve was fading fast. She was beginning to feel very sorry she'd ever thought about doing this. In fact, maybe she should switch her Christmas wish from a kiss to a big black hole opening up in the floor so it could swallow her.

"You *are* in there, aren't you?" she asked with a teasing smile to hide her embarrassment.

Slowly Santa turned and craned his neck, studying the plant in question.

Then looked back at her.

She smiled encouragingly, knowing her time was running out. Any second now, Holly was going to decide she wanted Matt for herself, and she'd have no such difficulties getting him—or any man—beneath that blasted mistletoe.

No, she couldn't fail. Take charge time.

Grabbing Santa's hand, she pulled him around the corner, noting his hand was big and warm and callused. At the first tug she also took in the fact that he seemed bigger and more powerful than Matt's lean physique had led her to believe, but now wasn't the time to dwell on that when she had him so close to her goal.

The noise of the party followed them, but they were completely alone in the hallway. Around them, all the office doors were shut, with not another soul in sight. The music and laughter from the party seemed almost surreal.

They were in their own little world.

Right beneath the mistletoe.

And he was staring at her from behind those ridiculous glasses and fake facial hair; the only real part of him available to her was his mouth.

Perfect, since that was all she happened to need at the moment.

Reaching up to touch his shoulders, she leaned in close. ''Merry Christmas, Matt,'' she whispered, and set her lips to his in the connection she'd been dreaming about all night.

She felt his startled jerk, felt the immediate tensing of his big body, but she just pressed closer and deepened the kiss, swallowing the growl of desire he made.

Of course it also could have been a sound of surprise, since she'd given him little choice in this kissing matter, but she figured if he hated it, he'd back off.

He didn't.

Instead, his hands went to her waist, tightening when she pulled off his glasses and tossed them over his shoulder. He tasted like champagne…like wonderful, delicious male…like *heaven*. It was better than her wildest dreams, and then he was tilting her head for better access and kissing her back. She nearly fell to the floor because it was the most blazingly, most pleasurable sensation she'd ever experienced in her life.

One of his large hands cupped her cheek, his fingers playing havoc over her skin as he slowly pulled back and stared at her.

She nearly staggered from the wonder of it all. Never had a kiss so rocked her world, left her so off balance, so dizzy with rocketing emotions. "That…was some mistletoe," she gasped.

"It had nothing to do with the mistletoe."

No, he was right, she could see that in his blue eyes, in the lines of his mouth, that wonderful, soft yet firm, incredibly talented, mouth.

Confusion had her taking a step back, so that Santa's hands fell to his sides. This was supposed to be just a kiss, she thought, not a life altering moment with the emotional impact of an 8.0 earthquake. "Gotta go," she managed to murmur.

Yeah, she definitely had to go. Maybe she really *was* just a chicken, but Lord have mercy, how could she have known what would happen to her insides over one silly embrace? It made her feel things; wild, reckless, *hot* things that she'd never felt before.

Had never wanted to feel. All she'd wanted was one kiss! A silly little Christmas wish. But she'd gotten much more.

"Katie."

She heard him call her name, in a voice made so thick by desire that she didn't recognize it, but she kept moving, had to keep moving.

Wow. Just wow.

Because she needed a moment to herself, she escaped into one of the darkened offices. It took more than a few deep breaths to calm her racing heart and throbbing body. It took a while longer before she realized she'd gotten far more than she'd bargained for.

By the time she reentered the party, Matt stood by the tree, the Santa costume gone. How did he get rid of it so fast? And why? When she caught his eye, she could only stare, still amazed by the connection they'd shared.

"Good evening." His voice was perfectly calm. Almost asleep calm.

Catatonic calm.

"It looks as though nearly everyone showed up tonight," he said.

How could he sound so...so *normal?* With one kiss he'd leveled her, and yet he stood there as if it'd been no big deal.

Was it possible he hadn't felt what she had?

And how humiliating was *that?*

"Matt, about what just happened—"

He looked at her blankly. "What just happened?"

"Exactly," she said, nodding. "About that—"

"Excuse me?"

"No, excuse *me*," came a low, husky male voice that made Katie's entire body tighten.

Bryan Morgan.

Head pilot and local daredevil. He was the hero of every man at Wells Aviation, and the center of every woman's fantasy.

Every woman but Katie. He was a jump-off-the-cliff type of guy, far too similar to her daredevil father who had gotten himself killed when she was just a teenager. As a rule she steered clear of him, though the reasons were so complicated she didn't often allow herself to think about them.

Especially now, when he was smiling at her, a wide, devastatingly charismatic smile that would have melted any other female in the room.

"You look lovely," he said, which was funny only because he was tall, leanly muscled, rugged, and the most gorgeous man ever to walk the planet, and *he* thought *she*, plain-Jane Katie, looked lovely. Right.

"Thank you," she said politely, pointedly turning away from him back to Matt. Darn it, she wanted to talk about their kiss.

"And the decorations," Bryan said, a small smile in his voice. "So tastefully done."

Great. He liked the decorations. Now could he just go away? She had a kiss to discuss!

"Especially all that strategically placed mistletoe," Bryan added, and Katie finally went still, giving him her one-hundred-percent undivided attention.

"What?" she whispered, her heart all but stopping.

Bryan just looked at her, his brilliant blue eyes innocent. And hot. Now she realized that was a complete contradiction, but it happened to be true. Something deep down within her unfurled, hesitated. "What did you just say?" she asked again.

He merely smiled. "Nothing. Nothing at all."

2

BRYAN MORGAN threw his plane into a spin, acknowledging he had about ten seconds to pull himself out if he wanted to live.

Nine...eight...

The image of last night's party floated through the haze in his mind. There'd been plenty of loud talking and even louder music, reminding him of his huge family. Growing up with six older sisters, there hadn't been a lot of quiet, or alone time. So he had a fine appreciation of both. Because of that, he liked his parties a lot more intimate and personal...but there had been one redeeming factor last night. A surprising one.

A woman. Now, Bryan loved women, he really did. All shapes and sizes. But in his mind, he already had a permanent force of at least seven in his life, if he counted his mother as well as his sisters. All of whom had bossed, charmed, coaxed and threatened their way for each of his thirty-two years. And since they showed signs of living another half a century at least, it wasn't often Bryan allowed another woman to play a serious role in his existence.

In fact, it was downright rare. Oh, he dated. Often. But things were always on a walk-away basis.

Always.

And yet last night he'd held Katie and his heart had sort of fumbled. Warm, vital, sweet, funny Katie, with her soft, wavy, whiskey-colored hair that matched her whiskey-colored eyes, eyes in the past that had always looked at him so aloofly.

Seven...six...

She'd looked amazing in that shimmery red dress. Who would have thought? He'd even dreamed of it, the way it had fallen over her curvy little body and trim thighs. So different from her usual prim-and-proper business attire, which suited her accounting position, but not the heat and passion he knew lurked just beneath her surface.

Well, to be fair, he didn't know for *certain* she had heat and passion beneath her surface, he'd known her all year and hadn't been able to tell... until last night.

In spite of the force of gravity pulling his face into a grimace, he managed a grin. Because now he knew, oh yeah, he definitely knew.

Five...four... But what he *didn't* know was why

she seemed so wary of him. Over the years he'd caused a lot of feelings in women, most of them pretty good, some of them not so good, but never once had he caused wariness.

Three…and the plane continued to spin. So did his head, bringing his thoughts back to the task at hand.

Now was not the time to be daydreaming about things that would drain the rest of the blood from his head to parts south.

He needed his wits.

He was good at flying, really good, and it wasn't cockiness that told him that, but fact. Yes, he was confident, but then again, a good pilot had to be, and Bryan was nothing if not a good pilot.

Two… He hoped they were getting the shot they needed below, that the cameras hadn't failed as they had earlier because he really didn't think he could pull off this particular stunt any better than he just had.

It was the perfect ride, glorious blue skies, not a cloud in sight and…

One. Just a flash second before hurtling both him and a very expensive plane into the ground, he pulled out of the spin and shook his head slightly to clear it.

"Got it?" he asked into his headset.

"Holy cow!" Ritchie yelled into Bryan's ear. "*Holy, ace,* that was absolutely amazing!"

"Gee, guess you got it."

"You're wasting your talents taxiing the rich and famous in expensive airplanes, you should be doing stunts *all* the time."

Ritchie Owens was a Hollywood producer. That's what he told women, anyway. Mostly he did beer commercials. The stunt Bryan had just pulled off would be shown in an adventurous, exciting, quick-paced, filled with loud music ad spot designed to raise a man's thirst.

Or so he supposed.

Bryan didn't really care; it gave him an excuse to fly, and to fly with abandon, and that was all that mattered to him. "I don't taxi people. I run a charter company."

"Yeah, yeah, whatever. Still a waste."

Bryan didn't bother to correct Ritchie. He didn't feel any particular need to defend himself, not when he truly did love his work. In his opinion, he had everything he would ever need, and Ritchie, all four and a half feet of him, driven by the materialistic meter of success of the film industry, would never understand.

"God, that was fantastic." Ritchie was clearly ecstatic. "The best I've ever seen! We're gonna get tons of feedback from this one, ace. *Tons.* I feel it in my bones.''

Bryan remained silent as he easily circled and came in for his landing. The sun was at his back, the wind was with him. On top of the world, he took a deep breath, as always awed by the glory of being in the air.

No problems, no stress. Life was everything he wanted, everything he made out of it.

But inexplicably, that wasn't the case today. And if he was being honest, something he always was to a fault—just ask any of his past girlfriends—he had to admit it had everything to do with last night.

The Christmas party.

And the surprise Christmas kiss.

It'd been a helluva great gift. Admittedly, the gift giver hadn't meant to give *him* the kiss, but he'd tried to tell her he wasn't who she thought he was, hadn't he?

Well...maybe he hadn't tried very hard.

Maybe he hadn't managed to say anything except her name, but he was only human. And yeah, maybe a better man might have told her the truth right then and there, but he wasn't out for any hero awards.

He just wanted the girl.

He'd been momentarily stunned into meathead status when Katie had touched her warm lips to his, not to mention dizzy as hell from those stupid Santa glasses he'd been wearing.

He still had a headache from them.

And anyway, what was a woman doing even *thinking* of kissing a guy as boring and predictable as Matt Osborne? It was a crime, in his humble opinion, a total crime.

Bryan completed his landing without incident, tied the plane down on his own even though there was a staff of linemen waiting to assist as there always was, and also a film crew who'd paid to use the tarmac for the morning. He tipped his head to stare at the sky.

"Already yearning to be back up there?"

He recognized the female voice and braced himself.

"We have a great staff, you know." Holly, who'd come up behind him, managed to casually brush her long, lithe, very toned body against his. "Why do you always insist on doing everything yourself?"

Seemed silly to tell her the truth, when she didn't care about the truth. What she cared about, what she'd cared about for the entire two weeks since she'd come to this place as the new office manager, was getting action.

Man action.

Apparently he was the man.

"Do you do all your own handling because you like to sweat?" Holly wondered, circling him until she was in front of him, smiling with all the innocence of a shark. "Or because you like the way all us silly females melt over you when you do?"

"Oh, definitely, it's because I like to sweat."

She laughed softly. "So big and tough."

"You should see me after I wash the plane."

His light sarcasm was a wasted effort. She merely smiled. "You're so exciting, Bryan. How did you manage to keep all those tipsy women off you last night? It wouldn't have anything to do with the…Santa costume?"

"I thought my being Santa was a secret."

Holly arched a brow and let out a mysterious smile. "Whoever told you that?"

"You know who. *You.* I got your note that Matt would be late and couldn't do it, so you needed *me* to do it, and to keep it quiet about it."

"Oh, *that* note." She purred and lowered her lashes. "I suppose I owe you now."

Oh, boy. "No. Consider that a freebie." Besides, he'd gotten his reward.

"A freebie?" Holly pursed her lips. "You wouldn't, by any chance, have gotten...*lucky* with that costume last night, would you? Maybe lucky with a certain accountant who thought you were...oh, I don't know, a certain vice president?"

Ah, now it made sense. He'd been set up. "You were responsible for that?"

"You're giving me far too much credit," she said serenely, studying her manicure. "And besides, everyone knows, Matt was supposed to be Santa."

"Yes," he said patiently. "But Matt *wasn't* Santa. I was."

"Right. So if a mistake was made—" she lifted her shoulders and sent him a guileless smile "—then...oops."

"You told her Matt was in the costume, didn't you?"

"Not exactly."

"Then what, exactly?"

"Are you telling me you didn't enjoy that kiss?"

"Okay, let's do this another way. Does she or does she not *now* know the truth?"

"Not." Holly grinned. "Are you kidding? Prim-and-proper accounting Katie kissing the wild, reckless, rowdy, untamable Bryan Morgan? She'd have a coronary. She definitely doesn't like guys like you.''

''She's not all *that* prim and proper.''

Holly bent at the waist and burst out laughing. ''Do tell.''

Bryan gave up and started walking toward the first of three hangars that made up Wells, knowing he had exactly one hour to take care of his paperwork before chartering a flight that would keep him out of the airport for the rest of the day.

Without a doubt, he was going to have to put that kiss right out of his head. Yes, the little accountant kissed nice, so what? She didn't like guys like him, so what? He didn't care, not when there were plenty of other women in the sea.

That he hadn't been looking was another matter entirely, he told himself. Between work and his loving but demanding family, he'd been busy, and hadn't needed the additional complication. And he knew all too well, women were definitely a complication, no matter how sweet yet sexy their light, expressive whiskey eyes were.

With that in mind, he made it to the hallway outside the postage-stamp-size office he rented from Wells, when he heard a very familiar voice.

''Matt? Matt, I know you're in there.''

Katie.

Katie back in her dull business suit with the too long skirt and the too full blazer so he couldn't so much as catch a glimpse of that lush body he now knew she had, knocking on the closed door of Matt Osborne's office.

She should look unappealing, but she didn't, not at all. Instead, she looked…huggable.

Damn, what was that about?

He attributed it to knowing that she kissed like heaven, and smelled like it, too.

Then Matt opened his office door and smiled absently at her. "Yes?"

She bit her lower lip, clearly expecting a different reaction. "I wanted…to talk about last night."

"The party?" Matt seemed surprised.

The nitwit had no idea what he'd missed. Bryan supposed there should be some guilt associated with that, but there wasn't.

"I thought it went really well," Matt said, then stole a quick glance at his watch. "Oh, look at that. I'm sorry, I've gotta go. I have a report to finish."

With an apologetic smile, he turned away to shut the door.

"But—" Katie's smile seemed forced, even to Bryan who was still a good way down the hall from them. "It's just that…the mistletoe…"

"Mistletoe?" Matt shrugged. "I noticed plenty

of the stuff scattered all around. The decorations were superbly done. Nicely and strategically placed."

"Yes," Katie agreed. *"Strategic."*

"It's got to come down though, or we'll have people taking advantage of it during office hours." His brow wrinkled. "Hmm...maybe I'd better write a memo."

"A memo," Katie repeated. "Remove the mistletoe to avoid mass orgies during work hours."

Matt nodded distractedly, and after a quick goodbye, closed the door in her face.

Clueless jerk, Bryan decided, even as he was oddly grateful for clueless jerks.

Katie just stood there. "Well wasn't I ever so memorable," she muttered.

More than memorable, babe. "Morning," Bryan said.

Katie nearly leaped right out of her skin and whipped around to stare at him. "What?"

"I said, 'Morning.'"

Her face was pale now. "Say it again."

Bryan wondered if his voice was confusing her. After all, he *had* spoken last night. But people heard what they wanted to hear, and she'd definitely wanted to hear Matt's voice.

She blinked.

"Morning," he said again, obliging her.

She shook her head. "I should have had some coffee."

And he should tell her the truth. *Should* being the key word here. "You were asking about the mistletoe," he said. "Is there something I can help you with?" *Like maybe kiss you again?*

She didn't answer, just narrowed her eyes.

"Is anything wrong?"

"Your voice...it sounds..."

"Familiar?" He grinned, he couldn't help it. "Well, it should. We work together."

"Right."

Poor baby looked so confused. His conscience, never the most righteous of creatures, reared its head for a moment.

A very short moment.

Because he knew if he came clean right then, she would either deny that the kiss had knocked her socks off, or she'd run like hell.

Neither appealed.

Not when his goal for the day had suddenly become to get another. "About that mistletoe," he said casually. "I bet it's still in the hangar. We could just walk on over there and—"

"No," she said quickly, backing away. "I'm... busy. Very busy."

He obviously made her nervous. He tested this theory by taking a step toward her.

Sure enough, she retreated…right into a file cabinet, which she hit with a loud thunk. The two flowerpots above teetered wildly, then fell. She caught one, then the other, and quickly set them down on the ground, whirling back to him with her hands behind her back as if she didn't trust herself.

She had a streak of dirt across one cheek. She looked unsettled. And adorable. He had no idea why that appealed, he'd certainly never been attracted to adorable before. Long-legged, full bottom-lipped sexpots, yes. Adorable, no.

"I'm fine," she said quickly when he came toward her. "I'm just fi—" The word ended in a gasp when he took her arms in his hands to steady her.

They were now in exactly the same position they'd been in last night, nose to nose, thigh to thigh.

"You—you have blue eyes," she said inanely. "When did that happen?"

"At birth, actually." He grinned. "Let me guess, you hate blue eyes."

"No, I—" Her gaze dropped to his mouth, and in a totally innocent gesture, she licked her dry lips.

Bryan nearly groaned, but managed to hold it together because he had a huge advantage—*she* might not know how good they'd be together, but he did. Dammit, what a dilemma, because despite himself, he never, ever took advantage of women.

Well, almost never.

"About that mistletoe..." he murmured.

"No! No, it was a bad idea! A stupid idea. A really idiotic—"

"I get the picture." He tipped his head to one side because her hands had come up between them to grip his shirt, whether to push him away or to keep him close, he had no idea. "You don't strike me as much of a risk taker."

"Absolutely not," she said quickly. Too quickly.

He smiled, because last night, for whatever reason, she'd done exactly that, she'd dropped her reserve and had made the first move on a man. On *him.*

"In fact, *risk* is a bad word in my book," she continued. "A really bad word, as bad as—as—"

"As...?"

"As...oh never mind!"

Above them, the intercom buzzed, then Mrs. Giddeon paged Katie to the front desk.

With a cry of what could only be relief, Katie

broke free, brushing against him as she ran off down the hall.

Good, Bryan decided. He shouldn't have teased her. He had absolutely no idea what had come over him. He could really care less that she wanted Matt, that she wasn't his type. It wasn't his problem.

Five minutes later he walked into his office and faced his two other pilots, both of whom looked at him and laughed. He looked down.

And saw two perfect handprints—made from dirt—on his white shirt. "Very funny," he said, but he wasn't annoyed, just strangely unsettled.

Katie might be a novice where men were concerned, but she'd accomplished something no woman other than his sisters and mother ever had.

She'd left her mark on him.

3

"LORDIE, would you look at that?" Julie murmured beneath her breath to Katie.

At the voice of her friend and co-worker, Katie looked up from her notes for the upcoming staff meeting, but she saw nothing out of the ordinary.

Cassandra and Eloise filed into the conference room, followed by Dale, Jack, Evan and Mrs. Giddeon. Everyone looked perfectly normal, even Holly, as she sauntered in.

Then she caught the newest arrival.

Bryan.

That her belly gave a little quiver really got to her. "Him?" she asked Julie, who was practically drooling.

"*Him,*" Julie answered breathlessly. "Wow."

Granted he was tall, dark and…okay, gorgeous. So what? And yet for some reason that only upped her annoyance factor, she couldn't take her eyes off him. Even worse, she was hit with a strange sense of…*awareness?*

She didn't understand it, but she didn't appear to suffer the enigmatic problem alone. Apparently every female in the room was afflicted. Even Holly, who managed to maneuver herself close to him.

Watch out, Katie wanted to warn him. Holly was looking as predatory as she had...oh, about one minute before she'd stolen Katie's fiancé three years ago.

Beneath her own Christmas tree no less.

Old times, she reminded herself. Forget it.

And anyway, *where was Matt?*

She'd been hoping for a few minutes alone with him to discuss their kiss. It'd been three days!

But still, she couldn't tear her gaze away from Bryan. She had to admit the man had a presence. The very air around him seemed to change, shimmer with an aura of excitement. Thrill.

Danger.

That presence wasn't put on, like it was with so many daredevils. Nope, all that edgy restlessness came utterly naturally to him.

Which was exactly why Katie didn't—couldn't—like him.

"There's something not quite tame about that man," Julie announced in a conspirator's whisper. She shivered with delight.

To Katie there was nothing even remotely exciting about it. Her father had flown stunts. He'd done things no one else would even consider and had *still* craved more, even putting aside the needs of his own family in order to get it. He'd been grown-up enough to have a family, but not mature enough to want to be with that family. Her father was always pushing the envelope, and always going full speed ahead. Always wanting, craving, yearning, burning for something just out of his reach.

He'd found it in testing experimental aircraft.

Oh, and it had also killed him.

Katie tried to swallow the nearly twenty-year-old resentment and only managed to swallow her last piece of gum, which left a heavy feeling in the pit of her stomach.

She could never fall for a man like that, one who wasn't mature enough to put fun on the back burner in the favor of a quiet, lasting, enduring relationship.

Julie looked at her. "Are you telling me you don't think he's spectacular?"

Well, she was human. *Female* human. She could admit Bryan's broad shoulders, so perfectly covered in his white pilot's shirt, were nice, very nice indeed. So were his long, long, powerfully built legs, which were in dark-blue trousers fitted in a way that might have made her sigh in feminine appreciation if she was weak enough to sigh over such things. He had his aviator sunglasses tucked in his front pocket, his sleeves shoved up instead of rolled, and scuffed work boots on his feet. His hair was tousled as if he'd been running his fingers through it.

Gorgeously rumpled, she supposed was the correct term.

But it was his face that held her; the rugged, tanned, lived-in face. The one that had laugh lines around his generous mouth and smile creases around his sharp eyes, eyes that told her what she needed to know—he actively recruited fun and trouble, and—

Darn it.

He caught her staring at him.

No surprise, no discomfort, not for this man, who was probably used to being stared at. He merely absorbed her gaze, gave her a quick wink and a slow grin.

And in spite of her embarrassment and irritation, something strange happened. Something…almost familiar.

What was it about him?

Why did she feel as if…they *knew* each other?

As if she'd kissed *him* instead of Matt? She nearly laughed out loud at that, because really, she knew who she'd kissed.

Matt stepped into the room then, a very welcome sight indeed. His hair was perfectly groomed, his shirt perfectly ironed, his trousers perfectly styled.

Everything about him was perfect.

Only, oddly enough, the little flicker of awareness, the one Bryan had caused, died. *Died.*

And Katie went cold.

She *had* kissed Matt. Right? Well, of course she had, what a ridiculous notion, one she put right out of her thoughts. Instead, she concentrated on smiling a welcome smile. Only Matt's nose was in his notes and without even glancing in her direction, he sat directly across from her. He was distracted, she decided, and very busy. She understood that. Still, her smile faded with the slight, unintentional as it was.

Yes, Matt was the perfect man for her, but she did expect to get noticed at least. Determined to get a reaction, she pasted on a new smile. "Hello, Matt."

"Hmm?" Matt lifted his head, blinked her into focus. "Oh. Hello." He even returned her smile, blossoming her hopes, but then he went back to his notes.

Sedate and mature were fine qualities, but this was getting ridiculous. "I was wondering about the party." This time he didn't so much as lift his head from his work, and Katie went from vexed to insulted. "And the decorations," she added. "Specifically the mistletoe."

Matt sent her an absent smile at that. His face was open, easy to read and utterly serene. Nothing bothered him, or very little. He was a peaceful, quiet, reserved man. *The perfect man,* she reminded herself.

So why did she feel like smacking him? Oh, yes, because he wasn't acknowledging their hot kiss!

"The mistletoe was a great idea," he allowed. "I already mentioned that."

"Yes, but—"

"For God's sake man, she's trying to ask you about the *use* of it." Bryan merely smiled sweetly at Katie when she stared at him. "Aren't you?"

"I…well…" *How did he know?* And why was she feeling *that* feeling again, the one that made her insides tremble, the one she had thought *Matt* would give her?

Holly laughed, the sound easy and infectious. "Wasn't it a grand party? I know for a fact that every single one of those strategically hung plants got good use.'' She smiled slyly at Matt, who blushed.

Blushed!

Katie stared at him in dismay. For days she'd been attempting to get a reaction from him and had gotten nothing. Then Holly says one little thing and he blushes! Frustrated, she glared down at her stack of notes, mail and various pencils and stuff she'd brought with her to the meeting.

Her heavy silver mail opener gleamed temptingly in the harsh office lights.

No, killing Holly right here would not be good office protocol, she decided, not even when the darn woman brushed part of Katie's paperwork off the table.

''Oops,'' Holly said lightly as everything scattered and entangled on the floor. She glanced over at Matt as she spoke to Katie. ''Sorry.''

Katie glared at her—she'd done that on purpose!—but Holly didn't notice, she was still staring at Matt. So Katie bent for the mess, and from her vantage point beneath the table, she had a front row seat of Holly slipping off her right heel and lifting her toes up to…Bryan's lap! Her bright-red polished toes cradled the spot directly between his thighs…and squeezed.

He made a sound, though it was muffled to Katie

because she was beneath the table. She watched as Bryan's hand grabbed Holly's ankle, his fingers gripping so hard his knuckles turned white.

They were playing hanky-panky, right here in the conference room and she had to witness it! Holly slid off her other heel, then lifted that leg up to Bryan's lap as well.

Katie jerked back...and smacked her head on the underside of the table hard enough to rattle everyone's water above. Whether it was the impact, or the resulting stars dancing in her head, or maybe the strangled sound Bryan made at the movement of Holly's toes, Katie bit her tongue. ''Ouch,'' she muttered, just as Holly played twinkle toes with Bryan's lap again.

Abruptly, he shoved back his chair and rose. He gathered his paperwork, and without another word, walked around the table.

Katie figured he'd sit right next to Holly, maybe for some more footsie action, but no such luck. He came around, passed Holly and sat...right next to Katie!

''Wow, he smells amazing,'' Julie whispered in her ear.

Holly leaned across the table to Katie. ''Switch spots with me, quick.''

Katie glanced at Bryan. He was looking a little

ragged around the edges, and more than a little tense. A very unusual look for Mr. Casual.

"If you switch with her," he said mildly, "I'll tell Matt why you keep bringing up the mistletoe."

Okay, switching was probably a bad idea.

But how did Bryan know that?

She blinked at him, considering, thoughts racing, and Bryan just sent her a slow, sure smile, a smile that tugged at every erogenous zone she had.

What was the matter with her?

Thankfully, Mr. Riggs, president and director of Wells Aviation, walked into the room then and Katie had other, more critical things to stress over.

Such as why she spent the next hour sniffing as unobtrusively as she could, obsessing over the fact that Julie had been correct.

Bryan did indeed smell pretty darn amazing.

BRYAN COULDN'T GET OUT of that meeting fast enough, couldn't get outside, in the fresh chilly air, soon enough to suit him.

With relief, he headed for his scheduled flight, loving every moment of the next few hours as he charmed his passengers, then flew high in the air, in sweet control.

All too soon he was back in the lobby.

So was Holly.

"What was that about back there?" he demanded in a quiet but dangerous voice most people had the good sense to answer.

She played her tongue over the very corner of her mouth in a way Bryan was sure rendered most males completely stupid. Fortunately he was only slightly less stupid than the average man. "Holly."

She smiled. "You mean when I put my foot on your—"

"You know that's what I mean."

"I could tell you liked it."

So she had talented toes. "I want to know why you're using me, and who you're trying to make jealous."

"Well that's flattering."

"Don't play games with me."

"But games are so much fun."

"I don't get it," he said, genuinely baffled. "Why don't you just go straight after whoever he is? I'm sure he'd fall right at your feet as all men do."

"*You* haven't."

"But you don't want me," he pointed out, exasperated.

"Are you sure?"

This was why he kept women at arm's length. But being the baby of a family with so many females, he'd been taught well. The last thing he needed was to let Holly—or any woman—get to him. Still annoyed, he looked through the glass windows and across the tarmac.

A figure walked behind the safety line toward hangar two.

Katie.

The most unusual thing happened. His heart stopped, then started again with a heavy beat. He found himself staring after her, which made no sense, no sense at all.

But there was something about her...

On impulse, he walked away from Holly without a backward glance and followed the flash of blue. He finally caught up with her in the long hallway between the mechanic's hangar and the supply warehouse.

"Hey there," he said.

She didn't slow down, and he had to practically run to keep up with her. "Nice office meeting," he said.

Nice office meeting.

Oh, wasn't he just the conversation master? Grimacing, he shook his head and tried again. "You look pretty today." Which was true, though he wished she would trade in those conservative outfits for something better suited to her petite yet curvaceous frame.

"Holly looks prettier," she noted, still walking at nearly the speed of light. "If you tell her so, she'll probably be so flattered you'll be able to grope her back this time."

"What?" He stopped to gape at her, but all that accomplished was to allow her to outdistance him. Her hips and sweet rear end were really moving now. Running to catch back up, he grabbed her arm to slow her down and turned her to face him.

"I said, if you tell her so," she repeated dutifully. "You might—"

"I heard that part!" He must have missed something here. Katie's face, usually calm, flashed annoyance, anger, even embarrassment.

The lightbulb finally clicked on in his dimwitted brain. "Holly told you about what she did—"

"No, I *saw* what she did, when she dropped my papers and I went under the table. I saw her foot— And then you— Oh, you know!"

Yeah, he knew. "Don't you see what's happening?" He was disturbed that she really didn't appear to. And even more disgusted that it mattered so much to him. Since when did he care what people thought?

But he cared what *she* thought, he realized, and figured he'd dwell on that shocking fact later. "You saw exactly what Holly wanted you to."

"What do you mean?"

He hated this. It was like being back in high school, and he'd really hated high school. He'd thought to wait to tell Katie the truth about the Santa thing, both because it amused him to keep the secret and because he took few things seriously other than flying.

But oddly enough, he was taking this very seriously. "I know you're trying to get Matt to discuss your Christmas party kiss, but there's a good reason he won't."

"I know." She grimaced. "It's because I'm Christmas cursed. I never should have made that stupid Christmas wish."

"You're…Christmas cursed?"

"Let's just say Santa seems to lose my address."

"And the Christmas wish thing?"

"It's no big deal."

"Oh, I think it probably is."

"Okay, fine, I made a stupid wish to…" She blushed. "Can I ask you something?"

"Of course."

"Well, you're a man…"

"Yes." He had to smile. "That was too easy, try another question."

She rolled her eyes. "Forget it, just forget it. It's not important."

Yes, it was, he could see that much. But so was this. "About that kiss, Katie—"

"I'd like to forget that, too."

"Sorry, no can do." He'd never forget it. "Matt can't discuss this with you. He can't, Katie, because *I'm* the one who shared that kiss with you."

Her mouth worked.

Opened.

Closed.

Opened again. "I kissed Matt," she finally managed to say. "In the Santa costume."

"No. You kissed me. In the Santa costume. And I think you already know it."

"No."

"Yes. Otherwise, how would I know about it?" He tried to smile, but truthfully the memory of her in that dress, pressed against him, her mouth on his, pretty much made it difficult. "I know if you think about it, you'll see the truth. You've nearly recognized me every single day since."

"In your dreams."

"Really? Then why are you always staring at me?"

"I am *not* always staring at you!"

When he only waited patiently, she blew out a frustrated breath. "Much," she muttered.

"I'm flattered," he said.

"Don't be! I did not kiss you!"

"I could prove it to you, if you'd like."

4

HE COULD prove it to her.

Oh, Lord.

Katie's palms were clammy, her heart raced.

The flu, she decided. It was just the flu coming on.

Which didn't explain why the thought of him "proving it" to her had her nipples hard and achy.

Bryan kept his distance, but she felt the heat of him, the power in his big frame all the same, and she knew if she slid her arms around his neck and pressed close he'd make a rough, appreciative growl—

No. This was most definitely a road she did not want to travel.

Normally she was an easygoing person. Quiet and reserved, maybe even a little mousy, but she was working on that. And yet she wasn't easygoing now. "How could you prove something that never happened?" she asked with remarkable—and totally false—calm.

"By kissing you again."

She stared at him, and it wasn't a loss of words that made speaking difficult, but that she had so much to say and no rationale left in which to say it. "No, you can't kiss me."

"Again. You mean I can't kiss you *again.*"

"There was never a first time!"

He leaned closer so that she was surrounded by him. "I have six sisters," he confided in a voice that managed to convey both his affection and love for his family. "That's six nosy, bossy, demanding and completely wonderful *females.*"

She did not want to know this about him. She wanted to picture him as wild, uncaring and...well, a jerk.

He felt safer that way.

But nothing about this man was safe. Nothing.

"So trust me on this one," he continued. "I learned early to never disagree with a woman, but I'm very sorry to say you're wrong."

Did he have to stand so close? She could see his eyes weren't just a *little* blue, but all the way, ocean-deep, drown-in-me blue. Terrific. Not only did he love his family, but he had amazing eyes.

Not fair.

He also had a scar that ran along the line of his dark brow, probably from doing something crazy.

Realizing she was staring at him, and that he was enjoying that very thing, she turned on her heels and moved toward the storage warehouse. She didn't need anything, but she felt so flustered, so uncustomarily unnerved, she opened it, flipped on the light and stepped inside.

Okay, think.

She'd kissed Santa Claus, she knew this much for certain. The rest was pure speculation. She knew what she wanted. She wanted Santa to have been Matt. Wanted *Matt* to have hoarsely whispered her name with longing. Wanted *Matt* to have been the one to put his hands on her and gently squeeze as if he could never get enough of her.

Nice, dependable, kind Matt. Grown-up Matt. Perfect Matt.

She had no doubt it had been him, none whatsoever.

None.

Mostly none.

This wasn't good. In fact, this was bad, very bad.

"You're thinking about it, aren't you?" Bryan whispered.

"No."

"Liar."

"If you have six sisters, you also know it's not exactly flattering to call a woman a liar."

He grinned.

"I bet you're the baby of the family," she said without thinking, and his grin widened.

"Oh, I am. Spoiled rotten, too. And you know what else? You're interested in me. I like that." He settled even closer and smiled at her. "What else can I tell you?"

"Why you'd want to play footsy with Holly."

His smile faded. *Honestly* faded. "Holly is the last person on earth I would play footsy with," he said. "That woman is dangerous."

"Men like that."

"Men like excitement, not danger, not in a woman anyway."

"Uh-huh," she said in a tone that could be construed as nothing other than sarcasm.

"Tell me this much," he said, strangely intent. "Did you see me egging her on? Or did you see me move away from her as quickly as I could?"

She thought about that. "You moved away from her."

"Like a mouse out of a snake's path."

That made her laugh. "You're hardly a mouse." But she could concede that maybe what she'd seen in the meeting *had* been one-sided. There were, however, other issues here. Personal issues. Bryan may be charming when he wanted, but he wasn't serious. At least not about women. And she *was* serious. She wanted a *serious* man.

"Ask me something else," he encouraged. "Go on, try me."

"Okay…why did you take that terribly dangerous stunt job yesterday morning?"

"It wasn't that dangerous."

"I watched you pull out of that spin with only seconds to spare." She hadn't meant to say it, hadn't meant to sound so worried.

"You watched."

Oh, yeah, she'd watched. Watched and bitten her nails down to the quick with anxiety she hadn't wanted to feel. "You fly with wild, reckless abandon."

"Thank you."

"That wasn't a compliment!"

"I'm careful, and highly skilled."

He was talented, she'd give him that. "I just don't know why you have to do it like that, as if each second was going to be your last."

"Katie, I *live* like that."

She backed up until she came up against a shelving unit, which she gripped at her sides with fisted hands. "*Exactly*. You live like that. Which is the reason…which is why—" Horrified, she broke off.

"Why what? Why you can't admit it was me you kissed?"

How to explain that she had a precise definition of what she wanted in a man and he was the exact opposite? She wanted the three *S*'s. Security, safety, stability. She didn't want to be afraid for his life on a daily basis. She didn't want someone who made her feel as if she were on a perpetual roller coaster.

She hated roller coasters!

As if he could read her mind, his good humor vanished, replaced by an intensity she didn't know how to handle, and he once again closed the distance between them. Now she could feel the warmth of his breath on her temple as he quietly studied her. "Was it that bad? The kiss?"

She studied her shoes. The ceiling. The wall. Anything other than his serious and oh-so-gorgeous face.

But he didn't give up.

"Did I kiss like a Saint Bernard?" he asked. "Did I have breath like a whale? What?"

She couldn't help it, she laughed. "I'm not admitting anything, mind you, but no, not bad breath. Not too much slobber. It was…"

"Yes?"

"A twenty on a scale of one to ten," she admitted.

He smiled, not a cocky one, but it still made her roll her eyes and look away. Until he caught her chin in his fingers and turned her back to him.

"Why don't you like me?" he asked softly, and when she opened her mouth to deny this, he gently slid those fingers against her lips.

At his touch, a bewildering tightness invaded her insides. Her eyes widened on his. She saw his jaw tighten, felt his fingers tense, and wondered if he felt the same confusion.

"Truth," he whispered. "For months and months now you've done your damnedest to avoid me. Changing directions in the hallway, sitting far away in staff meetings, dealing with my pilots when you need something, instead of dealing with me. Why, Katie? At least tell me why."

One last stroke with his fingers and then he lifted them away from her lips, but he didn't move, so that when she tipped her head up to look at him, her mouth was only inches from his. It shocked her to realize her body was straining closer to him, and once again she flattened herself against the shelving unit. "It's not that I don't like you. But we have nothing in common."

"How do you figure?"

"Well, other than us being day and night? Oil and vinegar—"

"*Concrete* reasons. No cheating with silly metaphors."

"Okay, well…I'm plain. And you're—" *Outrageously sexy.* "*Not* plain," she finished lamely.

"Neither are you."

"Then you're too tall."

He laughed. "Chicken excuse, but I'll let you have it. What else?"

"I like everything planned out."

"And I don't?"

"You'd jump off a cliff on a whim."

"If I had a good rope, maybe."

"See? Polar opposites. That's us."

"That's not completely true." His voice was low, husky, his direct gaze like a caress. "We both love airplanes."

"How—" How could he have known about her secret passion and love of planes? That she hoarded and devoured every book she could find, every picture, every magazine. That sometimes, late at night, she wandered through the hangars and just looked at the planes that so fascinated and terrified her at the same time?

"I've seen you." He lifted a finger and tucked

a wayward strand of hair behind her ear. The touch electrified her. "I've seen the look of longing and passion on your face as you've touched a sleek Lear, seen your yearning. Why don't you fly, Katie? What keeps you grounded?"

"My father," she confided before she could stop herself, and this time it was *her* who covered *his* mouth. "Don't. Don't ask, I don't want to talk about it."

His hand came up and circled her wrist. When he spoke, his lips tickled her palm. "We should."

"No. Look, it's nothing personal."

"I think it is."

"I just…" Lord, it was hard to think. She had her hand on his mouth, his very *sexy* mouth, and she couldn't tear her gaze from it, even when it curved with satisfaction. "I'm not much of a risk taker."

His eyes sparkled at that. "You're here alone in the warehouse with me, aren't you? Seems pretty risky to me. Tell me, what drew you to Santa that night? What made you want to kiss him?"

"I'm not going to tell you that!"

"Please?"

"This is silly. It doesn't matter to you."

"Tell me."

"It was Matt."

"Matt."

"Yes. He's dependable. Reliable. He's—"

"Mr. Perfect." He shook his head even as a smile tugged at the corners of his mouth. "I've heard the women talk about him."

"Then you already knew what attracted me."

"Dependability? Reliability?" He made a face. "Sounds like a car. A new one, when we all know it's the *used* models, the coveted and experienced and loved ones, that have all the nerve and personality."

"Bryan—"

His eyes flashed now, still with good humor, but with something more as well. "*I* was Santa, Katie. And I'm going to prove it to you."

"No!" Not stopping to think about her sudden, irrational fear, Katie ducked from between the shelving unit and his body, not stopping to look at him until she had the door handle firmly in her hand and opened.

Bryan lifted his hands. "I wasn't going to prove it *that* way."

"Oh." She felt dense. "I just thought—"

"I know what you thought. That I was going to kiss you again. But if I wasn't Santa that night, if I wasn't the one to give you that kiss—which must have been a helluva doozy, by the way, to have made such an impression—you have nothing to worry about, right?''

''Um…yeah. Right.''

He laughed softly then, a terrifyingly sexy sound that made the butterflies go to town on Katie's stomach again.

''How about I prove to you that it *was* me, but in another way?'' he suggested.

Warily she eyed him. ''How?''

''And when I do—'' he completely ignored her question ''—you're going to admit you were wrong. Out loud this time. To *me*.''

She still had one foot out the door. She was safe. Yeah, safe as a name caller in a glass house. ''I have no problem admitting my mistakes,'' she said so stiffly he laughed again. ''But I'm not wrong here.''

''Uh-huh. We'll see. Dependability. Reliability? Those are the things you need?''

''Yes,'' she whispered.

He looked slightly disgusted, but resigned. ''Damn. I was afraid you were going to say that.''

A FEW DAYS LATER, Bryan was in the middle of a final check, trying to get out of Wells for the day, when he heard a strange noise coming from the opened cockpit of his plane.

He set down his clipboard and walked around the Cessna, his mind a million miles away.

He was thinking fondly of mistletoe and sexy red Christmas dresses. He was thinking of warm, vulnerable, whiskey-colored eyes, and sweet-scented, shoulder-length hair brushing over his arms as he leaned into the kiss that had rocked his world.

Was *still* rocking his world.

It had been a week.

Seven days.

One-hundred-sixty-eight hours.

He didn't know how many minutes, but for an admitted adrenaline junkie, he was dying for another rush.

Another kiss.

He'd tried his damnedest to appear to be the model citizen whenever Katie was around. Dependable. Reliable.

He did it all.

He tried so hard his head hurt. What was he doing? Why did he even care? Was he that egotistical that he couldn't let it go?

So Katie wanted neat and simple Matt, who was sedate enough to put a gorilla to sleep without effort.

In contrast, she thought Bryan wild. Uncontrollable.

That sound came from the cockpit again, and he climbed up the landing stairs of the sleek plane to peek inside.

Nothing.

He went in, took a step toward the cockpit, then froze when the door slammed behind him.

"What the—" He turned back just as a soft weight plowed into him. "Oof." The backs of his knees hit a low seat, tripping him, and he crashed into the wall of the plane.

On the floor, with his legs still draped over the back of the seat and that soft weight draped over the top of him, Bryan shook his head and evaluated.

Hot flesh and overly scented skin? "Holly! What the hell—"

That was the last word he managed before she straddled him, leaned in and whispered, "Take it like a man, would you? I need to use you for a second."

"What—"

"Hush! He's coming. I want him to see!" And she took his mouth with hers.

Behind them the airplane door opened abruptly

and Katie's voice called into the dark depths. "Bryan?"

Both he and Holly swore.

"Matt's there, too!" Holly hissed. "Damn that man, he's so slow!"

"Bryan?" called Katie. "I need an invoice...."

Oh, perfect.

Bryan tried to jerk free, but Holly was quicker, and prepared. She pressed down on him, both with her knee in his windpipe and her mouth on his.

Worrying about Katie seeing the kiss became secondary to actually breathing. And still he heard Katie come closer.

Inanely, Bryan wondered if she would believe he'd passed out and Holly was performing mouth-to-mouth resuscitation. Certainly she'd never believe the truth, that he'd been attacked!

Hell, *he* hardly believed it.

"Bryan—" Katie's voice stopped short on an audible gasp as she caught sight of him—big, bad Bryan Morgan, being held to the floor by Holly's lips.

Dammit! Struggling to sit up, he shoved Holly off his thighs.

Katie was already halfway across the hangar floor.

Surging to his feet, he leaped for the door. "Katie!" he bellowed.

She turned, just as Bryan took a quick step, too quick, and promptly fell out of the plane, flat on his face.

When the stars and pain faded, he rolled onto his back on the cold concrete floor of the hangar and blinked Holly into view.

"Save your breath," she said with a sigh. "She's gone. For such a well-curved little thing, she sure can move. And apparently Matt wasn't with her."

Bryan spared her one quick glance as he surged to his unsteady feet. "You. *Stay.* When I get back you have some explaining to do."

"Oh, Ricky," she whined in a perfect mimic of Lucy Ricardo.

Instead of strangling her, Bryan shook his head and went after Katie, but Holly happened to be right on one score—Katie *could* really move.

By the time he figured out which way to go, she'd crossed the entire length of the tarmac, her low, economical heels clicking loudly, her long skirt flowing wildly in the breeze.

"Katie!"

Naturally she kept walking, even faster now, and he jogged up to her, passing her, running backwards in order to stay right in front of her, but she wouldn't even look at him. "Katie, I—"

"I'm busy," she huffed.

"You're also upset."

"Why? I don't care who you kiss."

Ouch, though it was a good point. She didn't care, he didn't care...so what was the big deal?

He wished he knew.

His face hurt from taking a dive on the hangar floor. His head hurt, too, and though he was in excellent shape, he could hardly keep up with her. "Can you stop for a moment? Or at least slow down?"

"Nope."

He glanced behind him to make sure he wasn't going to fall, *again*, and kept running backward. "About what just happened—"

"Forget it."

He'd like to. "I can't. You know, it wasn't really what you thought."

"Really?" Finally, she stopped, put a hand on her hip and lifted an eyebrow. "What did I think?"

"Um..." He was feeling a little slow on the uptake.

"That you're slime? That you're sick? That you're— You're bleeding!"

Why that softened her, he hadn't a clue.

"Your lip," she said and lifted a hand before she stopped herself. "You should tell your little girlfriend not to bite so hard."

"She's not—" Hell! How did this stuff happen to him?

They were on the far side of the tarmac now, the wind blowing fiercely, whipping Katie's hair into both of their faces. Her skirt rioted, too, tangling up in his legs as well as hers. They were close to the lobby door, close to the first hangar, but neither of them moved. "I suppose you won't believe the truth," he said.

Her gaze narrowed and now she did touch his mouth and stared at her finger. Then she stabbed it into his chest, hard. "That's not blood, it's bright red lipstick! Gee, I wonder how *that* happened? Oh, wait, I know." She let out a tight smile. "You're a closet cross-dresser."

"She jumped me," he said inanely, going with the truth instead of the resuscitation excuse, thinking he should get points for honesty. "Really. I heard this noise and went to investigate."

"In your parked plane."

"Yes."

"I imagine you thought it was a mouse or something."

"Or something, yes," he agreed, ignoring her

huff of disbelief. "Then suddenly there she was, kissing me."

"She plowed you to the ground, naturally," Katie said agreeably. "Straddled you. Forced your arms around her, then attacked your mouth."

Pleased by her compassion and understanding, he smiled. "Yes! Exactly!"

Katie's eyes went cold. "Someone ought to put out a bulletin. You men need a new story."

"What are you talking about?"

"That's exactly the same story my fiancé gave me, when I found him in the same position with Holly. Only it was under my Christmas tree, three years ago."

5

FOR THE FIRST TIME in Katie's life, her nice, logical world of accounting failed her. She had her computer up and running, a spreadsheet opened in front of her and yet all she saw were numbers leaping and jumping around, making her dizzy.

She found herself mixing her debits with her credits. Confusing her assets with liabilities. Twisting her expenses.

All because of a man. And not the man she'd so carefully picked out for herself either, but one who had the ability to turn her life upside down in a very unsettling way.

How was she supposed to face the fact that the kiss that haunted her dreams with its heat and intensity, the one that had awakened needs and yearnings she hadn't even been aware of, might have come from a man she could never let herself care about?

Never.

Bryan was everything she didn't want. Unpredictable. Wild. Uncontrollable.

Not to mention a woman magnet.

Anyway, it didn't matter, she'd kissed Matt.

She really had.

Oh, Lord. Her head hit the desk with a loud thunk.

Not Bryan, please don't let it be true.

She was happy with her life just the way it was. Mostly. Okay, she was working on the happy part. But what she wanted for the rest of it was quite simple—the exact opposite of what Bryan made her feel. Her three little *S*'s.

Security, safety, stability.

All three of those in one, Matt poked his head in her office door and smiled.

She lifted her head and smiled back, stupidly, *yearning* for his next words.

I'm sorry I've been teasing you, of course I remember our kiss.

Or better yet, *How about we try that bone-melting kiss again because for the life of me I can't stop thinking about it.*

Actually, if he could just haul her out of her chair, press his body to hers and plant one on her... Yeah, now *that* would be the best thing to lay to rest all these crazy doubts.

With that in mind, she waited earnestly.

"We need the general ledger," he said, shattering her hopes with quiet ease. "Do you by any chance have it ready?"

Maybe he was just shy. She could understand that, really she could. But right now she was desperately afraid she knew why he wasn't responding to her, darn one Bryan Morgan!

She had to know, without a shadow of a doubt, who she'd kissed.

"It's almost ready," she lied, purposely not looking down at her desk, where the thing lay out right in the open, finished. "Why don't you come in for a second while I get it?"

"Okay."

"Oh, and maybe you could shut the door?"

He did, and then leaned against her file cabinet, tall and lean. Handsome. Reliable. Dependable.

A mental image of a car salesman flashed in her mind and she shoved it out.

Matt was Mr. Perfect, and she was going to prove it to herself if it killed her.

As she walked toward him, some of her intent and purpose must have gleamed in her gaze because he straightened, his brow crinkled in question.

She kept walking, afraid she'd lose her nerve.

Matt abandoned his perch and backed up, until her extra chair hit the back of his knees, forcing him to sit. He gripped the arms and sent her a wary look. "Um...how about I come back later when—"

When she was in her right mind?

Not likely to happen.

"No need," she said, putting her hands over his as she bent, lowering her face, puckering her lips, not quite daring to close her eyes because she was nervous and deathly afraid she'd miss her target.

"Katie!" Matt scooted back as far as he could in the chair, but she had him surrounded. The chair made an alarming squeak, then started to tip with his efforts as she tried to soothe him.

"Just one more time, Matt."

"One more time? *What are you taking about?*"

Her palms grew damp with nerves, making them slip on the armrests. She fell across his lap full weight.

"Oomph," he said, and though she tried to smile a come-hither smile, he didn't put his hands on her as she imagined, instead arched even farther away from her as she fumbled. "Katie—"

That was the last word he managed before their combined weight proved too much for the chair. They toppled backward to the floor.

THE HOSPITAL waiting room had been painted a soft green, and decorated with warm paintings and drawings.

Probably to calm people.

It wasn't working, a half hysterical Katie was certain of that much. Nope, in fact that green was making her feel seasick.

Of course it could have been that she'd nearly killed the vice president of Wells Aviation.

"A concussion," Bryan said from his chair, watching her pace. "How do you suppose *that* happened?"

She cringed and kept pacing.

"He's a careful man," Bryan said thoughtfully. "I can't imagine him just…falling out of his chair."

"Um, yeah. About that…" Katie managed a little smile. "He didn't exactly fall on his own."

"I see." Though his mouth remained still, his eyes twinkled with what she was pretty certain was humor. "You mean something tipped him over?"

"Sort of." Katie closed her eyes in mortification. "You remember that Christmas party thing?"

Now one corner of his mouth quirked. "I think I do, yes."

"And that stupid kiss."

Bryan paused so long Katie opened her eyes.

"That stupid kiss," he repeated.

"It should have been so simple!" She forced a laugh. "It's really the funniest thing."

"Try me."

"Well, I got to thinking about what you said, you know, about it not being Matt."

Bryan just looked at her.

"Right. Anyway, I got to wondering—"

"If I was telling the truth? I thought we already established that much. If I wasn't, how would I even know about the kiss?"

"Well, I didn't say I was rational." She managed another smile. "I needed to know for certain if it was really Matt, even though of course it was. You were just somehow teasing me. All I had to do was prove it, so I just…"

"You just…what?"

"Tried to kiss Matt again." She rubbed her eyes. "And that was that."

"Not quite it wasn't. You left out the part where you nearly killed him."

"Oh, yeah." She sank to an empty chair and dropped both her bravado and head into her hands.

"The headlines should be interesting," Bryan told her sympathetically. "'Accountant Launches

Herself at Single Executive, Hoping for a Kiss and Knocks Him Out Cold.' You know, in some states you could probably get arrested.''

That thought hadn't even occurred to her, but it did now and Katie went weak. If it had been the other way around, and Matt had been the woman, and *she* the *he*... ''Oh, God, I sexually harassed him!''

Bryan grinned. ''Shame on you. Can you do it to me, too?''

''I'm going to be sick,'' she said faintly.

''Well, this is the place to do it.'' But he ran his hand over her bowed head in a soothing gesture.

The craziest thought went through her mind at his oddly welcome touch. She was resisting him because...well, he wasn't grown-up enough, didn't know anything but fun. And yet here he was, being the mature one in the face of her own stupidity. She might have warmed to him then. Might have, except for his next words.

''Look, it's not that bad,'' he said. ''At least now you know the truth.''

''No,'' she said miserably. ''I never actually kissed him before we fell.''

Bryan stared at her, then laughed. ''You poor baby.''

rousal, and had immediately taken over the kiss
until she couldn't so much as remember her name.

Not this time.

No fireworks, no heat barreling through her
veins, nothing except the short, dry, chaste kiss.

Matt immediately pulled back and frowned at
her. "What was *that* for?"

"Yes, Katie. Do tell."

Katie jerked around. *Bryan!* What? Was her
good karma on vacation?

Bryan lifted a mocking eyebrow, darn him, and
sent her a knowing smile.

"What are you doing here?" she demanded.

"Me?"

"Yes, you!"

"Matt asked me to drive him home." Bryan's
eyes sparkled, his mouth quivered suspiciously.
"Unless of course, *you're* going to do it."

"No!" Matt said quickly, too quickly, then sent
Katie an apologetic but terrified glance.

Katie could only sigh. Bryan's eyes were still on
her, she could feel them, but she'd streak naked
through the hospital before she'd look at him
again.

"Hope I didn't interrupt anything," he said
lightly, turning her, forcing her to face him.

"ARE YOU WAITING for Matt Osborne?"

Katie straightened in her chair and looked at the
nurse in surprise. "Me?"

"He's been released. You're driving him
home?"

Katie looked around, but there was no one else
the woman could possibly be speaking to. Bryan
had vanished a half hour ago. "Um...okay."
Guess she wasn't fired.

Yet.

She followed the nurse down the hallway past
the emergency room cubicles. Not all the curtains
were closed so she got an eyeful of moaning,
groaning, screaming, yelling people.

Not a happy place.

Finally they stopped before a cubicle that *did*
have a closed curtain. The nurse whipped it open,
and when Katie hesitated, the woman gently
pushed her inside and slid the curtain closed again.

Matt sat on the cot, holding his head in his
hands. When he saw her, he straightened, his eyes
widening a little.

Terrific. Now he was afraid of her. She forced
a smile. "Matt? They said you're free to go now."

"Yes." He looked at the closed curtain behind

her as if it were a bolted steel door and he was locked on the wrong side of it.

The awkwardness didn't fade when she found her feet and moved closer to him. With a barely perceptible movement, he shifted back, away from her.

She dropped to the cot next to him and sighed. Any second now he'd fire her. She'd take it like a man.

Probably.

"Katie?" He sounded wary but concerned, which made her sigh again.

Mr. Perfect was a gentleman, right to the end. Except that he was watching her as one would a poisonous spider. She supposed she couldn't really blame him; in his eyes she'd been acting pretty strange since the party.

"Why are you here?" he asked.

"I'm driving you home." She attempted a friendly, don't-worry-I'm-sane smile. "I'll have you there in five minutes tops."

He looked as if five minutes were a lifetime. Or maybe he was just worried she'd knock him down again and *really* injure him this time.

Well, that was her own fault, she supposed. And

she still wasn't any closer to the truth. handsome, and so darn right for her!

Why couldn't this be simple?

Slowly she lifted a hand toward him, he'd take it. He didn't, instead stared down fingers as if he expected them to separate fr body and yell *Boo!* "We really need to go, said.

"Just checking…" He gingerly took her fing studying them intently. Then he slowly craned neck and stared at the ceiling, and then the wa around him. "For mistletoe." He shot her an apo ogetic smile. "I'm sorry, it's just that you seem so obsessed…."

She tightened her grip on his hand and gentl tugged him up because she *was* obsessed. And sl wasn't finished; she had to know. She had to the wild, unpredictable and far too sexy Bryan of her head. "I have to try this one last time," whispered, more to herself than him. "I won' you, I promise." Going up on her tiptoe lightly pressed her mouth to his.

He stiffened at the connection, and she *Yes!* because she'd felt the same reaction at the party. But that night his hands had on her, he'd made a rough sound   li

Oh, yes, given that smug expression, he knew *exactly* what he'd interrupted, and she'd never live it down.

His cocky, wicked grin only reinforced the knowledge.

6

WELL, AT LEAST she had Tic and Toc, her cats. They'd never abandon her. They'd never look at her with soft reproach as Matt had, wondering why she was trying to ruin his life.

Darn him for giving her a complex anyway. All she'd wanted was one little kiss; it wouldn't have hurt him to cooperate.

Much.

"Meow."

Katie let out a long, shaky breath. "Well, I didn't *mean* to hurt him," she told the cat. "But really, now that I think about it, that concussion was his own fault. If he would've just stayed still, we wouldn't have fallen."

She sat on her porch, both cats heavy in her lap as she watched the sunset and sighed. "I'm still Christmas cursed, apparently. Big surprise there."

"I've heard you say that twice now."

She nearly dumped Tic and Toc to the floor at the unexpected sound of his voice.

Bryan stood below the bottom step.

In the growing dark, she couldn't see his expression clearly, and told herself it wasn't necessary. She didn't care. More than that, *he* didn't care. "We have to stop meeting like this," she muttered, trying to soothe the two orange tabbies as they both lifted their heads and stared with reproach at this newcomer.

Bryan stepped onto the porch and sent her his trademark crooked grin, the one that did funny things to her stomach in spite of the fact that she'd refused to acknowledge those things.

And not for the first time, she acknowledged somewhere deep down that Bryan was acting far more "mature" than she. Darn him.

"I hope you don't mind," he said. "I looked up your address in the computer."

"I mind."

His lips curved, but he said nothing to that, simply sat on the bench right next to her. "So. What's this about a Christmas curse?"

"It means I have yet to successfully manage a smooth holiday season."

"Ever?"

She didn't, couldn't, answer. Not when their thighs brushed, their arms touched, and his face, when he turned it toward her, was completely void of the laughter she'd been silently groaning over ever since he caught her trying to kiss Matt.

"I'm sorry you had to go through all that," he said, reading her mind with horrifying ease.

"Which? Nearly killing our vice president, or having him now be afraid of me?"

"That you didn't believe me the first time."

"Oh. That."

"Yeah." He nudged her shoulder with his. "*That*. Katie, is it so hard to believe? That you and I could have shared a kiss?"

"It wasn't *just* a kiss."

"No," he agreed with a rueful laugh. "It sure wasn't. And if I hadn't had that ridiculous costume on, if we hadn't been surrounded by dressed up, drunken fools, if..." His eyes gleamed with heat. "Well. Maybe it was for the best."

She was certain somehow his statement should make her feel better. It didn't.

"So...are you going to admit it?"

"Admit what?"

He let out a short laugh and shook his head. "You can't fool me, you know. I'm the master of avoidance techniques."

"You don't avoid anything. You jump into every single day with your eyes wide-open, one-hundred-percent ready for anything and everything. Don't tell me you know anything about avoidance techniques.''

''Ah, but the adventure and excitement of my job, that has nothing to do with what I'm talking about.''

''And what are you talking about?''

''*Heart* stuff. *Emotion* stuff. That's what I'm the master of avoidance at.''

She stared at him, and he stared right back, his eyes clear and open and honest.

''Why?'' she whispered. ''Why are you telling me this?''

''Because maybe I'm a big fake,'' he whispered back. Slowly, as if he were afraid to frighten her off, he lifted a hand. His fingers brushed her cheek in a soft, barely there caress. ''When it comes right down to it, I've never taken the biggest risk of all. I've never opened my heart all the way to a woman.''

''I find that hard to believe.'' Was that her voice, all whispery and light? Good Lord, she sounded as if she were having an attack of the vapors. But then he shifted a little closer and those long fingers cupped her jaw, and she became much more seriously breathing challenged. Her pulse raced. Her heart pounded. Her palms went clammy.

Wait, she *was* having an attack of the vapors!

"You're breathing funny," he said.

Well, so was he. "I thought you loved your carefree lifestyle," she said softly.

"I do. I'm just saying…hell." A self-deprecating laugh escaped him. "I have no idea what I'm saying."

"I've seen customers fall all over themselves to get your attention," Katie said. "I've seen half the staff—the *female* half, that is—do the same thing. And I certainly haven't seen you running away. In fact, I've *personally* witnessed you opening up one of your planes to at least a dozen different dates."

"I said I've never opened my *heart*. Not my planes, or…anything else."

"Really?"

"Really."

"Why?"

"Why? Because I have enough women in my life with my family. Because I never felt the need for another nosy, bossy—"

"Hey! We're not *all* like that."

"Then maybe I haven't met the right woman."

Oh, she didn't want to know this, she definitely didn't, because something within her softened, melted. Warmed.

Darn it. Darn *him*.

Her insides were going all molten on her, dissolving with each light stroke of his roughened fingers. "Bryan—"

Now those fingers spread wide, as if he needed to touch more of her, and his thumb slid slowly, languidly, over her sensitive lower lip until it quivered open.

His gaze darkened, his mouth opened, too.

"Bryan—"

"Mmm. Love how you say my name. Say it again."

She nearly did, but then realized her eyes were half closed, her body was straining toward his, and she was one touch away from doing what she'd sworn never to do. She could never become attracted to him.

Too late, claimed a little voice, *far too late.*

She not-so-kindly ignored her little voice, because after all, Bryan Morgan was not a forever kind of guy, no matter what he said. She straightened away from him, clicked her mouth closed and glared at him.

So did Tic.

Toc leaped gracefully from her lap and stalked off, clearly bored.

Bryan just waited patiently.

"Stop that."

"Stop what?" he asked innocently.

Making me forget why I don't want you. "Stop waiting for me to tell you what you want to hear."

"Which is?"

"That I kissed *you*."

He laughed softly, sexily, and her stomach tightened again. *Oh, Lord,* she thought frantically. *It's true.* No more fooling herself, because that's really what she'd been doing.

She'd known the truth all along. It *was* him, no matter how much she wanted to believe otherwise. Worse, she was helplessly attracted to *this* leanly muscled, sleek, sleepy-eyed, sensual man in front of her.

And she'd kissed him.

"Come on, truth now," he said huskily. "You know it wasn't Matt in the Santa costume."

She could only stare at him.

"Let me prove it," he said softly. "I can, you know." His eyes seconded the motion. His mouth curved invitingly, and Katie actually shifted slightly, instinctively moving closer.

"Right here, right now." His gaze was on her mouth. "Let me lay all these doubts to rest for once and for all."

Heat pooled in all the places in her body she'd ignored for so long.

"Katie?" His fingers toyed with her hair. Their

mouths were only a fraction apart, but he wasn't moving any closer, he was going to make her ask for it.

Her body was already begging.

"Come on," he whispered, his heavy-lidded eyes dark and sleepy and filled with promises.

So many promises.

But promises weren't good for her, she'd had one too many broken in her past, too many from the likes of a man like this, a man who had no intention of ever settling down.

There. That was the bottom line. She needed to remember that.

Saving herself from making a huge mistake, she jerked back, and in the process startled her cat.

Tic straightened from her lap, meowed softly, then leaped from her legs to Bryan's.

Whether or not the heavy cat missed on purpose—with her claws out—landing directly in the juncture between Bryan's thighs, and the intriguing bulge there, Katie couldn't be sure.

But she had to admit, it was quite a conversation stopper.

"That's two," Bryan said in a choked voice.

"Two?"

"Two men down for the count today." He

groaned and bent over. "That's got to be a personal record for you."

IT TOOK HIM A WHILE, but Bryan finally figured out he'd been going at this Katie thing all wrong. He wasn't usually so slow in the woman department, but to be fair to him, it had been a long time and he was rusty.

Not to mention—Katie was everything he'd *never* wanted. She represented stability, dependability, and…what else was it she'd said?

Oh, yes, reliability.

She probably wanted a white picket fence and two point four kids, too. And yet, he couldn't stop thinking about her, dreaming about her.

It was scary stuff and he vowed to get over it, and quickly.

The morning after nearly getting a vasectomy from Katie's cat, he flew a particularly tough stunt for a commercial—made all the tougher because in spite of himself, his mind kept slipping back to a certain soft-eyed, warm-spirited, strong yet vulnerable Katie Wilkins.

After the flight he sat for a long moment in his plane before pushing himself out of the cockpit. As he turned toward the aircraft's door, it was suddenly filled with a curvy grinning blonde.

"Don't even *think* about it," he muttered to Holly, remembering the last time she'd cornered him in this very spot.

She lifted an innocent brow. "Playing hard to get, Bryan? That's so sexy in a man. And so pointless. Every woman worth her pumps knows with the right...shall we say *motivation,* a man is putty in her hands."

Bryan sighed. "Why don't you give me a break and go ruin some other guy's chances for a change?"

She grinned. "Oh, did I ruin your chances with Katie? What a terrible shame, your actually having to work hard at getting something you want."

It was true. He hadn't had to work at anything, not once in his entire life, because up until now, it had all come easy—school, friends, lovers. *Life.*

Another reason to get over Katie.

"You poor, poor man," she said, tsking softly in her throat. "Trying to get a woman who has no intention of ever falling for a man like you. You're fumbling around in the dark on this one, trust me."

He narrowed his eyes. "Why is that?"

"I could tell you why she's so squirrelly about the attraction between you two, but...nah."

"You owe me one."

"I owe no one."

"I wore that damn Santa costume so that you could trick Katie into making a fool of herself in front of Matt, all so you could make sure he noticed no woman but you."

Holly rolled her eyes and looked bored. "What a convoluted idea *that* would be."

He matched her bored expression. "Of course, I could just tell Matt—"

Her eyes sharpened. "Wait. That...won't be necessary."

He smiled. "I didn't think so. So...spill it."

"You mean let you in on our little Katie's private torments? Tell you that her father was a daredevil stunt pilot just like you, one who made promise after promise to her that he always broke because a cool and thrilling job would come up? Tell you that after breaking her heart over and over again, he managed to *really* destroy her by getting himself killed on a job he had no business taking in the first place?" She lifted a negligent shoulder. "I suppose I could tell you all that, and all the sad little details that go with it, but... Well, that wouldn't exactly be like me, would it?"

Bryan stared at her, but for once could see no intent to deceive. "Tell me you're lying."

"Would I do that?"

Heart heavy, he closed his eyes and shook his head. *Oh, Katie.*

"Oh, please," she said with heartfelt disgust. "Don't feel sorry for her, she always made out in the end. She and her mother received a huge life insurance settlement. She went to the college of her choice. She got to become whatever she wanted—God knows why she'd waste it on becoming an accountant, but that's another story. Fact is, she came out smelling like a rose."

"And you didn't," he said quietly, finding himself pitying Holly, not Katie. What kind of a woman would look at Katie's life, and what she'd been through, and resent her?

But what he felt for Katie was far more complicated than pity. Compassion, empathy, yes. Definitely all that and more. Also a fierce pride for what she'd done for herself in spite of the obstacles she'd overcome. But there was a new understanding for what she saw when she looked at him.

And it wasn't pretty.

All this time, he'd been allowing himself to get caught up in the bafflement of why a woman with so much hidden passion and love for life would stifle herself. Why she would pretend she didn't feel, and even worse, pretend she didn't need someone to feel for her in return.

He hadn't considered the possibility her past had driven her to that.

Did she really believe she'd be happy going along with the status quo for the rest of her life, avoiding adventure and excitement, never knowing what she was missing?

Yes, he decided, because she *did* know what she was missing. Hell, she was missing it on purpose so as not to get hurt.

He was outside her office, his hand raised to the doorknob before he knew what he was doing. But her office was empty. He let himself in and stood staring down at her neat-as-a-pin desk, realizing that knowing Katie's past was only half the problem.

The other half was their basic differences.

Nothing was out of place here, not one piece of paper, not a single pencil, not even a paperclip.

Hmm.

Quickly he retraced his steps down the hall, needing to make sure, but—

Yep.

He opened the door to his own office and took in the wild, unorganized mess. Huge piles of paperwork were haphazardly stacked everywhere. Some had fallen over onto other piles, creating bigger mountains. When he'd run out of desk room he'd used floor space, nearly every inch of it.

No doubt. They were indeed opposites.

He attempted to straighten out some of the clutter, but no matter where he shifted a pile, the place still looked like a disaster area. Finally, he opened the large drawers on his desk and just shoved some of the paperwork into them. When they were full to overloading, he coaxed and jammed and threatened, and only slammed his fingers once, maybe twice.

Swearing, sucking on his sore fingers, he went to work on the files all over his floor, but he'd gotten exactly nowhere when he looked up at the shadow in his doorway.

Katie stood there, staring down at him with a bemused look on her face. "Did you lose something?"

He was on his hands and knees, surrounded by a mess he had yet to come close to fixing, even after hours of work. Worse, she didn't look surprised, and that really irritated him. Dammit, he could be neat if he had to. He could!

"No," he said stiffly, and casually kicked a pile

beneath his desk, hoping she didn't notice. "I know exactly where everything is."

"Uh-huh."

He ignored her, and when he looked again, she was gone.

The mess wasn't.

And he was very tired of cleaning.

Maybe, he figured, it was time to regroup. Shift gears.

Attempting to make himself more like Matt was a really bad idea. He didn't *want* to be like Matt. He liked himself just fine, and thought Katie probably did, too. She was just scared.

And with good reason.

He wanted to show her that risk could be good, certainly better than stability and neat desks. The scary part was, he wasn't even sure why it all mattered so terribly much.

Why *she* mattered.

Damn, this was getting complicated. Normally, he was good at complicated. But despite having so many sisters, he didn't really do well as it applied to a woman.

"Definitely need a new plan," he muttered, rubbing a finger along the thick dust on his desk. "A good one."

He mulled over the facts. One, whether she admitted it or not, Katie felt safe and relaxed with Matt. Two, she did not feel safe and relaxed with Bryan. She felt out of control, hot and itchy.

All he had to do was convince her that out of control, hot and itchy was a good thing.

How hard could that be?

7

MATT CAME BACK to work the week before Christmas.

The day he did, Katie hid out in her office, pretending everything was peachy, when of course it wasn't. How could it be? In her quest for Mr. Perfect she'd overlooked one minute detail—*his* feelings.

It went even deeper than that. She'd thought her needs simple—she wanted a nice, secure, happy life with a nice, secure, happy man. Someone who knew his goals and responsibly went after them, someone who didn't let fun run his life.

So why then had her dreams been taken over by a man who didn't fit the criteria, a man who lived his life the same way he flew his airplanes? With wild, reckless, adventurous abandon?

Now Matt was back and she was fairly certain her job was in jeopardy. Her stomach rumbled in spite of having bitten all ten fingernails down to the quick, which was probably a lot more nutritious then her usual breakfast of sugar-coated cereal.

Searching her desk, she came up with three candy bars and happily devoured them all. When she was finished, her skirt felt too tight, but at least the sugar gave her a sense of energy.

Holly poked her head into her office. "My, don't you look...stressed."

Suddenly Katie found a silver lining and managed a smile. "Be nice. This is probably our last day working together." She spared a thought to wonder how much unemployment benefits paid. Or how she'd explain the reason for losing this job. *Well, you see, ma'am, it all started when I gave our vice president a concussion while attempting to sexually harass him.*

Now wouldn't *that* look good on the old résumé.

"Why would this be our last day together?" Holly asked.

"I don't think giving Matt a bump on the head—" not to mention making him paranoid about mistletoe "—is likely to get me a promotion."

Holly laughed and perched a slim hip on the corner of Katie's desk. "You're making way too much of a little accident."

"Uh-huh. Oh, and by the way, thanks for tricking me at the party."

"I don't know what you're talking about. But then, I rarely do."

"I know what you did, and even for you, it was really low."

Matt walked by her office right then, his arms full of paperwork. He didn't so much as peek in. Actually, he sped up, nearly running by.

Holly grinned and looked at Katie. "Guess he's in a hurry." She rose and moved to the door. "Hello, Matt," she called, and Katie winced.

"Don't call him in here!" she whispered in panic, slipping out of her chair and onto her knees behind her desk. She ducked. "I'm not ready for the firing!"

"Well then, don't let him see you." Holly pasted a bright smile on her face as Matt reluctantly came back to the doorway.

"Don't worry," Katie heard her say to Matt in a soothing voice. "The big, bad accountant is gone."

"I thought I saw her...."

Katie crouched farther down and decided the heck with getting fired, she was going to end up in prison. For Holly's murder.

"Oh, she's long gone," Holly said sweetly to Matt, in a voice that said *I'll protect you!*

Katie rolled her eyes as they left together, and wished she had more fingernails to bite.

AT LUNCH Katie took her sandwich and soda outside to watch the planes landing and taking off.

Above her came the drone of an approaching Cessna. The wings gleamed in the sun, reflecting the spectacular blue sky. It swooped in close then soared upward again, the pilot apparently having a ball as he yet again dipped close, this time coming in for his final approach.

As she watched, the wind whipped her face, her hair, and still she just stood there, watching, knowing by the inexplicable tingle in her tummy who it was in the aircraft.

Bryan.

No man had ever given her that tingle before. Certainly not Matt, which, if she was being honest, was what had attracted her to him in the first place.

That tingle scared her to death.

But whether she liked it or not, the truth was very simple. Katie didn't want both Matt and Bryan. She wanted Bryan.

Only Bryan.

She couldn't even say for sure when she'd

stopped fooling herself, when she realized that she and Matt would be truly poorly matched. Yes, he was charming and intelligent. He was security and stability personified. Oh, and let's not forget the third *S*. He was safe. But he was safe only because he didn't make Katie's heart leap with excitement.

The plane came in for a perfect landing.

She sighed, in both appreciation for Bryan's skill, and with regret for what would never be. From deep within her came an ache, an old one. Her father had been that skilled, and that uncontrollable. Her mother had loved him anyway.

He'd nearly destroyed her.

Katie had witnessed it firsthand and yet here she stood, wondering, fantasizing... Had she not learned a thing? Did she think Bryan was any different?

She was a fool.

With a loud roar, the plane rocketed by her. At the end of the runway Bryan executed a U-turn and then headed back toward her for the tie-down spot.

He'd seen her.

Katie would swear it by the way her inner tingle spread, liquefying her limbs. She realized she stood rooted to one spot, practically quivering, waiting for the sight of him.

Then he appeared, his hair ruffled, his skin

deeply tanned, his eyes covered in aviator glasses that reflected her own wide gaze back to her. He hopped down with ease and grace and looked right at her.

Then he grinned.

She nearly responded in kind, nearly went running toward him, but she managed to restrain herself. Barely.

She was pathetic, melting because of a smile!

Over the loudspeaker on the side of the building, came her page. She turned away, so thankful she nearly tripped over her own two feet.

With not near the same amount of ease and grace Bryan had exhibited getting out of the plane, she escaped back to her reality—work.

HE CAUGHT UP WITH HER.

There were others in the large maintenance hangar; in fact it was fairly crowded, and with three large aircraft in the middle, she couldn't see everyone at once.

But she saw Bryan.

Surely he'd come to talk to one of the mechanics, or even another pilot. Maybe he was simply headed for the pilot's lounge.

He looked right and left, searching, though not for her. That would be silly, pretentious.

Ridiculous.

But then their gazes met. He went utterly still, then slowly reached up and tugged off his aviator glasses, carelessly hanging them on his collar by one earpiece.

Katie didn't so much as breathe. They hadn't spoken much since he'd been practically unmanned by her cat a week earlier. Up until then, he'd always looked at her with what could only be described as a hungry expression, as if she were a scrumptious dessert and he was a starving man.

But today he looked at her differently. With a good amount of hunger still, yes, but she had a feeling that look just might match her own. There was more though, there was—

"Mmm-mmm good," Holly said over Katie's shoulder, staring at Bryan and licking her chops.

Katie's mood shattered. "What are *you* doing out here?"

"Tracking down a stubborn vice president who forgot to pick up his messages." She smiled at Matt who was a plane length away. He had a stack of files in his hand, his glasses on his nose and his deep-in-work expression on his face, until he caught Holly's smile.

Flustered, he smiled back and...dropped his files.

Katie stared at him. Why was it whenever she saw Holly, Matt wasn't far behind? Or was it whenever she saw Matt, Holly wasn't far behind?

Before she could digest this, a beefy trucker lumbered into the hangar.

"Delivery," the man said gruffly, consulting his clipboard which had seen better days and had a sticker across the top of it that said Bite Me.

Holly gave the man the once-over as she walked toward him. "Sugar, don't you guys usually deliver parts to the *back* of the hangar?"

"Um...yeah." He swallowed hard, clearly rendered an idiot by Holly's wide, welcoming smile. "I don't have parts today, it's a truckload of office supplies. Ordered by—" he referred to his clipboard "—Katie Wilkins."

"A truckload?" Katie frowned. "But I only ordered the usual. Pencils, paper, stuff like that." She'd been distracted lately, sure, but could she have been *that* distracted? She glanced at Bryan, felt her pulse race, and admitted the truth. "It couldn't be more than a box or so," she said with one last hopeful protest.

"Not according to the order slip, lady. You've got an entire truckload of paper here."

Everyone looked out the front window, where the delivery truck had been parked. The back door opened with a loud clang and two more beefy men prepared to unload.

"I don't need that much computer paper," Katie protested.

"You ordered it, lady, not me. And it's not computer paper, it's toilet paper. A truckload of toilet paper."

BY THE END of the day Katie had heard every single toilet paper joke she could take.

Needing...something, she waited until everyone had gone, then made her way to hangar two where the overnight clients had tied down their planes.

The hangar was huge, and since the walls were metal, every little sound echoed. Dark had long ago fallen so she should have been nervous, *would* have been nervous in the past, but for some reason tonight, she wasn't.

She flipped on one low light and stepped inside to be immediately swamped by her senses. The hazy perceptions from the low light, the scent of aviation fuel, the chilly breeze that always raced through because of the high ceilings, she experienced them all.

If anyone could see her right now they'd wonder at her strange urge to come stare into the darkness at airplanes. But she didn't care what anyone thought—a first for her. She simply wanted to please herself, and the heck with all the others.

Another first.

At least five silent planes greeted her, maybe more. She couldn't see into the far stretches of the yawning hangar. They drew her, these sleek, fast aircraft. Strange, given it had been a plane that once upon a time had destroyed her entire life.

But irrational and terrifying as it was, she did indeed harbor a secret passion for airplanes. Bryan had seen that passion in her and that had terrified her too. He'd seen past her guard, had been able to read her so well when no one else ever had.

Scary stuff, indeed.

She realized she stood in front of Bryan's plane, her hand on the metal like a lover's touch as she was gazing up, wondering what it felt like to sit inside, what it felt like to be high in the sky, soaring wild and free without a thought or care.

"It takes both," came a deep, familiar voice behind her, assuring her that she'd spoken out loud. "Thought *and* care."

8

"SORRY," Bryan murmured, looking anything but.

Katie had been so wrapped up in her thoughts she hadn't heard him come up behind her.

His dark gaze settled on hers, full of a whole host of things that made her heart race. "I'd pay big bucks for whatever you're thinking right now," he said.

"Me? I'm just thinking..." *What?* That he was the most startlingly beautiful man she'd ever seen? Most definitely. That she was beginning to be sorry he wasn't the type to settle down? Yep, that too. That she wished with a sudden shocking urge she could kiss him again, without the white beard and fake belly? Oh, yeah. "I'm just thinking it's probably past time I get on home. I—"

Bryan laughed and moved even closer, his broad shoulders blocking out the one low light. "Just thinking about home, huh?"

Yeah. Home. Which had a bed. Which she could imagine Bryan in, the sheets twisted around his naked body. He would have a beautiful physique to match that beautiful face, she thought, and given his personality, and how he attacked life with full gusto, she could only imagine what a fabulous, giving, earthy, uninhibited lover he'd be.

He let out another low, sexy laugh. "You sure that's all?"

"Yes."

"The way you're stroking my plane, Katie, makes me think you're not telling the truth."

With horror, she glanced down at her hand, which was indeed still moving over the side of the plane with slow, methodical, loving strokes. With a small, choked sound, she jerked her hand back, but Bryan took it in his and brought it up to his mouth.

"Tell me," he whispered against her skin.

"M-my thoughts?"

He nodded, and nibbled at her knuckles, then soothed the spot with a soft, surprisingly tender, openmouthed kiss.

She let out a shaky breath, but it ended in an uncontainable moan when his tongue darted out and drew her finger into his mouth, which he slowly sucked while holding her gaze captive in his.

Her knees, which she'd firmly locked at his first touch, turned into jelly.

"Your thoughts," he reminded her.

"Bryan, when you put your hands and mouth on me, I can't think at all."

She'd expected a flare of triumph at that, but he simply closed his eyes, slipped an arm around her waist and dropped his forehead to hers. "So honest," he murmured. "So sweet. I want to taste you, Katie."

Quickly losing touch with her rational side, she searched her brain for something to slow down the moment, to give her some breathing room. "You seem to feel that way right here a lot. I've seen you in action."

"What?"

"Holly. Remember that? Her lips locked on yours? Not to mention her legs wrapped—"

"I remember." He dropped his hand from her side. His eyes went curiously flat. "I didn't kiss Holly."

"No, she kissed you."

"You trust me that much at least."

"I understand there's a difference between kissing and being kissed."

"Do you?" he murmured. "I wonder."

The sudden flicker of amusement in his gaze confused her.

"Come here," he said abruptly, and shouldered open the plane. He tugged her along behind him, until they stood inside.

"I'm going to tell you something I wouldn't admit to anyone else." He lowered his voice as if he were parting with a state secret, his voice husky with mirth. "I've *never* kissed a woman here." He still held her hand tightly, as if he thought she'd bolt at the first opportunity. *"Never."*

"But you've been *kissed* by a woman here. Is that it?"

"As you said, there's a big difference between the two." He leaned back against the wall, put his hands down at his sides, open-palmed against the wall. He should have looked helpless and vulnerable in that position, but he looked about as helpless as a lion out for a hunt. He spread his legs a bit so he and she were the same height, but other than that, he remained perfectly still, not making a move to touch her. "Come here," he said again.

As odd as it seemed, it excited her, seeing all his strength so carefully restrained. "You...want to kiss me?"

"No, I want *you* to kiss *me*."

Her heart nearly parted company with her chest. She managed a laugh, but he didn't so much as crack a smile. His dark eyes were filled with the challenge.

Could she kiss him?

Oh, yes, she could, she most definitely could. Slowly she leaned closer, careful not to touch him with any part of her body, though she had no trouble detecting the sudden tension that seized him when she came within a breath of him.

Heat shimmered through her again at the sense of all his leashed power and passion.

"Kiss me," he whispered.

She did, once, lightly brushing her lips over his. The jolt she felt at the connection shook her to her toes, but she wiped her face clean of expression and leaned back. "There."

"Hmm," he said with a lift of one shoulder.

"Hmm, what?"

"Nothing."

"It's something!" she insisted. "I kissed you, just like you asked." Defiant, her body humming, she did it again, leaned forward and touched their mouths together, only this time she lingered for one second longer, unable to control herself. "See?" she asked a little breathlessly, noticing that his hands were now fisted tightly as if he'd had to hold back from reaching for her.

"What I see is that you're holding back big time." He pushed away from the wall, setting his hands on her shoulders and putting her in the same position he'd just vacated. "Now."

Her stomach clenched. "Now *what?*"

"Now *I'm* going to kiss *you.*"

Panic skittered up Katie's spine because she knew perfectly well she could resist one little kiss, even if her knees were still quaking from the last one, but resisting a *big* kiss, when she knew exactly how thrilling, how hot, how everything, one of Bryan's kisses could be…well, he might as well ask her to jump into Niagara Falls without a life preserver. "I'm not sure this is such a good idea," she said faintly.

His hands had rested on her shoulders. Slowly they slid down her arms to the very tips of her fingers, then back up again, up, up, up, until he cupped her face in his big, warm hands. "It's just the difference between giving the kiss and getting it, remember?"

"Look, I realize you want to show me that *Holly* kissing *you* isn't the same thing as *you* kissing *her,* but—"

"No. I want to show you that Holly kissing me isn't the same thing as what we shared the night of the Christmas party, when we were kissing each other."

"Oh," she breathed, and though she held herself very still against the wall, just as he'd done, she could feel her entire body pulsating with anticipation.

"You're shaking," he whispered, his hands on her waist now as he gently drew her up against him. "Am I scaring you?"

"No! No, I'm just..." How to put words to what she was feeling inside when she didn't even know herself? "I'm nervous," she admitted.

"Don't be."

"Right." But her voice still wavered with that shimmering, uncontrollable anticipation. "We're just proving a point anyway."

"Uh-huh. A point." His voice was deep, husky, barely audible. *Thrilling.* His mouth hovered near hers, his breath soft and warm on her face.

She wanted to be kissed so badly she nearly met him halfway. *Now,* she thought, *please, now,* but still he just hovered, his gaze steady and intense on hers.

"Bryan..."

"Hmm?"

Do it! Kiss me!

"Yes, Katie?"

"Aren't you going to...?"

"Don't want to rush you," he murmured.

"You're not!"

"Because you're still shaking," he pointed out.

"I'm just ready," she said. "*Really* ready."

"Sure?"

"*Yes!*"

He came a fraction closer, so close she could feel the heat of his firm yet so soft lips, and she let out a little helpless sound of desire before she could stop herself.

"It's just me," he assured her, mistaking the sound for distress. "And you know me now, Katie, or you're starting to. You know it'll be good."

Yes, she knew that. And yes, she knew she wanted this kiss.

But what she didn't know was if she could trust him, *really* trust him, with her heart, with her needs, with her tender, new, burgeoning emotions.

His hands slid around her, then up and down her spine while, unable to keep herself entirely still as he'd done, her own hands moved over his shoulders to his neck,.

In the end, she lifted her mouth and met him halfway. The kiss started off slow and deep, and her toes curled as desire heated her from the inside out. She welcomed his tongue, and thrilled to his low moan when she opened to him. His grip on her tightened pleasurably, as if he couldn't help himself, and the kiss exploded with sudden urgency.

Again her senses swamped her, this time with the heady scent of an aroused man, the almost overwhelming feel of being sandwiched between Bryan's muscled weight and the even harder wall.

He lifted his head and stared down at her, his chest moving with each ragged breath, his eyes dark and so opaque she could see herself reflected there in the deep, heated depths. "There," he said thickly.

"There...?"

A whisper of a smile crossed his face. "Yeah, there. I know I was trying to prove something, but damned if I can remember what it was. You've scrambled my brain."

"I...really?"

"Most definitely."

"Well then...maybe we could do it again. You

know, just until we remember why we're doing this.''

"Sounds good." He bent his head.

She wrapped her arms around his wide shoulders, sank her fingers into his dark hair and hugged him even tighter to her, needing to be as close as she could possibly get. Incapable of holding still, she slid her hips to his. It embarrassed her how they undulated of their own free will, but she couldn't seem to control herself.

At her movement, he made a low sound in the back of his throat and pressed her back against the wall, pinning her there with his body, freeing his hands so that he could slip open the buttons on her blouse. When the silky material parted, he looked down as he slowly slid his hands over her shoulders, taking the material with him. Her breasts were covered by a very plain white bra, but it was thin and her nipples had long ago hardened into tight, hard peaks, thrusting out, begging to be freed, to be touched, kissed.

At the sight of her he made that sound again, then again when he brought his face forward, nuzzling her bra aside. His mouth slid across the soft curve of her breast to a beaded nipple, and he sucked her hard into his mouth.

chore, she drew a deep breath and wondered at the insanity of what had just happened.

It was supposed to have been just one kiss.

Simple, right?

Only it'd been anything but, and she had no doubt, if that plane hadn't just interrupted them, they might have made love.

What had come over her? Unable to believe it, she made her way out of the dim hangar. Actually, staggered was more like it, as if she'd just polished off a glass of wine. *Drunk on lust,* she thought, and let out a laugh that sounded hysterical to her sensitive ears.

At the door, she realized the night had grown cold, icy cold, which she hadn't noticed since she'd been steaming up the air with that kiss.

Kisses, she corrected. Definitely plural kisses.

Bryan was talking to someone. She stepped closer, then was very sorry. Standing in front of her were two of their staff members, both part-time mechanics. With them was Holly, who grinned when Katie showed herself.

"Well, well," she said, her grin widening. "I suppose you were just…what, maybe catching up on some work?"

"Um…" Katie's brain was still fogged with passion. "Yes. Work."

She heard Bryan groan, saw him move toward her, blocking her from view, but she didn't understand why until she heard Holly say, "*Work*. Yes, that explains why you're buttoned wrong."

Katie looked down at herself.

She'd mismatched not one, not two, but *three* buttons. "Oh, boy," she whispered.

Holly just laughed. "Yeah. Oh, boy."

9

ONE DAY LATER Katie found herself craning her neck for a better view of Bryan.

He flew by.

Then again.

And again.

In the long, torturous moments between those appearances, Katie knew exactly what he was doing, even if she couldn't see him.

Stunts.

Dangerous ones.

Upside down, sideways, a roll, he would do them all. And even though she told herself he was free to do as he wanted, that she had no hold on him, and he no hold on her, she still felt like grabbing him right out of the sky and locking him in a safe dungeon somewhere.

She realized she stood at her office window with her nose pressed up against the glass. With effort, she forced herself to relax, even as he finished filming.

She'd known, hadn't she, what he did for the thrill as well as the extra money? Somehow she'd forgotten that basic fact. That it was slammed home now when she stood quivering on the ground while he so foolishly risked his life, didn't improve her temper.

He was so totally wrong for her.

All men had a long list of faults, but Bryan had more than his share. First, he gave her hot looks that fried her brain. Second, he gave her hot kisses that fried her brain. And third, *everything* he did or said fried her brain.

Oh, and he was passionate about everything, including her.

Wait. Those weren't exactly faults, were they?

No problem, she could come up with others. He was startlingly tender and gentle, and he made her laugh at things, at work, at herself.

At life.

Darn. Those weren't faults, either.

How had this happened? He brought out the worst in her. He did! She'd sent an entire truckload of toilet paper to the maintenance hangar, for God's sake.

It had to stop.

She just didn't know how. So she went back to what had become her own private spectator sport.

She plastered her face to her window and watched him fly.

AS WAS HIS PREFERENCE, Bryan tied down his own plane, only this time his mind was not on the job at hand.

He'd nearly lost it up there.

"Ace! That was fab, man, absolutely—"

Bryan lifted a hand to Ritchie to ward him off. He didn't want to talk about his latest stunt, he didn't want to talk at all.

He passed right by the film crew, who were still congratulating themselves on a job well-done, as if *they'd* risked their lives for a stupid beer commercial.

The fact was, Bryan was disgusted with himself. Hell, he was disgusted with the whole world at the moment, and needed to be alone to think.

One wrong move up there and he could have died. It was a thought that had rarely occurred to him before, even on hundreds of previous, more dangerous flights, and yet he couldn't stop thinking about it now as his long stride churned up the tarmac. He entered the lobby and made a beeline for his office.

It wasn't as though his plane had malfunctioned or failed him. No, it had been his own hands, when he'd held the spin for a fraction of a second too long.

He'd had control at all times, but still, for the first time in his life, he'd imagined the *could have,* the *might have,* the *almost.*

Then imagined himself dead.

And it wasn't his own pain he thought of, but his family's. He was the baby, the joy of his parents' hearts. How would they take it?

And Katie. God, Katie.

It would kill her.

All for a stupid beer commercial.

He passed the women at the front desk, each of whom grinned and sent him the thumb's-up sign.

He passed several clients milling around in the lobby, who wanted to comment on his expert flying.

He passed Holly in the hallway, who managed to annoy him with one easy smile. "Do you make love the way you fly?" she wondered, her eyes laughing. "Because if you do…wow."

Bryan moved faster, needing solitude, needing, for some inexplicable reason, to touch base with his family and hear their voices.

Needing…

He moved by Katie's door, which was ajar. She

stood with her slim, straight back to him, staring out the window at the tarmac.

At his parked plane.

He stopped so fast he nearly tripped.

She'd watched.

"Katie." He'd whispered it before he could stop himself and though she stiffened, she didn't move. "I'm sorry..." Sorry for what exactly? "That you had to see that. That—"

She didn't turn to him. "I've been watching you fly stunts for months, why would you apologize now?"

He wished he could see her face, wished she was in his arms, straining against him as she had last night...he wished for so much he didn't know where to start.

"I'm really busy," she said pointedly, still not looking at him.

"Yes, I can see that."

"Then you'll be sure to shut the door on your way out."

Well. That couldn't be any more clear, could it? No matter that he didn't want to walk away, instead wanted to make her relax, even smile.

He was a man of action though, not of subtlety, and she wasn't ready for action.

Or that's what he told himself as he backed out of her office and shut the door.

Two minutes later he was in his own office with his oldest sister on the telephone, and just the sound of Mandy's voice made him smile.

"What have you done now?" she asked. "You only call me when you're feeling guilty about something."

"I do not."

"Uh-huh. When did you call me last, Bry?"

"Well..."

"Let me refresh your memory. You'd just forgotten Mom's birthday and you wanted *me* to call her up and tell her you'd been held hostage on some remote island."

"Hey, she would have believed it coming from you!"

"And the time before that," she continued, undeterred, warmth and love and affection clear in her voice, "you called because you'd just beat up Cindy's boyfriend and you didn't know how to tell her."

"I didn't beat him up. Exactly."

"I suppose he got that black eye by walking into a door."

Actually, he had. His sister's no-good boyfriend had cheated on her with a close friend. When

Bryan had run into him in town, the boyfriend had taken one look at Bryan's furious face and whirled to run, smacking himself on a door so that Bryan didn't have to.

"And don't forget when you crashed Dad's prized '69 GTO into the mailbox because you were busy yelling at me for wearing too much makeup."

Bryan laughed. "I was sixteen."

"And let's not forget our famous trip down the driveway—our steep driveway—on what you so lovingly called a rocketship, but was really just a cardboard box?"

"Hey, my arm healed and you can see almost perfectly out of that right eye!"

She laughed. "And who, in spite of her pain, covered for you?"

At her soft voice, he smiled. "You. Always you." Suddenly he felt better. Warmed somehow. "Thanks, sis."

"For what? Don't you hang up yet, you haven't told me what's—"

"For loving me," he interrupted, because it was the only way to cut her off. She'd talk forever if he let her. "I love you, too."

"Bry! Don't you dare hang up on me—"

Gently, he set the phone down, and when he looked up and saw Katie standing in his doorway, her hands clasped tightly together, nervousness so clear on her lovely face as she offered him a hesitant smile, his heart stuttered.

"You're busy," she said. "I'll just—"

"Stay. Please?" he added, walking toward her.

"You love your family."

"Always."

"They love you back," she said, retreating as he came toward her.

"Mostly," he said with a smile as he cornered her.

"Even when you do crazy stuff."

"Uh-huh." Their bodies brushed. She was breathless, and he was getting there. "That's how family stuff works."

"I was rude before," she said quickly, lifting her hands to his chest when he reached for her. "I wanted to apologize..."

"Katie—"

"I never meant to kick you out like that, but I was watching you fly and—"

"Katie—"

"And it reminded me of—"

"I think about you all the time," he said, dipping his head to slide his cheek over her hair. "Even when I'm flying. You should know that."

"My father—" She stopped abruptly, finally allowing his words to sink in. "What?" she whispered. "What did you just say?"

He stared at her, shocked at himself. "I think about you too much. Tell me about your father."

"No, wait." Katie had put a hand to her heart, absently rubbing there as if she ached. "That thinking about me thing. Why can't you just *stop* thinking about me?"

"I've tried."

"You're not trying hard enough."

"Do you want me to stop?"

"Yes. No. *I don't know!*" Her hands fisted in his shirt, probably to push him away, but she held on. "You're sidetracking me." She stared down at her fingers clutching him, and as if she just realized what she was doing, she loosened them and smoothed over the wrinkles she'd caused. "I came in here to apologize and you're going to make me forget that, or even why."

"Sorry." He had no idea what for, but if she wanted to hug him and apologize, who was he to say no? "Go ahead, beg for my forgiveness."

"For what?" she asked, annoyed.

"I don't know exactly, but I'm certainly going to let you do it."

"Bryan...darn it! You ruffle me."

"You ruffle me, too. Do it some more."

"This is crazy. I can't...do this. Not with you."

"Because of what I do?"

"Because of *who* you are. You remind me of—"

"Your father?" he asked, gently nudging her. "Come on, Katie, open up. Tell me. He hurt you, I know he did, and you never talk about it, it's not healthy. It'll make you explode, or—"

"Or cause me to be unnecessarily rude to you?" She let out a smile. "Too late."

"You haven't been rude, just...a bit prickly."

She laughed at that, then set her head on his chest. "I'm so sorry, Bryan, for so many things."

He didn't need another reason to draw her close, to tuck her body against his and hug her tight. That she let him was a bigger thrill than any flight he'd ever taken. "Come with me."

"Where?"

Bless his sweet and totally untrusting Katie. "If I said to the end of the earth, would you follow me?"

"I'd have to be pretty far gone to do that."

"So, will you?"

She hesitated, then let out a rueful laugh. "Apparently, yes."

Smiling, he led her to hangar three. When he walked up to one of his Cessnas, she held her breath. And when he took her inside, she let the breath out shakily. He strapped her into the copilot seat, sat next to her, put on his sunglasses, and she went more than a little pale.

"Tell me we're just checking out the new leather seats," she said.

"Yep. From twelve thousand feet."

"Oh, my God." She bit her lower lip. She looked as though she tried really hard to contain a sudden rush of excitement, but he knew her now. Yes, she was afraid, but she was also ready to do this.

"Okay?" he asked.

"Oh, sure. I'm great. Really. Couldn't be better." She looked nervously out the window.

"No stunts," he promised, thinking she shouldn't look so appealing, that it shouldn't be so thrilling to be doing this, with her. "Nothing but straight flying, wherever we feel like going."

"Just like that."

"Just like that. Spontaneity, sweetheart. It doesn't have to be dangerous."

Her gaze slid to his mouth and he nearly groaned. "Do that again," he murmured. "And I'll be happy to delay this little fun until I kiss us brainless."

"This is crazy."

"No. This is fun. Simple, easy, good fun. You've not let yourself have enough of it." He got them off the ground gently, took them into the right altitude gently, did everything as gently as he could, and nearly laughed out loud in triumph at the sheer pleasure on her face. "Breathe," he instructed with a smile. "Or you'll pass out."

"Oh!" She laughed a little nervously and drew in her first deep breath. "Yeah, that helps." After a moment she said quietly, "You're much more complicated than I thought."

"Because I can remember to breathe without instructions?"

"No, because..." She turned and looked out the window again, exhilaration and a sort of terrified joy shimmering from her every movement. "It's incredible up here, amazing. I had—" she turned back to him, her eyes full of so many things, incredible things, she took his breath "—I had no idea," she whispered. "You know, how it would be."

"It's good, isn't it?" he whispered back. "Being so high, soaring through the clouds, riding on the wings of air so crisp you can feel it humming through your veins with every breath."

"Yes. Exactly, yes." She swallowed hard and sent him a shaky smile. "I guess it's not such of a stretch to admit I was afraid to give in to this, because then I would have to admit I can understand some of my father's compulsion to do this. He was a stunt pilot.''

''I know,'' he said gently. ''And I'm sorry. But flying doesn't just have to be about wild stunts.''

''No, I can see that now.'' She tilted her head and studied him. ''I think maybe I can see you more clearly now, too.''

At that, their gazes met and held, and Bryan sent her a slow smile that she returned. It warmed him from the inside out.

And terrified him at the same time.

''I'm sorry it took me so long to admit I knew it was you, Bryan,'' she said.

''Me, what?''

''Beneath the mistletoe.''

At least they were high above the tree line, or he might have crashed. ''I'm sorry.'' He shook his head to clear it. ''Could you say that again?''

''I know it was you I kissed.'' She sent him another shaky grin. ''I've known since...probably that night. About time I admit it to you out loud, huh?''

''You wanted it to be Mr. Perfect, I understand that.''

''I'm sorry I let you think that, too.'' She grimaced. "I let *myself* think it, when the truth is, I really didn't want him at all, I just thought I did. I'm sorry, Bryan, so sorry I made you feel as though you had to change your entire lifestyle in order for us to—"

She went silent while he lay on a bed of pin nails, waiting, waiting, not breathing...still waiting. "In order for us to what?" he asked very softly.

She swiveled in her seat and looked deeply into his eyes. "It doesn't matter. You're not the set-tling-down type and I accept that. Just as I accept this irrational attraction."

"Irrational?"

She nodded. "Absolutely."

"How so?"

"Look, Bryan, let's be honest at least."

"Always."

"I loved my father with all my heart. So did my mother, but nothing we could do or say was ever enough to make him happy. He had to get out there, *up* there, had to push the envelope all the time. Had to risk his neck without a thought as to how we'd feel. Always. And then..."

"He died," Bryan finished gently. "He left you angry and hurt and afraid of letting yourself enjoy life."

"Yes. I understand you, Bryan, I understand, but I can't live with it. I hope you can accept that."

Like hell. "You don't know me very well yet," he said mildly.

"I meant what I said. I understand you, but I don't have any no intention of taking that understanding any further."

"Because of your past."

"Yes."

"I'm sorry, but that's just absurd."

"But—"

"But what? All pilots are crazy, wild thrill seekers? *No.* Some of us value our lives greatly, no matter what you think. Some of us plan to be around for another hundred years."

"A hundred?"

He had the sudden and ludicrous picture of himself at 130 years old trying to make love to Katie.

Oh, yeah, no doubt, he could do it. He let out a little laugh and she glared at him.

"What?" she demanded.

He grinned.

"You're thinking of something dirty," she accused. "I know it."

"It was that old-age thing you just laid on me. I was wondering if you'll still want me when we're really ancient."

"I don't want you now!"

"Oh, sweetheart, don't tell a lie I can disprove with one touch of my mouth to yours. You know you want me, don't you?"

She glared at him as if he were no better than pond scum, which pretty much gave him his answer.

10

It was the day before Christmas and not a creature was stirring.

Except Katie.

She was more than stirring, she was frantic. Somehow she'd fallen woefully behind in all her paperwork, not to mention year end preparations.

Somehow.

She knew exactly how. She'd wasted the past few weeks making an idiot of herself on a regular basis. Then yesterday she'd spent most of the afternoon in the air.

In the air.

It gave her a secret thrill even now. It worried her, how she'd acted. One smile from Bryan and she'd followed him wherever he'd wanted to go.

So much for being the grown-up, mature one.

The airport was hopping with travelers. The staff watched the clock, and for some reason they all looked so darn merry it drove Katie crazy.

"You may not have heard," Julie said halfway

through the morning, "but we're about to have one of those happy holidays. Lots of hugs and kissing and making jolly. It's called Christmas. You might have heard of it?"

"Funny."

Julie studied her for a moment. "You need another Christmas party," she decided. "More mistletoe."

When Katie's head whipped up, Julie's eyes were sparkling with amusement. "You could have told me you kissed Santa. I had to hear it through the grapevine. Was it yummy?"

"Who told you?"

"Holly. She said—"

"Don't tell me."

"—that you jumped Santa."

"Oh, my God."

"Did you really try to kiss him *again?* Is that how Matt got a concussion?"

Katie closed her eyes and groaned.

"Cool!" Julie grinned. "You're a goddess among us office women, you know. We're all trying to figure out what we'll use at the Valentine's Day party to kiss whoever we want."

Katie sighed and bore the moment. But as soon as she was alone again, she picked up the phone and dialed her mother. "Hey, Mom. Yes, I'll be there tomorrow night for ham, wouldn't miss it. Oh, and, um, Mom? Why didn't you ever marry again?''

Her mother was silent for a full ten seconds. "Well that's a loaded question."

"I know, I'm sorry," Katie said quickly. "I don't mean to pry, I know Daddy really destroyed your heart—"

"Damn right he did. No one should die that early."

"I meant because he was never there for you."

"What on earth ever gave you that idea?"

"Well—" Katie let out a little laugh "—he was always flying."

"Because that was his passion. But I was his passion, too."

"You…were?"

"I loved him heart and soul, no one else ever came close to giving me what he did." She sighed. "What a beautiful man he was."

Had she really gotten it wrong all these years? How could that be possible? Her mother had accepted her father, faults and all, and had loved him with a fierceness few ever experienced.

Could she do the same?

She said goodbye, and stared at the phone for a

good long time. Finally she rose and headed down the hall toward the soda machine.

She needed caffeine, lots of it, especially if she was going to finish by a decent time. Tomorrow she'd go to her mom's house, maybe they'd even talk more, but tonight she wanted to be home with her pretty little tree, her adoring cats—okay, not exactly *adoring*—and her annual video of *A Christmas Carol*.

She wanted to be alone to think.

Unfortunately Holly was standing at the soda machine, a huge cinnamon bun in one hand, delicious-smelling hot cocoa in the other, a secret smile on her lips.

Katie put in her three quarters, pushed the button for orange soda and eyed her nemesis. "Ruin anyone's life today?"

"Now *that* hurts." But she didn't look insulted. "We could be friends, you know."

Katie laughed. "Yeah. Right. *Friends*."

"I care about you."

"Don't take this personally, Holly, but I find that really hard to believe."

"Why?"

"Why? Gee, maybe because you're always making a fool out of me?"

"You're still upset about that fiancé thing."

Holly actually stuck out her lower lip in a pout. "I did you a favor. He was a quiet, mousy man."

"So quiet and mousy he dumped me the moment you flashed him some cleavage." Katie had thought it still hurt, but she realized as she said it out loud, nothing happened. No little pang in her heart, no resentment twisted her nerves.

Nothing.

"Well it took more than just a little cleavage—" Holly broke off at Katie's frown and cleared her throat. "The point is, I was just saving you some heartache down the road."

"And what about the Barbie vacation house? When we were six? You told my mother I didn't want it, that I hated it, when it was all I really, *really* wanted. She gave it to *you* instead." God, she couldn't believe that popped out of her mouth.

Holly couldn't believe it, either. "You've been holding a grudge for nearly twenty years? Over a—a *Barbie* house?"

Apparently so. How pathetic. "Never mind."

"No," Holly said slowly. "I think we should talk about this. What else is going on in that mind of yours?"

"The Christmas party."

"Oh, jeez…are you going to harp on that? Get

over it, would you? You ended up in the right man's arms.''

''How can you say that?''

''Bryan Morgan is hot, hunky, smart and funny—not to mention in-your-face magnificent— and he can't keep his eyes or his hands or his mouth off you. I have no idea what you're complaining about.''

Funny thing was, suddenly neither did Katie. But this confrontation needed to be handled, and now that she'd started, she might as well take it to the end and make a total jerk out of herself. ''You didn't know it would work out this way. Why did you encourage me to kiss the wrong Santa? I've been over it and over it, and it doesn't make any sense. Why would you willingly let me kiss Bryan, when you want him for yourself?''

''But I don't want Bryan, I want—'' She broke off, looked down at her roll, then took a large bite.

''You want…who, Holly?''

In a surprisingly open moment, Holly looked at her, her gaze guileless for once. ''Mmhphmm,'' she said around her mouthful.

''Who?''

But Holly just took another large bite, then suddenly tipped her head into flirty mode as her eyes focused on someone coming down the hallway behind Katie.

Katie glanced over her shoulder, saw Matt, and winced. He'd been avoiding her, ever since The Incident, as the staff lovingly referred to it.

She whipped around to tell Holly she needed to hightail it back to work, mostly because she was a chicken, but Holly had flattened herself next to the soda machine so that Matt couldn't see her.

Katie's eyes narrowed suspiciously, but before she could speak, Matt saw her.

The expression of pure terror on his face as he realized he was alone in the room with her might have been comical, if Katie had any sense of humor left about the situation.

"Oh," he said, stopping abruptly. "Hello," he added, polite to the very end.

Katie wished just once he'd say what was on his mind, but then again, since what was on his mind undoubtedly involved her early demise, maybe his political correctness was good thing.

Katie took a step forward, intending to go around him and back to her office where she would once again willingly drown herself in work.

Matt jerked back.

"I'm just going around you."

"Oh." He let out a shaky smile. "Sorry."

At that moment, Holly peeked out and sent Matt a sultry smile. "Hey there, stranger."

Matt looked at Holly. Holly looked at Matt.

The air seemed to thicken.

"Well, this is fun," Katie muttered.

But Matt didn't so much as glance at her. Instead, every ounce of his concentration was on Holly, and how she ate her roll as she slowly walked toward him, making a big production out of licking her fingers clean. "Mmm," she said with a secret smile. "Mmm, good."

Matt's eyes widened, and when Holly did it again, sucking her first finger into her mouth, the poor man nearly fell over in his haste to get closer. He recovered his balance, then walked directly into the wall.

The calm, restrained, quiet Matt blushed wildly, straightened and jammed his hands into his pockets, all the while staring at Holly's mouth.

"You okay?" Holly asked him, her eyes half-closed, smiling sexily. "You hit pretty hard there, maybe I should…kiss it and make it better?"

"I— You— *Well*." Matt closed his stuttering mouth and blushed some more. "If you'd like," he finally said, his voice a little husky.

Holly's smile spread across her face as she

moved toward him. "Where should I start, Mr. Vice President? Where does it hurt the most?"

"Everywhere," Matt said fervently.

Katie couldn't believe it! She knew for a darn fact she'd never come *close* to making Matt lose his composure, and she'd pulled out all the stops! She'd certainly never, ever, seen him flirt, and he was most definitely flirting now. "What's going on?"

Katie didn't realize she'd asked the question out loud until Holly, her gaze still on Matt, said lightly, "You had your Christmas wish, and I have mine."

Holly wanted Matt.

Holly had always wanted Matt.

It had never been about Bryan at all, but making sure Matt had been free for Holly. *"Oh,"* she said, but neither Holly nor Matt spared a glance for her. The two silly fools were staring at each other with stars twinkling in their eyes.

Well...good. They deserved each other. Disgusted, Katie turned away from them and went back to her office, trying to get her mind back on her job, but it was difficult. Seeing the way Matt looked at Holly, and seeing the way Holly looked back, had caused an odd ache inside her.

She still wanted what she'd always wanted, a

nice, happy, cozy future. Only there wasn't one coming.

Given her luck and aptitude for scaring men with mistletoe, there might never be one coming.

Bryan came into her thoughts. Bright, funny and most vexing Bryan. And because she was very human, she wished that she could...that he would...that they might...

She had no idea what was happening to her. They were completely unsuited, she knew this. And yet, she wanted to see him, darn it, irrational as it was. She wanted to see his crooked grin, hear that bone-melting voice. She even wanted to kiss him again.

But—and this might be a blessing in disguise—she had no idea what his itinerary was. Good. To go into the control room and actually check would require her facing how far-gone she was.

She went anyway.

Chet, one of the maintenance crew, was sweeping the empty control room. Casually, she flipped through the flight records searching for Bryan's entry... Ah, there it was—

"Whatcha looking for?"

What was she looking for? "Um...just checking."

"For...?"

For what? Good question. Her sanity, maybe.

"Bryan is already back," Chet said helpfully.

"Sure am," came that deep voice she couldn't stop thinking about.

She whirled and faced him. He wore his pilot's uniform. His aviator sunglasses hung off his collar, and his mouth curved in that welcoming just-for-her smile. "Want to greet me properly?"

"Uh…" Just like that, every single thought flew right out of her head.

Why had she needed to see him? For the life of her, she couldn't remember. She could hardly remember her name.

Bryan laughed softly, and mindless of their audience, tugged her close. Instead of the heated, passionate, wild, out-of-control kiss Katie half expected, he tucked her in tight to his body and simply hugged her. "Missed you, too," he whispered, and nodding to Chet, he led her out of the room.

"I did not miss you," she said, stiffly.

"Okay."

"I didn't."

He turned her to face him. He was grinning, the jerk. "You were looking for my flight plan."

"So?"

"So...you want me." His eyes went hot. "I want you back."

Her resistance deserted her. "Look, Bryan, it's not that simple."

"Yes, it is. Spend tonight with me, Katie. Let's ring in Christmas Day together."

"That's for New Year's. The ringing."

"Okay, we can do it again next week. Say yes. Let's banish your Christmas curse and have a great time while doing it."

"You mean sleep together."

"I didn't say anything about sleeping," he said wickedly.

"Bryan."

His fingers lifted to caress her cheek, his gaze softened. "You're nervous. I won't hurt you, Katie."

But he would. He could. "I can't."

"Yes, you can. Come on, it'll make Christmas morning special."

"I...don't have a present for you," she said lamely. As if that was her only concern! She had a million of them! "I can't think of anything in the world you could want that you don't already have."

His eyes darkened, and for a moment she thought he was going to say *you.*

How silly that would be. This man could have anyone, anyone at all.

"No presents," he said quietly. "No pressure. Just you and me."

"Bryan—"

The intercom buzzed. Katie was needed at the front desk for a "disturbance."

Saved by the bell from her own hormones.

Bryan followed her.

Two of their biggest clients waited for her, Rocky and Teddy. They'd been both best friends and enemies for nearly sixty years. Short, chunky and balding, with matching deep squint lines from long days in the cockpit, not to mention identical perpetual scowls, they could have been twins separated at birth, except for the fact that Rocky had lily-white skin and Teddy was African American.

They never agreed on anything, unless it was how much they detested everyone else. Both of them held envelopes and glared at her as she came closer.

"Merry Christmas Eve, gentlemen," she said. "Is there a problem?"

"You betcha, little girl," Rocky grumbled, waving his envelope, which Katie recognized as the monthly statement she'd recently sent out in the mail. "You charged me the going rate for fuel last month."

She didn't understand the problem until Teddy grinned. "I got the favored customer discount." His amusement dissolved as he, too, waved his bill. "But I got charged full price for tie-down fees, and missy, I *never* get charged full price."

"I didn't get charged full price there." Rocky beamed. "Because *I* got your preferred customer discount."

"You—" Teddy's face turned beet red as he grabbed for Rocky's bill, but Rocky lifted it high over his head, chortling as the portly Teddy leaped up and down like a bullfrog, trying to grab it. Rocky wheezed with amusement, coughing from his forty year old cigar habit as if he intended to lose a lung.

Bryan grinned at the spectacle, and when Katie glared at him, he only laughed. "They'll get it out of their systems in a minute," he told her. "Once they get in a good punch or two. Happens all the time."

"Well, I can't let them duke it out here," she said firmly, thinking of insurance premiums and lawsuits.

"Katie—"

"I can handle this."

"But—"

"Let me do my job," she insisted. "Gentlemen!" When they didn't appear to hear her, she reached over the counter for the envelopes, which were being waved by two greedy fists, high over the men's heads as they danced up and down trying to outmaneuver each other.

"Katie, I could just—"

"No," she said to Bryan over her shoulder. "Believe it or not, I can take care of this on my own."

"I realize that, but if you'd just—"

"Please." Envisioning two heart attacks, or even a stroke or two, Katie reached out farther, but the counter hampered her. Teddy and Rocky weren't just grabbing for their bills now, but actually starting to wrestle, and picturing the calamity when one of them clobbered the other, she became all the more alarmed. "Come on now, let's settle this reasonably—"

That's when Teddy slid in low and punched. Rocky evaded, and in a comical twist that rivaled any raunchy television wrestling show, Teddy swiveled with the follow-through that ended up going nowhere. He fell on his butt on the lobby floor. With an enraged bellow, he went for Rocky's feet, wrapping his pudgy arms around them just as Katie leaned all the way over the counter and grabbed both envelopes. Her toes left the floor, making her gasp at the loss of balance. She felt Bryan grab her legs, heard his worried voice calling her name.

But naturally, as this day was not one of her best, she overcompensated for her leap up. And as the laws of physics state, what goes up, must come down.

So it was only a matter of a second or so after Rocky tumbled to the floor in a heap over Teddy that Katie lost the battle for balance.

She would have toppled headfirst over the side of the counter, except that Bryan held her legs.

So actually, the only thing that fell was her skirt.

Right around her ears.

As she hung there, held by Bryan, his arms around her thighs, his face only an inch from her proffered tush, her plain white serviceable underwear flashing him, she was fairly certain that nothing else could possible go wrong for the rest of the day.

Naturally, she was wrong about that, too.

Because that was the exact moment that Holly and Matt made their reappearance. No one seemed to notice that Holly's lips were pleasantly swollen, or that Matt had untucked his shirt to cover the front of his pants.

Why should they, when the upside down, dress-flapping-in-the-breeze Katie easily stole the show?

11

BRYAN SHOULD HAVE followed his heart's desire. He should have taken a bite out of Katie's tight, curvy and oh-so-temptingly close rear end.

But he hadn't, he'd actually followed society's unspoken rule—do not bite a lady's bottom unless invited to do so.

And now he was alone on Christmas morning.

Christmas mornings were typically pretty darn good for him. They had been all his life. For one thing, he was the baby of a very large family who believed in lots of love and laughter.

And lots of presents.

Because he wasn't the most organized of men, he sat on his bed and wrapped the things he'd purchased for everyone. Better late than never, he figured with a smile as he unrolled some festive paper and dug in.

He wasn't getting together with his family until dinner, which was good. He wanted to see Katie first.

The nerves surprised him, but as soon as he finished wrapping, he showered, dressed and got into his car.

Getting to her place took no time at all, but he wasted another moment in rare angst, staring at the dark windows and wondering what the hell he thought he was doing. She'd made it clear over and over again he wasn't what she wanted in a man. Not that it mattered; he didn't want to be any one woman's man anyway.

He really didn't.

So why was he here, sitting in his car staring at her house like a fool?

Because he *was* a fool.

Was she even there?

Last night he'd been hoping they'd leave work together, maybe have dinner, and indeed spend Christmas Eve together, just the two of them, but those hopes had gone up in flames at Katie's vanishing act.

She hadn't answered her phone, and he wondered now if she'd skipped town. He knew so little about her, really, and yet he felt her knew her so well.

How could that be?

And even more startling was how much he wanted to spend time with her. Wanted to talk, wanted to share stuff, wanted to hear *her* share stuff. He wanted to laugh with her, wanted to make her laugh. Wanted to just...*be* with her.

And yet she was doing her damnedest to make sure it didn't happen.

Drawing a deep breath, he got out of his car and knocked on her door. From inside came an unmistakable meow, and he relaxed, knowing Katie wouldn't leave town with her cats alone in the house.

A few seconds later he could tell she was looking out her peephole. "Hello," he said to the still-closed front door. "Merry Christmas, Katie."

The door remained firmly shut, and he set his palms on the wood as if he could feel her right through it. "Katie? Let me in. It's—it's cold out here," he improvised quickly, setting his forehead against the wood now, needing to be close to her. "You wouldn't let a man stand out here and freeze to death, would you?"

"Go home, Bryan."

An apology, he decided brilliantly, staring at the door. Women liked apologies. "Katie? I'm really sorry."

A rueful laugh escaped her at his soulful tone. "What are you apologizing for?"

"Um...being a man?"

"I'm not mad at you," she said through the door. "I'm just—" he heard a clunk and knew she'd set her head against the wood "—just feeling stupid here."

He had to press his ear up to the wood to hear her. "Why?"

"See! This is just what I mean! It'll seem really silly to a man who's never doubted himself for a single second."

"I've doubted myself plenty."

"Uh-huh. Over what?"

"You," he said bluntly. "Over you."

"I'm just one of too many women."

"That's pretty much my point."

Another short laugh. "Was that supposed to make me feel better?"

"What I mean is, this has never happened before."

"What hasn't?"

"I can't walk away. I can't stop thinking about you. I dream about you, ache for you. I need you, Katie."

"You…need me?"

"Open the door and let me show you." At her silence, he sighed. "Please? I have a present." Another trick learned from his sisters, all of whom could be bribed. There wasn't a woman alive who could resist a present.

Except this woman, apparently.

"You said no presents," she said accusingly.

"Open the door, Katie."

She cracked it. "Why?" she asked warily, one cautious eye greeting him.

"Could you maybe open it just a bit more?"

"Well...okay. Just for a— *Hey!*" she cried when he used his superior strength to let himself in.

"Sorry," he said, anything but as he gazed down at her. She was rumpled, her hair wildly rioting about her sleep-flushed face. She wore a pale-rose bathrobe that swallowed her up. Two bare feet poked out beneath the full hem.

He loved bare feet.

"This is crazy," he said, wanting to devour her sleepy, mussed self on the spot. "Tell me what's wrong."

"You mean besides everything?"

"Well...yes."

She looked heavenward, then studied her feet.

"Katie?"

She rolled her eyes. "It's about yesterday."

"I figured out that much."

"You're going to make me say it specifically?"

"Well, since I'm clueless, yes. You'll have to say it. Specifically."

"Okay. You saw...my panties."

He stared at her, wanting to laugh, needing to laugh, but at the glare on her precious face he didn't quite dare. "Well, since I've been wanting to see your panties for some time, preferably on the floor, on the door handle, on the ceiling fan, anywhere but on you, I can't apologize."

Her mouth opened, as if she had to do that to breathe. He took the opportunity to reach for her, haul her close and put his mouth to hers. To help her breathe, of course.

She let out a little sound, which he swallowed. Then she grabbed fistfuls of his shirt. He liked when she did that, a lot, but this time she happened to get a few chest hairs in with the material of his shirt and he was surprised at how much a few little hairs, slowly pulled out of his skin, could burn like fire. "Uh...Katie?"

"Mmm." She buried her face in the spot between his shoulder and neck, and he decided he liked that, too, so much he could live with the fire in his chest.

For her, he'd do anything.

Which pretty much terrified him now that he thought about it. "It wasn't the panty thing," he whispered, holding her as tight as he could. "Admit it. You're just scared. Hell, so am I."

"I don't like being scared."

That made two of them. Not knowing what else to do, he kissed her again, a hot, wet kiss that had them both breaking off, panting for air.

"Where's my present, Bryan?"

Uh-oh. Damn, he should have known better. "Um...close your eyes." When she did, he reached inside his pocket for a scrap of red ribbon from wrapping his family's gifts. He'd intended to let her cats have it. "Okay," he said after a moment.

Katie opened her eyes and took in the red ribbon tied in a crooked bow around his neck.

He sent her a crooked smile to match it.

"*You're* my present?" she asked, her voice soft and hesitant.

"Don't tell me you want to return it. I didn't save the receipt. Plus, I bought me on sale, so—"

"Is it for keeps?"

Oh, boy.

"Never mind," she whispered, covering his mouth with her fingers so he couldn't deny, couldn't sooth away that slightly stricken, embarrassed light in her eyes. "I don't want for keeps, either.'' Then she replaced her fingers with her mouth.

Katie kissed him hard, her heart squeezing so tight she thought it was a miracle she could kiss at all. She'd take what she could get with him and be okay with it. She'd be more than okay. She'd thought she'd never get over her humiliation from yesterday, but somehow he'd done it, he'd made everything okay, just as he had from the moment she'd made her Christmas party mistake.

Only maybe it hadn't been a mistake at all. ''Keep kissing me,'' she murmured, and the words were barely out of her mouth before his head descended again. He kissed her over and over, until they were panting, straining against each other. He ran his hands down her back to her bottom. With a hoarse murmur, he drew her to him, burying his face in her hair.

''I can't feel anything but warm woman under this robe,'' he said, his voice so hoarse it was nearly gone.

''I was just about to get into the shower,'' she admitted.

He groaned, and with characteristic bluntness, opened her robe. Never reserved or shy, he bent his head and looked at her, his eyes so hot she was surprised she could stand so close and not get burned.

A flash of doubt hit her, because it had been a very, very long time for her, and because she'd never felt particularly comfortable in her own skin. "I'm sorry," she whispered, feeling his sudden stillness like a weight. "I'm not— My body isn't— I really hate to exercise," she finished lamely.

His unfocused gaze met hers. "What?"

"I'm not exactly...you know, perfect."

His eyes blinked and focused. "Are you trying to tell me you feel the need to apologize for this body?"

"Well..." Miserable, she nodded.

"You're kidding me."

"No. My tummy isn't flat." He touched it and her breath faltered. "And my breasts...they're not exactly...perky."

He switched his attention to them now and she could hardly speak. "And my hips..."

"Your hips?" he encouraged, but she didn't want to even go there.

"Forget it," she muttered.

"Never." He studied her, apparently not in the least disturbed by her curvy figure because he made a low, rough sound in the back of his throat, almost a growl, and hauled her close. "Perfect," he murmured. "Soft, round, sweet and perfect. You're beautiful, Katie."

"But—"

"But you do talk too much," he decided sinking to his knees and taking a love bite out of her belly before he dipped even lower, effectively shutting her up. Without another word, he opened his mouth on her. His hands, splayed wide over her bare bottom, drew her closer, then closer still as he nibbled, sucked and licked her halfway to heaven.

Unable to help herself, she cried out, because what he was doing to her simply caught her on fire. She had started to shake the moment he put his mouth on her. When she could no longer stand, he simply scooped her up and, following her breathless directions, took her to her bedroom. He set her down on the bed, but not before he spread her robe wide, gently tugging it away.

Morning light streamed in the windows, streamed over her nude body, but the last of her doubts faded in the light of his naked and fierce desire. Then he began to undress and she forgot all about herself. His shirt fell to the floor, revealing wide shoulders molded to a broad, muscular chest. Desperately ridding himself of clothes as fast as he could, his jeans hit the floor. His belly was flat, his thighs powerful. Between them he was heavy and hard.

"Oh, my," she whispered, staring, and he let out a groaning laugh. "Bryan, that's not going to— You're not going to be able to—"

"Fit? Oh, yes I am." He crawled onto the bed and reached for her, running his hands over her breasts, her stomach, her thighs and in between, all the while murmuring husky, sexy, earthy promises that mixed with his greedy and oh-so-talented fingers, arousing her to the point of no return.

He kneeled between her legs, his eyes hot and hungry, watching her closely as he put on a condom. He touched her then, making her cry out his name. He said her name, too, on a tight breath as his fingers slid over her hot, glistening center, and then opened her legs farther and entered her. "See?" he whispered roughly, covering her with his deliciously heavy body. "I fit."

Perfectly.

And then he started to move.

Instantaneous combustion.

It had never happened to her before, immediate orgasm, but it happened now. Endless ripples of pleasure rolled over her body, and her mind continued to reel as he thrust into her again. Then again. Time stopped as he raced toward his completion, and she raced right along with him.

Vaguely she realized Bryan had braced himself above her, his arms trembling violently in the aftermath, his whole body trembling, breathing as harshly as she.

As if to savor the last of his pleasure, he pressed his hips to hers. A low sound escaped him, one that somehow conveyed all she was feeling, and answering it, she reached up for him just as he reached down for her. She pressed her face to the base of his throat, where his pulse still raced.

One big hand came up to cup her head and he held her close. "I had to come," he whispered.

She smiled against his skin. "So did I. And we could always do it again, right?"

He went utterly still, then laughed. "I meant I had to come *see you.*"

"Oh."

He snagged her tight when she would have rolled away in embarrassment. "I like your idea of doing it again," he said with a grin. "I like it a lot." His hands slid over her body, holding her hips still so that he could rock against her.

He was already hard, making her hum in helpless pleasure as his fingers came around and slid between her legs. "Yeah," he said in a rough whisper, finding her hot and wet. "Definitely again." Before she could say anything, he lifted her up to straddle him, and in one powerful stroke buried himself deep inside her. "Ahhh." His eyes opened, held hers. "I felt lost this morning. Until you opened your door, that is."

She could hardly think. It took every bit of energy to open her eyes on his.

"I've found what I was missing," he whispered.

"Me?"

"You." He arched up, filled her even more, and she had the terrifying feeling that maybe she'd found what *she* had been missing, too.

THE DAY AFTER Christmas at any airport tended to be a wild one. It was no different at Wells Aviation. Planes coming and going, office staff trying to deal with end-of-year stuff, people milling everywhere, mechanics running like crazy, half-dazed in their after-Christmas glow, sluggish from overeating and overdrinking and not enough sleep.

Bryan felt half-dazed, too, but it had little to do with overeating and everything to do with not enough sleeping.

He'd been with Katie instead.

Thinking about it now had a foolish and idiotic grin on his face. Actually, the grin had been there for a full day now, and he couldn't swipe it away.

Nothing could.

Had he actually...fallen in love?

Okay, *that* took away his grin. Easily.

It couldn't be true. Yes, he cared about her, greatly, but...love?

God, no. How wrong that would be.

But what if she thought herself in love with him?

No. That would be impossible, too. She couldn't love him. He was unsuitable for that kind of relationship. He didn't know how to do love, and not for anything would he hurt her.

But what if she didn't realize that?

He'd just tell her so. Only she wasn't in her office. She wasn't in the lobby, or in anyone else's office, or on the tarmac.

Damn. By now, he had a plane full of passengers, ready for his chartered flight to San Diego.

"Check the mechanic's hangar," Holly suggested, when she came upon him standing forlornly in the lobby.

"How do you know who I'm looking for?"

"Oh, please," she said with heartfelt disgust. "It's all over your face."

He left for the maintenance hangar at a fast clip.

Holly followed.

"Don't you have work?" he asked, annoyed.

"Uh-huh."

After another fifty yards he tried again. "It's pretty chilly out here."

"I'm fine."

Exasperated, he turned to her. "Look, I don't know why you interfered in the first place, but I really think I can take over my life from here."

"Well, being a man, you would think so." Holly smiled serenely. "And as much as I'd like to take credit for that stupid grin you've been wearing on your face all day, I should tell you, I did it for purely selfish reasons."

"So why don't you go away for selfish reasons?"

"What? And miss the fun?"

"How do you know I'm heading for fun?"

"I didn't say *you*, big guy, I said *me*. *I'm* heading for fun. And you're it."

Bryan sighed.

The hangar was opened to the chilly day on both sides. Wind whipped noisily through. No less than four planes were tied down, being worked on by their team of mechanics. Power tools whizzed and whirled, accompanied by the steady drumming beat of a hammer, a compressor and the buzz of men shouting to be heard over all the ruckus.

He saw Katie immediately, and moved toward her. She couldn't have heard him approaching with all the din, and since she was turned away from him, she couldn't have seen him enter, either.

And yet, as if she felt him, she looked up. Across noise and clutter their gazes met, and a smile curved her lips.

Bryan went all warm and fuzzy.

Wait a minute! *Warm and fuzzy?* What was wrong with this picture?

Everything!

Dammit, he was here to tell her not to look at him like that. That if she thought she was in love with him she should just think again. That she should have stuck with Mr. Perfect...

No. God, no. He didn't want that, either.

Confusion was totally unwelcome, and he made the mistake of looking at her again.

She held a clipboard. There was a pencil in her teeth and another behind her ear. She wore a modest navy-blue business suit that had her looking mightily professional, and so adorable his fingers itched to grab her.

His heart squeezed and his confusion tripled, and of their own accord, his feet took him to her.

Gently he tugged on a lock of her carefully restrained hair. "So put together." He had to shout to be heard over the roar around them.

Katie blushed, clearly remembering how only the day before she'd been sporting a radically different look. Hair wild, completely naked, she'd straddled his equally naked body as she'd driven them both to ecstasy.

With not a blush in sight.

"I need to talk to you," he shouted, frustrated at the noise. "Can we…" He gestured outside, but she shook her head.

"I'm stuck here for a while," she yelled in his ear. "Invoicing."

And he had a plane full of people waiting on him. "But I—"

Another compressor joined the first. More hammering. And a new whine of a power tool upped the volume to beyond loud.

"Yes?" She smiled at him, an angelic, sexy smile in complete contrast with their annoying, overwhelming surroundings.

Tell her. "I…" *Tell her now, that her first instincts were right, he wasn't Mr. Perfect, and never would be. He wasn't a man she could bank on, didn't want to be a man she could bank on.*

"Bryan?" she yelled.

Oh, that sweet smile. "I..."

"You..." she shouted encouragingly.

"Katie...I..." Damn. *"I love you,"* he yelled at the top of his lungs, just as by a twist of fate, maybe his own Christmas curse, the compressors and all the banging abruptly stopped.

So did his heart as those three huge terrifying words rang out in the silent, stunned, amused, *filled* hangar.

Applause rang out. So did whistles and catcalls. *"Woo-hoo!"*

"You go, boy!"

"Bryan and Katie sitting in a tree," sang a group of mechanics. *"K-I-S-S-I-N-G!"*

Bryan stood there, rooted by shock.

He dared a peek at Katie, prepared to face her laughter, as well. But she wasn't laughing, she was staring at him, agog, as if she'd swallowed a toad.

Given the blockage in his own windpipe, he knew the feeling.

"You...what?" she whispered.

Oh, sure, *now* they could whisper. "Nothing," he said quickly. "I didn't say anything."

She didn't believe him, of course. And then she walked away, and with each step she took, his poor overwrought heart constricted.

12

WHEN KATIE TURNED on her heel and walked across the hangar toward the only chair she could see, she wasn't exactly thinking. She couldn't. The ringing in her ears and the pounding of her pulse took over.

Driven by a need to sit before she fell, she sank to the seat and closed her eyes.

"Katie."

He had the most wonderful voice, it should be illegal to have a voice like that. He also had the most wonderful scent, a warm, sexy male sort of scent.

That should be illegal, too.

"Hey! Are there going to be wedding bells?" one of the men called out. "Because I think we could do the wedding right here, right in the hangar."

"Yeah! We could part the planes to make an aisle," someone else called out.

"And we could throw O-rings instead of rice!" came yet another brilliant suggestion.

"Touching," Holly said. "Every girl's dream, right Katie?"

Bryan groaned, and Katie opened her eyes. Yep, his expression matched the misery in his voice.

Because of their audience, she wondered, or because he'd blurted out something he hadn't meant to?

Both, most likely.

The intercom system crackled again, making Katie jump. Mrs. Giddeon's voice echoed through the hangar, calling for Bryan to come charter his flight.

Clearly annoyed enough to forget they had clients and passengers listening, the woman threatened to personally hunt Bryan down if he didn't get his "fine-looking behind" to the front, and pronto.

"Would you look at that timing," Holly said with a tsk. "Can't leave passengers waiting, and you certainly wouldn't want Mrs. Giddeon hunting you down. No telling what she'd do to that 'fine-looking behind.'"

"I'm sorry," Bryan mouthed to Katie.

"No biggie," she said, shrugging, as if men mistakenly told her they loved her all the time.

Hey, she'd at least have a memory to keep her warm at night.

"No biggie?" he repeated, looking upset. "I—"

"Bryan," droned Mrs. Giddeon. Unhappily. "You have a mutiny brewing here."

"You'd better go," Katie said.

"But—"

"Oh, please," Holly moaned. "It's just a flight. You'll be separated for what? Maybe four hours? Cripes, children, hold it together, would you? Some of us would like to keep our breakfast down."

Then he was gone, and Katie was still sitting. *Had* to be sitting, since her watery legs refused to hold her. Around her the staff fell blessedly silent. Out of respect, she figured, grateful.

That's when she was hit with a shower of O-rings.

Arms slung around each other, her so-called friends and staff came forward humming—off-key—the wedding march song.

"I SUPPOSE you're going to pretend you don't want to talk about it," Julie said sometime later.

Katie feigned disinterest. *"It* being...what?"

"Helllooo...this morning's declaration? By the wild and hereto uncommitted Bryan Morgan?"

"Oh, *that* it."

Julie grinned. "How totally romantic was that! He declared his love in front of everyone."

"Yeah. Romantic." She was still pulling O-rings out of her hair. Obviously no one had heard him tell her he'd said nothing.

"Come on," Julie encouraged. "Tell me how Mr. Risk came to announce his love for Ms. Security."

Was she *that* easy to read? And anyway, it was no longer a matter of risk versus security. Yes, she'd probably always hesitate before taking a risk, but suddenly—or maybe not so suddenly at all—she didn't want to settle for status quo, either.

Bryan had claimed to love her.

Good Lord, the most wonderful, exciting, thrilling, fascinating man on the planet had thought for that one brief shining moment that he *loved* her.

Julie grinned because she'd spoken out loud. "And now back to our regularly scheduled programming, which apparently you're just tuning into. Do you love him back?"

Oh, yeah. "No."

Julie grinned. "Your dreamy smile answered differently."

"It's lust, not love," Katie said, frowning down at her clenched hands. She'd seen the horror on

Bryan's face, she knew he wished the words back. *"Lust."*

"Well, either one of them works as a hell of a bed partner on a cold winter night."

Maybe. For a while anyway. But lust wasn't ever going to be enough for Katie, there had to be more.

Bryan was what he was. She knew and accepted that. Maybe he wasn't flying stunts at the moment, but he would be soon, and that was scary, but okay. His sense of wonder at life, his love of excitement and adventure, it had all led her to this point. For that alone she loved him.

And he must never know.

She'd learned a lot about herself in these past weeks. She'd learned that being grown-up and mature is fine, but there had to be room for fun, too, that fun was okay. She'd certainly learned that maybe risk is part of what makes life so worthwhile.

Loving Bryan was certainly the mother of all risks. But she'd get over it. Maybe even try again someday.

And yet…she had the need to prove to herself that she wouldn't lose her nerve, that she would indeed risk again.

In light of that, filled with determination, she

marched into the mechanic's hangar. After all, it didn't have to be her *heart* she put on the line, right?

At the sight of her, everything and everyone went momentarily silent. "No show this time, guys," she announced.

"Bryan loves Katie, Bryan loves Katie," came a singsong voice from the back of the hangar, and trying to maintain her calm, she headed toward it, knowing it was Steve, their head mechanic and also part-time flight instructor.

"Unfortunately," she said in the face of his wide grin. "It's *you* I want to talk to. I want flying lessons." Behind her, everyone gasped.

Katie ignored them. This was *her* risk and she was sticking to it.

Because, really, Bryan had nailed it. All her life she'd been both fascinated and terrified by planes. Getting a job in an airport, however small, had been a step in the right direction. Learning to let a man like Bryan into her life had been another. "I want to start right now," she said quickly, before she lost her nerve. "You have a problem with that?"

"No, ma'am." He grinned. "Does Bryan know you're doing this? Because he might want to be the one to teach you..."

"Can you go right now or not?" She was in a huge hurry to do this now, to prove to herself she could. Without Bryan.

"Well…" Steve took off his hat and scratched his head.

"I'll pay double the going rate," she said rashly, and Steve lifted his brow, nodded and off they went. Just like that, with everyone left gaping in her dust.

Beat that, Katie thought with giddy wonder. It felt great. Better than great. It was almost as good as—

No, nothing was as good as making love, not now that she had Bryan to use as a scale.

But this was indeed a close second.

BRYAN HADN'T EVEN set his feet onto the ground when Julie came flying out onto the tarmac, her shirt flying up to alarming heights in the sharp wind.

"You're not going to believe this," she said, huffing and puffing. "But—"

A plane buzzed them, and Bryan scowled. "*Idiot.* That was too damn close."

"Yeah, about that—"

"Hey." His frown deepened as he gazed upward, shielding his eyes from the sun with his hand. "That's Steve's plane. Is he teaching some idiot to fly like that?"

"Maybe you should come with me," Julie suggested with a tight smile. "To the control room."

"Why?"

"Because that idiot? It's Katie."

BRYAN PACED the small control room like a caged tiger. He alternatively swore at the controls, swore at the sky, swore at the plane as it occasionally came into his view.

All the while Holly, who apparently had nothing to do except torture him, laughed, unperturbed when he turned on her with fire in his eyes.

"Oh, relax, *ace*. She's only taking a flying lesson."

"Yeah."

"And anyway, you probably have work to do." She smiled. "Why don't you vacate?"

He wasn't going anywhere until Katie was down.

"You're sweating, Bryan."

"Holly?"

"Hmm?"

"Shut up."

She only grinned. "Don't you see the irony of this? All these years you've been flying with reckless abandon, never worrying about what it did to the people who care about you.''

Bryan stared at her. God. How could she be so right? ''Well, waiting really stinks.''

''Bingo.'' And she softened. ''You know, whoever said *all* men are stupid wasn't quite accurate. You're not stupid, just slow.''

Bryan shook his head and grabbed the radio headset. ''Katie,'' he barked. ''Come down. Now.''

''That's not proper radio protocol,'' Holly pointed out.

As if he cared. ''Please,'' he added into the headset while Holly just laughed at him.

KATIE WAS HAVING the time of her life when Bryan's command came over the radio. She leaned back from where she'd had her nose pressed to the window, practically giddy with the thrill, and looked at Steve.

''Was that…a command?'' she asked, shocked. ''Was he *commanding* me to come back down?''

''I don't think a command includes the word *please*.''

''He *demanded*, Steve.''

''But he said please. I heard him.''

She'd heard something else, too—an inexplicable quaver in that deep, familiar voice, one that instincts told her was fear.

For her.

"Steve, would you say I did well for my first lesson?"

"Well..."

"Okay, forget about that little tower problem on the takeoff."

"We nearly hit it. Twice," Steve reminded her. "I wouldn't call that a *little* problem."

"Other than that, how did I do?"

Steve's lips quirked. "I suppose I should forget about that little dipping problem, as well."

"Hey, nothing wrong with a little roll."

"On your first lesson?"

Katie couldn't help it, she laughed. She felt so incredible, so excited, and she was flying. *Flying.* Up in the air, with the wind beneath her wings, and loving every second.

"Katie." It was Bryan again. *"Now."*

She borrowed the headset from Steve. "No," she said succinctly.

"We need to talk," Bryan said in his sternest voice.

She wasn't sure she liked his tone. "I don't think so."

"Yes, we do. Now, as a matter of fact."

Katie sighed. "Look, you said something you didn't mean. You said sorry. I accepted. If *I* can get over it, so can you."

Total radio silence.

Then he spoke again, his voice not nearly as calm, "Come down, now."

"You know, Katie, I really like you," Steve said. "But I really, *really* like living, so..."

"Bryan wouldn't hurt you! Well, probably not," she amended.

"Steve." Bryan again. Voice carefully controlled. Very tense. "Get her down here or—"

Steve flicked off the radio, but shot Katie a reluctant grin. "It's time, sweetcakes, let's take it home."

Yeah, it was time, she'd done what she'd wanted. She'd proved to herself that there was more to life than fear. That she could indeed put it all on the line and take a risk.

But now there was a man down below, waiting for her, and he was the biggest risk of all. One she wanted with all her heart and could never have.

"Let's go," she said, determined not to let anything ruin her happiness.

She waited until Steve landed. "Oh, I can park it!" she cried.

"No, I think—"

"Please? Let me have my crowning glory." With careful concentration she followed Steve's terse directions and pulled straight in, toward the hangar and its opened doors. The small figures standing there gradually came into focus. One by one she made out each of the mechanics. Then Matt. Even Holly. She saw Bryan, standing in the open hangar door, his pilot's uniform gracing his tall, leanly muscled body. He looked right at her, and though not one of his muscles seemed to relax, she would have sworn his eyes filled with relief.

Cocky now, she waved to him.

"Katie!" Steve yelled. "Keep both hands on the—"

Too late.

On the slight incline, the plane veered to the right. Three mechanics dove out of her way. Matt stood there a moment longer, his mouth hanging open in disbelief, terror in his eyes, before Holly tackled him and pulled him down to safety.

"Katie!"

"Steve, stop hollering, you're distracting me."

"But—"

"Hush!"

He only groaned and ducked.

She whizzed by without killing anyone.

That was her last thought as the plane's wing

clipped the steel hangar side wall, buckling it like a cheap toy as the plane skidded to an abrupt halt ten feet short of her tie-down spot.

When the plane shuddered still, Katie opened her eyes and risked a peek at Steve.

He straightened, looked out the window and grimaced. "Hey, remember last week when you almost killed our vice president and you didn't get fired?"

"Yeah?"

"Hope your luck is still holding."

13

HEART IN HIS THROAT, Bryan hauled Katie out of the plane. Before her toes could even touch the ground he had her buried in his arms and he was never going to let her go.

Never.

It shocked him, scared the hell out of him, but he could no longer deny the truth.

He loved her.

Because his legs were weak, he pressed his back against the other side of the hangar, the good side, on the steel wall that wasn't buckled like a tin can, and sank to the ground with her in his lap.

"You're shaking," he whispered.

"No, that's you," Katie whispered back, holding him tighter. "Bryan..."

"No." Fear and anguish and panic all rolled together into temper that overcame him now that he was sitting. "What the hell was that, Katie? What got into you?"

"Well, I—"

"What were you doing up there taking a flying lesson, and from someone *else?*"

"It's—"

"Dammit, how could you risk yourself that way, in a plane that isn't mine, and then that—that *approach*, though I use the term loosely! What the hell was *that?*"

"My life is my own, Bryan."

"Yes, but I want in."

"You…want in. My life?"

"I meant it," he whispered. "I meant what I said in the hangar. I didn't realize it, God who would have thought, but Katie, it's true. I love you. Enough to give up stunting, enough to know that I'll never want another woman, enough to promise forever. But please, *please* don't ever fly again."

He shouldn't have asked it of her, he had no right to ask anything of her when she hadn't asked anything of him. Misery and regret washed over him. "Wait. That didn't come out right."

"You don't want me to ever fly again," she repeated slowly. "Interesting."

"Katie—"

"Whoops," she said, covering his mouth again when he would have spoken. "Still my turn." Ignoring the commotion around them as everyone picked themselves up and took inventory of the damage, she looked deep into his eyes. "I thought I wanted safety. Security. Stability."

"The three *S*'s," Holly said with disgust, dusting herself off. *"Boring."*

Katie ignored both her and the baleful glance Matt shot her as he wiped at his filthy trousers. She looked only at Bryan. "I wanted everything I never got from my father as a child."

When he softened with remorse, when his hands slid over her arms in a caress, she shook her head sharply and kept her hands firmly on his mouth. "Please. Let me say this, I have to get it out. I thought I wanted *safe* love. The quiet, reserved kind that isn't really love at all, but just a teaser for it." She sighed and smiled into his eyes. "I was wrong, Bryan, that's not what I want at all. I want true, heart-pounding, butterflies-in-the-stomach, *real* love."

He pulled her fingers away from his mouth. "I can't tell you how glad I am to hear that. But dammit, you risked your life today!"

"Exactly." She grinned at him proudly. "So now I know I'm capable of taking a risk. I know I can do this."

"Do...what exactly?" Damn, was he always going to be clueless around her?

"Silly man. Now I know I can love you." She

cupped his face and kissed him softly, so very softly his heart caught.

"You...love me."

"Yeah." Her eyes filled. "I tried to save the best for last."

"Katie, sweetheart, do me a little favor." He could hardly speak. "Say it again."

"I saved the best for last."

"The other," he said as patiently as he could. *"Repeat the other."*

Her eyes filled. One tear spilled over and as he gently swiped it away with his thumb, she said the words he'd been dying to hear.

"I love you, Bryan Morgan, with all my heart. Will you be mine? Forever?"

His own eyes stung, his throat burned. "That's supposed to be my line."

"Well then, say it already."

Another tear spilled over his fingers and he had no idea now which of them it belonged to. "Will you be mine, Katie Wilkins? Forever and ever?"

"I will," she promised, and they sealed the vow with a kiss.

"I guess your Christmas curse is over," Holly said behind them.

Julie was also there, and she smiled. "From this point on, she's Christmas blessed."

Around them the rest of the staff gathered ooh-ing and aahing over Katie's erratic—and expen-sive—parking job.

Katie looked deeply and lovingly into Bryan's eyes. "Next time, I promise to let *you* teach me to fly, in *your* airplane. Okay?"

He gazed into her beautiful eyes as he stroked her cheek. Behind them he could see the damage to the hangar, the torn wing on the airplane and quickly calculated the expenses. He thought lov-ingly of his own planes, and how much they were worth. Behind her back he crossed his own fingers. "Next time," he said, and kissed her.

The Harlequin Reader Service® — Here's how it works:

If offer card is missing write to: Harlequin Reader Service, 3010 Walden Ave., P.O. Box 1867, Buffalo NY 14240-1867

NO POSTAGE
NECESSARY
IF MAILED
IN THE
UNITED STATES

BUSINESS REPLY MAIL
FIRST-CLASS MAIL   PERMIT NO. 717   BUFFALO, NY

POSTAGE WILL BE PAID BY ADDRESSEE

HARLEQUIN READER SERVICE
3010 WALDEN AVE
PO BOX 1867
BUFFALO NY 14240-9952

Play The Lucky Hearts Game

and get...
FREE BOOKS & a FREE GIFT...
YOURS to KEEP!

Yes! I have scratched off the silver card. Please send me my **2 FREE BOOKS** and **FREE MYSTERY GIFT**. I understand that I am under no obligation to purchase any books as explained on the back of this card.

Scratch Here!
then look below to see what your cards get you...

311 HDL C6J6   111 HDL C6JW

NAME   (PLEASE PRINT CLEARLY)

ADDRESS

APT.#   CITY

STATE/PROV.   ZIP/POSTAL CODE

Twenty-one gets you
2 FREE BOOKS and a
FREE MYSTERY GIFT!

Twenty gets you
2 FREE BOOKS!

Nineteen gets you
1 FREE BOOK!

TRY AGAIN!

Offer limited to one per household and not valid to current Harlequin Duets™ subscribers. All orders subject to approval.

Visit us online at
www.eHarlequin.com

Hug Me, Holly!

JILL SHALVIS

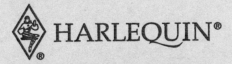

HARLEQUIN®

TORONTO • NEW YORK • LONDON
AMSTERDAM • PARIS • SYDNEY • HAMBURG
STOCKHOLM • ATHENS • TOKYO • MILAN • MADRID
PRAGUE • WARSAW • BUDAPEST • AUCKLAND

Prologue

LOST IN THE DEPTHS of hell, Holly pulled over, tossed back an Evian water and contemplated her next move. She could consult the map that lay open on the passenger seat, but then she'd have to admit she didn't know how to get to Little Paradise, which was the same thing as admitting she didn't know where she was going, and she hated that.

Holly Stone *always* knew where she was going. Okay, and maybe because of that, she'd always been a tad bit stubborn, but she couldn't help it. *Much.*

She could get out her cell phone and call…who? Her family? They'd get far too big a kick out of her being lost. *Oh, there's Holly, proving a beautiful blonde can't find her way out of a paper bag again.* That would be from her parents, who'd been patting her on the head, then shaking their own heads behind her back for years.

There she goes again, racing off without a plan

and blowing it before she even gets started. That would be from her oh-so-loving siblings, who'd never taken her seriously, not once, not even when she'd really needed them to.

No, she wouldn't be calling her family.

She could try a friend, if she'd managed to keep any over the years, which she hadn't. Holly didn't open up easily. For years this had disturbed her, but she learned to at least pretend it didn't matter.

Bottom line—she didn't play well with others, and she'd probably known it as early as kindergarten. It'd been reinforced in every job she'd ever had, and there'd been many. She'd been a banker, a photographer, a bookkeeper and most recently, an office manager for a private airport. She'd even almost had a boyfriend there, *almost* being the key word, though she'd worked very hard to get him. But then the boss's daughter had caught the jerk's eye and he'd decided he had bigger fish to fry. That was fine, because so did Holly.

At none of her jobs had she been particularly popular, which all came back to that getting along with others thing. Maybe she tried too hard, always pushing in order to accomplish her own agenda. People, especially men, didn't seem to like that.

But she was who she was. With a fatalistic shrug, she got out of the car, stretching legs that had been protesting the long drive from Southern California to this godforsaken part of Arizona over the past eight hours. Her heels crunched on the sun-hardened sand. The material of her clothes immediately stuck to her. Ugh. To avoid squinting in the unbelievable glare of the sun—why court wrinkles before she was even thirty?—she slid on glasses and considered her options.

Unfortunately, they seemed to be few and far between.

There wasn't another car in sight on the shimmering horizon.

The air felt thick with heat, despite the fact it was two days after New Year's. And her silk skirt was wrinkled, dammit. Time to get a move on.

A very large lizard zipped across the ground, far too close to her toes. She might have screamed and jumped back a little, but since there was no one around for what looked like a gazillion miles, Holly would have denied it to her dying day.

Just because she was out in the middle of the Arizona desert, with nothing other than lizards and cacti and rolling tumbleweeds for company—oh, and no one under the sun to call if she needed to— didn't mean she had to lose her cool.

She'd just do as she always did and take care of

herself. She was good at that. She'd consult her map and finish her trek. It shouldn't be far now.

Inside the car was much more livable than outside, and she cranked the air-conditioning again, spending a moment to lift some of the hair off her neck to cool herself down.

She'd always heard Arizona was hot, hot, hot, but this was a different kind of heat than she'd ever experienced in California. This was a weighted, dry sort that seeped right into her bones. It would destroy her skin in a week.

But she'd made a vow, and one thing Holly never did was back out on a promise, even if it was only to herself. She'd told her parents she'd be there, and though she knew they probably didn't really expect her to come through, she intended to do just that. This was a turn in the crossroads for her, a new leaf. All her life she'd been blond, decent enough looking that she wouldn't be cracking any mirrors...and seriously underestimated. She had to work hard to gain people's trust and respect, something she'd never been willing to do.

Until now.

Putting the car in Drive, she put her hands on the wheel, doubly determined to see this thing through.

And that was when she saw it, the small green sign that read: Little Paradise, population 856.

Seems she wasn't lost at all, but right where she was supposed to be. *Little Paradise.* The name must have been someone's idea of a joke.

Because Little Paradise looked just like her vision of hell.

1

WHEN SHERIFF Riley McMann's stomach rumbled for the third time in as many minutes, he finally gave in and looked at his watch.

Two o'clock. No wonder. He hadn't eaten since dawn, when he'd been called out of bed to help rescue a cow from a ravine.

Just one example of his fine, exemplary duties.

Actually, he preferred climbing down a sharp, rocky cliff, eating dust, and nearly being kicked in the head by a panicked cow that was going to end up as the Tuesday special than doing paperwork, as he was now. Maybe being sheriff in a ranching community like Little Paradise wasn't exactly challenging law enforcement, but he got to be outside most of his day, which he loved.

The slow-paced country life also gave him plenty of opportunity to work his own small ranch, which he also loved.

His stomach went off again.

With a sigh, he shoved away the mountain of

paperwork surrounding him, stretched his long legs and wished he'd remembered to pack a lunch that morning.

He could have asked Maria to do it. After all, it wasn't unreasonable to expect lunch to be a regular housekeeper's chore.

But Maria was no regular housekeeper.

So he was hungry. Very hungry. With longing, he glanced through his small office window across the street at Café Nirvana, the one and only restaurant in town.

It had been there since the beginning of time. At least since the beginning of Little Paradise. But after fifty years of feeding the town, Marge and Edward Mendoza were calling it quits. They'd put the place on the market for their retirement money so they could move to Montana and be with family.

It was rumored that their daughter, who cleaned house for some rich doctors out in California, had arranged for someone to run the café until the place sold. No one had shown up yet, but supposedly they were due to arrive any day now. Riley, who liked a change as much as any other guy, had to admit he wished this was one thing that didn't have to change.

Café Nirvana was the heart and soul of Little Paradise.

"Oh, stop staring at it and go on over there." This from Jud, his sixty-five-year-old deputy, who came into the office. He hitched up his continuously falling pants. "I can hear your stomach growling from the front room."

"I don't have time for lunch."

"Yeah, you never know when another cow emergency is going to come up."

"I have paperwork," Riley said with dignity.

Jud stepped around the potted cactus that currently sported a string of popcorn, making it the office Christmas tree. He shook his head. "You've had paperwork since the day you set your butt in that chair two years ago when your dad retired. He spent twenty-five years fighting that paperwork. It's never going to change."

True enough. Riley's stomach growled loudly. Pork chops sounded good. So did meat loaf. So did…anything. "What's the special over there today?"

Jud looked out the window and let out a long, soft whistle. "Looks like leggy blonde. Curves on the side."

"What?" Riley moved next to Jud, and saw the older man was right. That was definitely a leggy blonde pulling herself out of a red Jeep. Tossing back her perfectly coiffed hair. Smoothing down the blouse and skirt that screamed sophistication. Grabbing the small, elegant handbag that matched her ridiculously high heels.

She might have stepped right off the glossy pages of a magazine. Not that Riley had a problem with looking at a woman like that, no sirree. After all he was a very healthy, red-blooded, thirty-two-year-old American male, but she seemed as out of place here as a white, snowy, icy Christmas would have been.

"Well ain't she a fancy one." Jud hitched up his sagging pants again.

Fancy was hitting the nail right on the head. The woman walked like she owned the planet, with her bodacious hips swaying gently, her long, toned legs striding with unfaltering confidence.

Riley disliked her on sight. Not very gentlemanly of him, and it wasn't personal, but this woman had *big city, big trouble* written all over her, and he'd learned a woman like that and a place like Little Paradise didn't mix. He had his mother as a fine example. She'd lasted in this small town until he'd been a whole week old.

"What do you suppose she wants here?" Jud asked.

God only knew. "Maybe she heard about the good food at Café Nirvana."

Jud laughed. "That girl don't look like she eats much. But there's gotta be a reason someone like that would come to a place like this. She wants something."

Definitely. But Riley couldn't imagine what. "I'd better go see who she is."

"Yeah." Jud lifted an eyebrow. "She could be armed and dangerous."

Riley shook his head and moved toward the door.

"Well, she could! Hey, better frisk her. You know, just in case." Jud laughed at that, laughed so hard he had to bend over and wheeze for a bit.

That's how Riley left him, bent at the knees, pants sagging, breath wheezing in and out as he cackled to himself.

BY THE TIME Riley got outside, blondie had walked around the Jeep and was staring at the front of the café. She was taller than he'd figured, and as Jud had pointed out, definitely leggy and curvy. Her body was hard to miss in that form-fitting skirt and blouse she wore, both in notice-me red.

At her feet sat Harry. Harry was at least ten

pounds overweight, ugly as sin and the town beggar, but everyone in Little Paradise loved him.

"Shoo," the woman said to the huge orange tabby cat.

Harry just blinked at her and slowly lowered himself to the ground. With a grunt, he sprawled on the sidewalk, belly up. This was his demand to be stroked, but the woman just waved red manicured nails at him.

"Shoo!"

Harry yawned, and Riley grinned. "Can I help you?" he asked, coming up behind her. "Sheriff Riley McMann, at your service."

She turned her head, allowing him to see for himself that she looked even more beautiful up close and personal. Her hair fell to her chin, accenting a stunning face and the most icy light-blue eyes he'd ever seen.

She gave him the once-over, too. Slowly, she looked all the way down his body, then back up again, her gaze lingering on his badge. "Is this town actually big enough for a sheriff?" she asked.

Her voice was smooth as honey. And cultured. Everything about her screamed city, and though he should have been deferential and majorly polite to the newcomer, he was far too hungry for that. Besides, he knew the type. Polite would only get him walked all over. "We're big enough to court trouble," he said lightly. "Can I help you find something?" *Like the highway?*

"Is this really the only café in town?"

Riley glanced at the big, picture window. As far as places in town went, the café was Social Central. Proving the point were faces pressed up against the glass from the inside, staring at both him and blondie with avid curiosity. He could see Mindy, the librarian. Dan, the one-and-only mechanic for two hundred miles, maybe more. Lou, post office clerk and resident computer expert. Mike, the local contractor and wanna-be artist. All watching their exchange with great interest.

"Tell me there's another café," she said, watching them watch her.

"Not for at least fifty miles," he told her. "Café Nirvana is it."

She let out a small choked sound that might have been a laugh or genuine distress. "Café... *Nirvana?*"

He didn't try to hold back his amusement at her shock. "That's right."

"*Café Nirvana,* in the town of *Little Paradise?*"

She looked so horrified he laughed out loud. "Yep."

Tilting back her head she studied the stark blue

sky, then the wide, open landscape. Finally, she shook her head. "It's some sort of joke. It's got to be."

When she leveled those light-blue eyes on him with what could only be described as hope, he slowly shook his head. Nope. No joke.

He figured she'd go running right then, even though he knew nothing of why she was here.

Briefly she closed her eyes. "Cosmic justice," he heard her mutter. "Fate. Karma. You name it, I seem to court it."

Then she was walking away from him, but not out of his life. No, she went into the café, her look of determination as strong as her stride.

THE HUMUNGOUS orange cat was following her. "Shoo," Holly said again, but he dashed between her legs to beat her inside Café Nirvana, and nearly tripped her in the process.

"Gee, let me open the door for you," she said to his quickly retreating hind end.

But then she promptly forgot about the rude cat as she was assaulted by the scent of food. Bacon, steak, eggs, onions, peppers…mostly things she would never consider putting past her lips.

Not that she was a food snob, though she'd been accused of that before, but because she had the great luck of having a metabolism that worked with the speed of a snail. If she didn't stick to purely low-fat foods, she blimped up to the size of Miss Piggy. It didn't stop her mouth from watering helplessly as she considered the price her perfect size eight body cost her.

The audience she'd had a moment ago, the ones who'd had their faces plastered against the window while she'd gotten out of her car, shifted the moment she walked in the door. With unity, at each of their tables, they suddenly became busy with their own business, shoveling food into their mouths, talking, doing everything but look at her.

Small towns, Holly thought. Granted, everything she knew about them came from old reruns of the *Andy Griffith Show,* but apparently she hadn't been far off the mark.

The café was exactly as she'd imagined from the outside—tacky and nothing like the posh, elegant restaurants she preferred. Stark white walls, faded red vinyl booths with rips in the seats that would irritate the backs of everyone's thighs, not to mention destroy her stockings, and old chipped tables with mismatched chairs. The decor was...non-existent, unless one counted the cheap wood frames on the walls, showcasing pictures of what looked to have been bought at a blue light special.

Lovely. Her worst nightmare. Her heels clicked noisily across the cheap but thankfully clean linoleum floor as she headed for the counter, and the waitress wearing the ridiculous hot pink uniform behind it.

"I'm looking for Mr. and Mrs. Mendoza," she said, working hard at ignoring all the stares she was getting now that her back was turned to the room. Her spine tingled from all the blatant interest.

What was that about? Did she look like she was from Mars? She felt like it here, surrounded by nothing but dust and heat. She was used to Los Angeles, the land of palm trees, coconuts and friendly faces.

The waitress, an older woman with a huge gray bun piled precariously on top of her head, put her hands on her substantial hips—emphasized by that not quite subtle uniform—and gave Holly a serious once-over.

"Who's asking? Because if you're the I.R.S.—"

"No, I'm Holly Stone."

"And that name should mean something to me?"

"I'm here because Mr. and Mrs. Stone, my parents, sent for me to run this place for them as a favor to their maid, and her parents, the Mendozas, until it's sold."

"*You're* Mr. and Mrs. Stone's daughter?"

"Yes."

The waitress burst out laughing and Holly cast a glance heavenward. She was used to this, at least. All her life people had been amused by the total and complete lack of things in common between her and her parents.

Just another fluke of fate. Her parents were doctors and had spent their entire lives helping others. Their latest charitable act had been to urge their housekeeper's parents to retire early, before this hole in the wall sold, so the couple could get their first break in nearly thirty years of working.

Holly's two older sisters had followed in her parents' footsteps and were currently bringing immunizations to some tribe in Africa, otherwise they would have come here instead. They always helped out. Oh, and then there was her brother. He hadn't wasted his life doing anything selfish, either. No, as a brain surgeon, he was the pride and joy of her family, one who certainly couldn't be expected to take the time to serve omelettes in this godforsaken southwestern town.

And what had Holly become?

The screwup.

At that moment, and just to brighten her already oh-so-bright day, the sheriff strolled in the front door. He was the picture of the American cowboy; jeans faded and soft from constant use, scuffed boots, hat shoved back on his head to show a face tanned and rugged from long days in the sun. She doubted he'd shaved that morning, doubted even more that his wayward, thick, light-brown hair had seen a comb.

He had a calmness about him, and seemed very different from the men she was used to, men who spoke just to be heard, men who were into how they looked, how they sounded.

And yet despite his easy air, there was a wildness, a toughness to him, a sense that he was always poised for action.

Oh, and he was gorgeous. *Seriously* gorgeous, with all that out-of-control sun-kissed brown hair, even browner sinful eyes and a smile meant to make a woman's knees weak—if a woman was so inclined. Which Holly wasn't.

It wasn't that she didn't like men, but more that she didn't trust them, not with anything important anyway. The sheriff's easy, long-legged stride might exude charm and a laid-back sex appeal, not to mention he had to be the sexiest, most physical male she'd ever seen, but she was completely immune to it.

For the most part.

When he saw her, he didn't so much as falter, which might have been a direct hit to her ego. After all, men had been noticing her since puberty, but not this man. Still, something told her he'd come inside because of her. When she narrowed her eyes at him, wondering, he simply grinned and winked.

Winked!

She attributed her increased pulse rate to annoyance and firmly reminded herself cowboys, no matter how big and magnificent, did nothing for her. *Nothing*.

"Are they here? The Mendozas?" she asked the waitress dressed in obnoxious pink, ignoring Cowboy Sheriff with the same ease she ignored her growing audience.

The woman waved at the sheriff as if they were long lost buddies.

He cheerfully waved back.

Finally, the woman returned her attention to Holly, whose patience had worn thin. "My daughter said her lovely, *lovely* bosses were sending me help so that my husband and I could move to Montana where my sister lives. Is that you, then? You're the help?''

At that, everyone in the café stopped pretending to eat and listened with unabashed interest. Even the cat lifted his head and looked at her.

The sheriff, now leaning negligently against the counter, sipping at a mug the waitress had handed him, waited as well.

Holly's composure faltered briefly. *The help?* Is that what her parents had blithely told everyone? She'd given up her life and job in California to come to the depths of the desert of all places, without a Chinese takeout or dry-cleaning place for hundreds of miles, hoping for once and all to finally gain her family's respect, and they'd called her *the help?*

''They left a message for you, by the way,'' the woman told her.

Okay, good. A message was good. Holly hadn't seen her parents all year, partly because they were so busy saving lives, but mostly because she'd been avoiding them. It wasn't something she was entirely comfortable thinking about, but she knew they never took her seriously and even though she pretended it didn't matter, it did.

She was hoping things would change now. She was hoping other things would change, too. That maybe she would someday find her niche, her home, her place in life. And though she'd deny this, she secretly wished for things like love and a soul mate. Someone who would understand her through and through.

But there'd never been anyone like that in her life, and there probably never would be.

She needed to remember that.

She waited for her message, but Mrs. Mendoza seemed to relish hanging on to it. Luckily Holly was the most stubborn, determined woman on the face of the planet, well used to getting her way. Pinky here didn't have a shot.

Sure enough, after a full moment of strained eye contact, the woman relented. She took off her apron and hung it on a hook on the wall with great ceremony. "They said, and I quote, 'Tell her if she shows, thank you for handling everything, it should only be a month or so.' You can stay upstairs until the place sells."

So many questions flew through Holly's head she got dizzy. "What do you mean *thank you for handling everything*?"

"Everything as in…everything."

Holly tried to not panic. "There's no one else…but *me?*"

"Nope."

"For a *month?*" This was bad, very bad.

"Or so."

And then the woman walked away! She went to the entrance of what Holly assumed was the kitchen and yelled, "Eddie! We're done here. Let's hit it! Montana here we come!"

A man came out of the kitchen and removed his white chef's hat. He was grinning from ear to ear. Together they headed toward the door, stopping to give every customer a big hug and kiss.

"Wait!" Holly called, and when they looked at her, she couldn't think which of her thousand questions to start with. She pointed to the big, fat orange cat laying in the aisle asleep. "Your cat! What about your cat?"

"Harry belongs to the café," the man said, but both of them stopped to pet the cat, lavishing the sleepy, purring creature with affection, which he soaked up.

"He can't stay." Holly looked around her in horror. "He'll get *hair* everywhere."

"Don't be silly," the man said in baby talk, addressing the cat. "Everyone loves Harry, isn't that right, big guy, everyone *wuvs* you."

Great. Everyone "wuvved" Harry.

Everyone except for Holly, who'd never owned an animal in her life. "But I don't know anything about cats,'' she protested. Not that it mattered. When it came right down to it, she knew nothing about running a café by herself, either.

But the thought of caring for an animal somehow seemed a lot more terrifying than caring for a place.

''We can't take him,'' Eddie said firmly but sadly. ''He's yours now.''

''No—! Wait!''

The door shut behind them. Holly could only stare at it, the sinking feeling in her stomach growing to huge proportions.

She looked down at the cat, and would have sworn Harry smiled at her.

Chaos, panic and disorder, she could imagine him thinking. *My work here is done.*

And with that, he rolled over, stretched and yawned so wide she thought his head would turn inside out, then closed his eyes.

His purr seemed to echo throughout the entire dining area, mocking her with his happiness.

''Excuse me, miss?'' One of the customers lifted his mug toward Holly. ''I need a refill.''

''And I need my roast beef,'' called another.

Holly stared at them.

''I think they're talking to you,'' the sheriff said

helpfully. "And I could use some cream, if you don't mind."

Holly looked at the bright-pink apron hanging off the hook, imagined it against the creamy red silk of her skirt and blouse, and stood there, flabbergasted at the turn of events her life had taken.

"Better hurry." The sheriff lifted an eyebrow at the growing murmurs from the customers. "This isn't a patient sort of crowd."

Good Lord. What had she done?

2

THOUGH HE WAS snowed under with paperwork, Riley took a seat on one of the stools at the counter because this was going to be too good to be missed.

City Woman had wasted no more than ten seconds staring after the Mendozas. Then she lifted her chin, chilled her dismay into a cool calm and looked around her regally, as if she had everything under control.

It was fascinating to watch. *She* was fascinating to watch.

Riley had no idea what made Holly Stone tick, but he figured she was a spoiled-rotten socialite with nothing else to do with her time. Bored, she'd decided to see how the other half lived by agreeing to work as a waitress.

But that didn't really add up because a spoiled-rotten socialite out slumming wouldn't pick a place so far out of the way as Little Paradise. She'd want to be closer to home in case she broke a fingernail.

He knew she wasn't a dirt-poor relation of the city doctors with no choice but to work for a living. All that attitude and snootiness didn't come from being poor.

Maybe it was none of the above; maybe she was running away from something or someone.

That didn't fly, either. She seemed too ornery and too tough to let anyone boss or bully her around.

Slowly, she reached for the hot pink apron Marge had worn for decades. Holding it in her fingers as if it were a soiled diaper, she looked down at her own designer outfit, clearly attempting to decide which was worse—the hot pink or a stained blouse.

"What's your plan here?" Riley asked her.

"Haven't a clue," she answered, staring down at herself. "And isn't this just too lovely for words."

"I'd go with the apron if I were you," he said helpfully. "Cooking is a messy business."

Her gaze whipped to his as if the thought of cooking had yet to occur to her.

He laughed. "You do know how to cook?"

"Well…"

"Excuse me, miss?" It was Dan, the mechanic, holding up an empty coffee mug. He looked hopeful. "Are we going to get more coffee over here sometime today?"

Before she could answer, Lou, the postal clerk, waved his hand. "And I need my order," he called out. "Preferably *before* my next shift is over."

Riley had to give her credit. For someone he suspected had never waited a single table in her life, she didn't so much as flinch. But it was the oddest thing. For one minute there he thought she seemed uncertain, vulnerable, but then she turned back to him and her gaze was as cool as ever.

He had to laugh at himself. Though it was second nature to him to rush in to help or save people—anyone, even women who annoyed him—*this* woman didn't need his help. She'd probably never been uncertain or vulnerable in her life. "Looks like you're going to have to start serving sooner than later, princess."

"Princess?" Her eyes went glacial. "Did you just call me...*princess?*"

"It seemed to fit."

She shook her head and stared around her in bafflement. "It's official. I've stepped into the twilight zone."

"Miss?"

This time it was Mindy, the librarian. Her

glasses slipping nearly off her nose, she raised her finger and smiled hesitantly. "Can I get—"

"Hold your horses!" Holly told her. Slamming her arms into the apron, she then glared at Riley. "And what are you smiling at?" she demanded.

"Your lovely bedside manner."

She growled at that and proceeded to ignore him. It wasn't often he was ignored by the opposite sex, but in this case he didn't mind. Holly Stone was most definitely not his type, though he did understand her. All too well.

Riley had grown up with a sheriff as a father. Ted McMann had been warm, loving and, given that his wife had left him for the faster city life, stubborn and tough to a fault. As a result of that unrelenting authority, Riley had spent a good part of his youth tearing up the town and racing with a fast crowd. Hurting his father. Still, it hadn't taken Riley long to figure which side of the law he wanted to be on—the side without the bars. His father was still grateful.

Now Riley enjoyed the slow, sweet country life very much. He loved his ranch, he loved his job, and he loved the wild, open desert that had been his home since birth. But he didn't fool himself. He wasn't likely to find a woman suited to this life, not for keeps anyway. In his experience, both with his mother and the few women he'd gotten serious enough about to even contemplate settling down with, women craved far more than what small-town living could provide.

Not Riley, not anymore. Yes, he'd left Little Paradise for college, but after four years, he'd missed it with all his heart and soul. He loved the huge, open spaces, the quiet, the sense of freedom he'd never found in a place teeming with too many people and things. Yeah, he'd been ready to come home.

Princess here, on the other hand, didn't look ready for a break from where *she'd* come from. She was glowering at her customers as if this was all their fault.

"I almost hate to butt in here," he said with amusement. "Because honestly, it's so much fun to watch you work this out by yourself. But I feel the need to point out that this is what some would consider a *people* job."

"Do I look like a people person?" She yanked the apron strings around her waist and tied it. With an air of dignity better suited to royalty than a tiny café out in the middle of nowhere, she studied the mess behind the counter.

Marge had been an excellent cook, an even better people person, but cleaning up after herself hadn't been her strong suit.

The place was a disaster area.

Behind them, the clientele grew restless. From the kitchen came utter silence, the meaning of which obviously didn't escape Holly, because she chewed on her bottom lip and stared through the service window, clearly wondering how she was going to manage both serving and cooking.

"So, what's the plan?" Riley asked her.

She ignored that, too, so he stood, then moved behind the counter. The area was small. Holly was close enough that he could see her eyes weren't completely light blue, as he'd first thought, but had little specs of darker blue swimming in them. And though he was tall, she came up past his chin, so that he could look into her eyes without stooping.

Surprised when he did just that, she backed up a step, then lifted her chin again. "What are you doing?"

He smiled, enjoying her queen-to-peasant tone. "Just looking at you."

"Well…stop it. And why are you back here anyway?"

Hell if he knew. She was as annoying as any woman he'd ever met and yet for some reason, she stirred his blood. "Don't you want help?"

She looked horrified. "From *you?*"

Oh, yeah. She was definitely annoying.

"What does a cowboy, much less a sheriff, know about running a café?" she asked.

"What do *you* know about running a café?"

He had her there, he could tell. She just glared at him, apparently her standard response when she didn't know what else to do. Riley imagined she alienated quite a few people that way, but for some reason, it only amused him all the more. "What's the plan?" he asked again, tying on Eddie's old apron, which was thankfully dyed beige, not hot pink.

"Why should I tell you?"

He smiled at that. "Because in case you haven't noticed, you're about to handle this place all by your little lonesome. In fact, if I were you, I'd be super-extra sweet to me."

Her gaze was glacial. "I don't do sweet."

He laughed and went for the coffeepot to pour himself a cup, watching as she vanished into the kitchen. "Don't I know it."

HOLLY STOOD in front of the huge grill, staring down at the congealing fat surrounding the burgers, which good old Eddie had been cooking for who knew which one of the customers out front.

She supposed she could go out there and ask, but then she'd have to admit she was clueless, and she'd have to admit it in front of Riley McMann, the first man she'd ever met with the unique ability to completely ruffle her feathers.

No man did that to her. *She* did that to *them.* But not in this case, damn him anyway.

Things were definitely out of control.

Frustration swamped her. She felt as if she were floundering in a situation, scrambling to get what she wanted.

And what she wanted was so simple. It always had been.

Acceptance.

Compassion.

The *L* word. *Love.*

She deserved those things, didn't she? Sure, she'd always been a bit of a troublemaker, but that was only because she knew what she wanted, and knew if she didn't go after it full-steam ahead, no one was going to hand it to her.

No one had ever handed her anything. Instead they took one look and judged her on looks alone. So she had good genes, so what? Being blond and smart didn't mean jack diddly unless she was respected for it, which she wasn't.

From out front, someone called for the waitress.

Ha! She knew even less about how to be a waitress than she did how to cook.

But if she was going to make this work, if she was going to prove her worth to her family for once and all, she needed to learn both, and quickly.

So, what first? Where to start?

"You turn on the stove."

Damn, but she already knew that low, husky voice all too well. She turned and, yep, sure enough, there stood Riley. He touched a hand to his hat, setting it back on his head so that she could get a good look at his rugged, tanned, far-too-good-looking face, and the grin that went with it. "Let me guess," she said in the most alienating tone she had. "Your doughnut break isn't over yet."

He just laughed good-naturedly. "Actually, I prefer ice cream to donuts, thanks."

"Don't you have some bad guys to catch or something?"

He walked straight toward her, still smiling. A lock of hair had fallen over his forehead and his dark eyes were sparkling with good humor.

He was invading her space again.

And he just kept coming, his wide shoulders taking up most of her view, his long jeans-clad legs closing the gap between them with alarming speed.

She stood her ground and lifted her chin, daring him to come closer.

He did. Then closer still.

When he was within a foot of her, so close she could see the tiny laugh lines fanning out from his eyes, she caved and backed up.

At her movement, his grin spread and he reached out, brushing her hip with his long fingers. Forcing herself completely still was one of the hardest things she'd ever done, though she didn't understand why. He was just a man. She wasn't afraid of him.

"What are you doing?" she asked, cool as a cucumber and proud of it. He didn't have to know her heart had nearly accelerated right out of her chest.

All because of a touch.

He flicked the knob on the range, heating it. Then he looked at her, mischief in his smile, in every inch of his strong, masculine, sexy, slightly dangerous-looking body.

Dangerous because she liked strong, masculine and sexy.

Too bad she didn't like *him*.

"Just getting you started," he said.

"Oh." Her voice was breathless, and irritated. She cleared her throat.

He was *still* far too close.

"What did you think I was doing?"

"Um…" The phone on the wall rang and Holly dove for it, pathetically thankful for the diversion. "Hello!"

"Is this Café Nirvana? I need to speak to my daughter."

"Mother!" Holly gripped the phone tight, never in her life so happy to hear anyone's voice, even her mother's. "Where are you?" she asked, hoping the answer was *close*.

"Your father and I have decided to take a vacation."

"But…you've never taken a vacation in your life."

"I know. It's definitely time, don't you think?"

No. No, she didn't! "Mother, I'm glad you've decided to take some time for yourselves, but don't you think maybe now is a bad time?"

"It's the holidays."

"Exactly my point," Holly said, relieved her mother was coming back to her senses. "You can't take a vacation over the holidays. It's…too crowded."

"Which is why it's so perfect. We're going to avoid all the crowds by taking a cruise."

"A cruise."

"A month-long cruise of the Greek Islands, isn't that exciting? We'll be back before Valentine's Day."

Holly's stomach sank to her toes. "That's a very long time. What about the café?"

"Oh, the Nirvana? You said you would handle it. It'll sell sooner or later."

Holly gripped the phone tighter. "You said a month."

"Give or take. And you're always saying you wish we would take your exploits more seriously."

"Yes, but—"

"And as we've been telling you for years, there's no time like the present."

Over the line Holly could hear the murmur of a crowd, then the unmistakable horn blow of a ship, a very *large* ship.

"Gotta go, dear."

"But—"

"Take care of that place. We promised you would."

"Yes, but—"

Click.

Holly stared at the receiver in her hand and felt as if she'd been run over by a Mack truck. "Gee, Merry Christmas. Happy New Year."

She was on her own in this.

A small part of her felt like running. It wasn't an alien feeling; she'd been running from things all her life. And all of it came down to her own fears. When the tough got going, so did Holly. That had always been her motto.

But no longer. It had to stop, *now*. Especially when her parents probably expected her to do just that.

Which meant she had to swallow the urge to make for the door, and figure this mess out instead. By herself.

"Everything okay there, princess?"

Damn, *he* was still here. Probably waiting for her to fail, just like her parents. He'd pegged her as a spoiled, stubborn, selfish city girl.

Well, she *was* a spoiled, stubborn, selfish city girl. But she was here, it was done, and she was going to come out on top.

And she wasn't going to let anyone see her struggle to get there, that was for damn sure. With a cool smile in place, she turned and faced Riley McMann.

He stood there looking for all the world as if he'd been born in that tacky apron he'd put on.

"Why are you still wearing that?"

"Someone's got to carry out all that food you're going to be cooking."

She was going to have to cook. And she could barely boil water. This just got better and better. "I need to hire a chef like yesterday," she said to herself, considering. "I could place an ad—"

"No go." Riley smiled sweetly—she was beginning to mistrust that smile—and said, "The local paper comes out only once a week."

"Let me guess…and today's the day?"

"I've got it spread across my desk as we speak."

For some reason, his tone and words combined to create an incredibly naughty picture in her head, one of the sheriff standing in his office, looking down at what he had "spread across his desk," and it wasn't a newspaper, it was…*her.*

Okay, clearly she'd been too long without sex.

But now that the picture was in her brain, she couldn't get rid of it. She glanced at him to see if maybe he'd been provocative on purpose, but he only looked at her from those fathomless, innocent eyes.

Only problem was, no man that breathtaking, that sure of himself, that in charge of his emotions, could ever be innocent. In fact, given his looks, charm and personality, plus his authority in Little Paradise, she'd bet that good Sheriff Riley Mc-Mann hadn't been innocent for a very, very long time. He probably had every single woman—if there even were any—falling all over themselves to catch his attention.

They were welcome to him. Holly had put herself out for a man before; she'd even gone to great lengths to keep him. She'd *still* gotten hurt. Numerous times, in fact.

Never again.

The next man in her life, if there was one, would be a man who couldn't get enough of her, who loved everything about her, unconditionally.

The next man in her life would *not* be one Riley McMann.

"You could place an ad for next week," he said helpfully.

Great, wouldn't that just be nice. An entire week without help. "Terrific. Thanks." She gave him her best I-could-give-a-damn-everything-is-in-control smiles. "I'll just get started cooking."

He sent her the smile right back, though he was watching her with a look too personal, too direct, for two complete strangers. "I'll serve your customers coffee, and whatever you manage to wrangle up," he said.

Neither of them moved. Around them, the air seemed to sizzle, which confused Holly. She'd never felt anything like this. He was just a cowboy, rough-edged and far too casual for her tastes, and yet already he'd somehow gotten under her skin.

He glanced at his watch. "After that, though, you're on your own. I need to get back to my office by three for a phone call."

"I'd rather be on my own right now." Brave words, not such a brave heart, but she meant it. She wouldn't accept help, especially his.

"You're kidding."

She shook her head and reaching out, untied the ribbon he'd put around his waist. It meant she had to touch him, but she'd touched plenty of men before, so it should be no big deal.

But it was.

The minute her fingers brushed against his belly, her entire body tightened. It was only because he was an exceptionally fine male specimen, she told herself, careful to not meet his mocking gaze as she hung up the apron.

"You're going to refuse my help?" He looked shocked, as if no one had ever turned him down before.

"Yep."

"Well then, princess—or maybe I should be calling you Ms. Stubborn?"

"Just...go."

He stood there for another moment, watching her. "You're going to be okay."

"I always am."

His lips curved. "Yeah. I guess you'd better get busy."

He seemed so calm. Of course he did! He wasn't about to cook and serve a room full of strangers!

"Call me if you change your mind."

And admit she was wrong? Not likely.

He left her alone.

Alone.

With a stove.

Well, wasn't this just a fine and dandy mess? But with the determination and grit that had gotten her through far worse disasters than this, she got busy.

Busy destroying pan after pan.

3

WHAT AN IRONIC twist of fate. Holly had spent much of her adult life flitting from one job to another, gaining a myriad of experiences that she could use in life, and yet the one thing she needed now—okay, the *two* things—were both something she hadn't a clue about.

Cooking and people skills.

Anything else, *anything,* and she might have been able to wing it. Well, cooking she could learn if she *had* to. After all, they did have a little invention called a cookbook.

But the people skill thing... Being sweet and kind and warm to complete strangers who didn't know her from Eve? Serving them whatever they needed, and doing it with a smile so that they'd want to come back? That involved trust, lots of it, and Holly didn't trust easily. She didn't trust at all.

This was going to be the biggest challenge of her life.

But she wouldn't give up, even if it meant gritting her teeth and forcing smiles until her jaw was tired. Whatever the people in Café Nirvana wanted, she would find a way to give them. The business would thrive, the Mendozas would eventually sell it, and her parents would look at her with stars in their eyes.

And she could go home.

Home.

That she didn't really know where home was had her smile faltering there for a moment, but she'd figure that out, too. Soon as she got this serving thing down.

Since Holly had burned just about everything she'd ever attempted to cook, she decided to go with the theory that it was late afternoon by now, and therefore between lunch and dinner, when no food was required.

And what would she do about dinnertime? Well, she'd cross that bridge when she got to it. For now, though, she'd been hiding out in the kitchen long enough. She picked up a pitcher of ice water, pasted a smile on her face and headed out to the lion's den—er, dining area. Show time.

The first thing she did was scan the counter.

Not that she was looking for the tall, rugged and annoyingly handsome sheriff, because she wasn't.

And anyway, he wasn't there. A good thing, because he both distracted and flustered her.

And no one was allowed to live once they'd flustered her.

She was doubly glad she hadn't let him help her because she really hated to be indebted to anyone. Holly Stone made her own way in this world, and she always would.

The tables had practically emptied out, not a positive sign. With her smile still glued in place, she walked to the closet table and nodded to the man who sat there glaring at her.

He weighed 250 pounds minimum, and looked as if he lifted cars for a living. His striped uniform shirt was streaked with grease and the tag on his right collarbone said his name was Dan.

"Hello, Dan," she said in what she hoped was a pleasant voice. She'd read somewhere people liked to be called by name. She started to fill up his water.

"I wanted food," he said. "An hour ago."

"I know," she said in her nicest voice. "But there's a small problem with that. There won't be any more food served until dinnertime. Not today."

"*What?*" He was not only unpleasantly surprised, but angry on top of that. "You're kidding me. What kind of restaurant doesn't serve food?"

This didn't bode well for her tip. She kept pouring, determined to make things okay. "Well, you see—"

She broke off when he let out a high-pitched, very girly scream and stood up, dancing around, flailing his arms, looking like Tinkerbell on steroids.

She'd overfilled his cup. Ice water right in his lap.

Well, darn it, he'd distracted her! She whirled to grab a towel off the counter—and wasn't it ever so wonderful to see that Riley was back, sitting there as if he didn't have a worry in the world.

"Problem?" he asked.

Holly ignored him to rush back to her dancing customer. He had a huge water stain across the front of his pants. "Here." She tossed the towel at him because she wasn't about to dab at his lap herself.

It hit him in the face.

He stopped bouncing, yanked the towel away from his mouth and glared at her. "You," he said.

He towered over her, really, *really* unhappy about having ice water poured over his…parts.

"Now, Dan." Riley stood up, a friendly smile on his face. "It was just an accident."

Dan didn't respond to that, just gave Holly one of those looks that made her nervous for her own body parts.

"And with it being such a hot one outside," Riley continued easily, "I'd think all that cold water would cool you right off, just like a nice swim in a stream. Don't you think, Dan?"

Dan drew in a deep breath before he grimaced at Riley. "Yeah, a cool stream."

"That's it. Why don't you just sit on back down now and relax?"

"Don't worry, Sheriff." He shook his head. "I like you too much to cause any trouble here. You can sit back down, too."

Riley nodded and smiled warmly as he did just that. "Good man, Dan."

"But I ain't coming back. Not without Marge serving me. She never spilled water on me that made my d—" He broke off and cleared his throat. "I miss her already."

Holly was just relieved that she was still among the living, and that Dan didn't do anything else but finish drying off before walking out.

Without tipping her.

The entire room had fallen silent, which wasn't

saying much since she had only three other tables with people at them.

Oh, and the grinning sheriff—she couldn't forget him.

Without a word, she went into the kitchen. What an idiot, she told herself. Spilling water like a nervous little ninny. She wasn't nervous!

And she wasn't a ninny! She was Holly Stone, woman with nerves of steel.

Determined, she searched the huge refrigerator and came up with a fresh apple pie—*thank God*. Renewed with hope, she went back out to offer it to her dwindling customer base.

"Looking good," Riley said as she passed him.

She wondered if he meant the pie or her, but then she figured he must have meant the pie because she was still wearing hot pink over red silk, for God's sake, not to mention she was beginning to sweat.

She looked about as far from good as you could get.

"Uh...Holly?" Riley called out to her. "Holly!"

He spoke earnestly, but knowing he just wanted to rub her failures in, she kept going. With her hands full she couldn't see her feet, and in the aisle between the counter and the tables, she tripped over a lump that screeched "meow!"

The pie flew through the air and landed on the lap of the woman with the perpetually slipping glasses.

Mindy, the librarian, she told Holly, swiping the pie off her glasses.

She didn't tip when she left, either.

On her hands and knees, Holly scrubbed at the floor, trying not to acknowledge the self-pity threatening to swallow her whole.

Only three feet away from her were the long legs of the sheriff. He still sat, calm as you please, at the counter.

With all her might, she wished she'd spilled the pie on *him.*

Harry, who was freshly awoken from his nap, thanks to her, leaped to the counter. Right in front of her, only inches away from Riley's drink, he sat down and began to wash himself.

Oh, perfect. Her customers were dwindling fast, and she had a big, fat, ugly cat sitting on the counter, cleaning his paws.

Disgusted, she stood and tried to shoo him off.

Clearly insulted, Harry leaped again, aiming for the closest table. According to Murphy's Law, this was naturally one of the few tables actually occupied by a paying guest.

The man there stroked Harry. "Don't worry about that mean woman who hates cats," he crooned, glaring at Holly.

From behind Holly came something that sounded suspiciously like a laugh. Whirling, she glared at Riley, but he was just sitting there, looking guileless.

She sent him a long look for good measure, but he simply leaned back, stretched his lean, toned body out, put his hands behind his head and winked at her.

The man who Harry had practically attacked was heading for the front door.

"I'm sorry," she called, but he just lifted a hand and kept going.

He stiffed her, too.

Let's see...she'd probably just cost the café an entire day's wages, all in an hour. Had to be a personal record for failure, and exhausted at just the thought, she sank into the nearest chair.

And sat on Harry.

RILEY WOKE UP a hungry man. *Really* hungry.

He hadn't gotten lucky last night. Holly had closed Café Nirvana—his usual dinner haunt—

early. He could have whipped up something in his own kitchen, except for the fact that he really hated to cook. He could run an entire ranch practically by himself. He could patrol a county that had more square miles than he could count. He could bring peace to a room faster than he could blink, with just a smile and some sweet words, and enjoy all of it.

But ask him to so much as boil water for tea and he would find something, *anything*, else to do. Even go hungry.

Apparently Holly felt the same way, which gave them something in common, an uncomfortable feeling for him. He felt much easier when he didn't like her. She was just playing here, just passing through.

So why couldn't he stop thinking about her?

Hopefully she'd run for the hills—or the nearest city—by now. Yeah. Given her success rate of exactly zero yesterday, she'd probably done just that. The entire town would be grateful.

So would he.

He came into his house after doing some chores and stopped short in the doorway of his kitchen. Standing by the work island was Maria, his housekeeper. In front of her was a breakfast fit for a king, and also a bagged...lunch? His mouth watered at the thought, even as he knew it couldn't be true. Maria didn't like him enough to cook for him, *twice*.

"What are you doing here?" he asked, knowing she came only twice a week, *if* she was in the mood, to clean up after him. He wasn't particularly proud of the fact that she was necessary.

But she'd been there just the day before. He knew because he'd had clean sheets, fresh towels and the dishes he'd stacked for the past few days— he kept meaning to get to them but somehow never managed it—had been washed and put back in the cupboard where they belonged.

Maria ignored his question and shoved him into a chair, a considerable feat considering she was barely four feet tall to his six plus. Her wide girth apparently gave her the strength of four men.

Without a word of greeting, or even a smile, she set the plate of delicious-smelling food in front of him. "Eat," she commanded in heavily accented English. "I do not have all day to clean your dishes."

No one had to tell him twice. Riley started shoving the most amazing food in his mouth. Omelette smothered in cheese, a mountain of bacon on the side, crispy just the way he liked it, and another mountain of sourdough toast, slathered in butter.

"I've died and gone to heaven," he said, then moaned around another mouthful. "This is the best food I've ever tasted."

"You're half-starving, what does a half-starving man know?"

"I know good food," he promised her. "And this is it."

"A man who works as hard as you cannot go without eating. That Holly What's-Her-Name is going to be the death of you."

No doubt. "You've never worried about me before."

"You had the café before," Maria pointed out. She slammed a pan into the sink and turned on the water. "What were the Mendozas thinking, letting someone like that take over?" She switched to Spanish then, letting off a rapid-fire monologue Riley couldn't begin to follow.

"Why are you here?" he asked when she'd run out of steam. "Not that I'm complaining," he added quickly when she glared at him. "I'm grateful for the food, more than you know, but—"

"I heard about the Nirvana shutting down."

"It's not shutting down, it's just—"

"Not serving food a dog could eat."

"Well, I think there's a mix-up. I'm sure it'll get resolved."

"She doesn't know how to cook."

"Cooking isn't everyone's strong suit." He flashed her a grin. "Not like you."

She sniffed, as if not being able to make a meal was the greatest sin a woman could commit. "I know how much you count on that café, and I could not let you go hungry." This last was spoken gruffly as she removed her apron. "Everyone in town is talking about her. There is a bunch of unhappy, hungry people around."

"Yeah."

"She is big city. She does not belong here."

Riley didn't need the reminder that Holly came from a world entirely different from his, that she was restless, and probably looking for something in Little Paradise that didn't exist outside her imagination.

"She is too beautiful."

That wasn't a problem for Riley. He loved beautiful women; he loved all women. But he didn't need an attitude-ridden, trouble-causing princess, that was certain.

"Soak your dish, Sheriff, do not leave it all week for me. Enjoy your lunch."

And with that, she was gone.

Interesting. Maria liked him, she really liked him. But after he indeed soaked his dish, he saw the note she'd left him by his front door. "Wipe your feet. The sheriff of Little Paradise should not live like a pig."

Okay, maybe *like* was too strong a word.

BY THE TIME Riley pulled up to his office, he was running late. But at least his belly was full. He could last all day on the feast he'd had. Bring on the lost cows, the occasional town drunk, a speeding tourist…he was ready.

Holly's Jeep was still parked out front of the café, assuring him she hadn't run for the hills.

Or the nearest big city.

He'd give her until the end of the week. Hell, he'd give her until the end of today.

He walked into his building and surprisingly enough, there she stood by the front desk, with containers of food.

She let out a tight smile at the sight of him. "Hungry, Sheriff?"

He could see that she expected him to be. He could see also that she hadn't lost her inherent…cityness. She wore a two-piece number today, with a snug top and a short, wide skirt that screamed fashion. He had no idea who the maker was, or even the material, but he had no doubt it was the latest fashion, made by someone expensive.

"I brought breakfast," she said.

Tearing his attention away from the way the ice-blue color of her outfit emphasized her eyes, he looked at the food she'd put out. Steaming eggs, sausages, cinnamon buns...the works. "Wow." He didn't know which stunned him more—her little smile, which made her seem young and vulnerable in a way he'd never imagined, or the fact she'd actually brought *him* food. "You cooked?"

"Don't look so surprised." She lifted a blond eyebrow. "Food is the way to a person's stomach."

"I thought food was the way to a man's heart."

"I don't care about your heart. All I care about is you liking the food."

"Why?"

"So you can influence the people in town, of course."

Thinking she was kidding, he laughed. Leaning against the desk, he crossed his arms and studied her.

She looked the same as ever; cool, calm and collected. And very sure of herself. But he was beginning to think maybe that was all an act. If she was so sure of herself, she wouldn't be here.

"Excuse me for being cynical," he said. "But yesterday I got the distinct impression you didn't like me much. Why do you really care what I think of your food?"

"Actually, I don't care what you think. But like I said, the people of this town do, and since I didn't exactly bowl them over yesterday—"

"You yelled at them, you spilled on them, you treated them like they were dirt beneath your heels," he pointed out.

"Yes, well, maybe I could use a little honing up on my people skills. So are you going to eat this damn food and tell everyone you know it's good, or what?"

He shook his head at her audacity, but she didn't back down in her quest. She actually expected him to help her.

Jud walked in the front door, saw the two of them and stopped short. Pulling up his slipping pants, he lifted his nose and sniffed. "What's going on here?"

Holly looked at Riley, expectation and hope in her gaze. It was so far and away from the mistrust and sarcasm she'd been showing him since yesterday, he could only stare at her.

"Well?" Jud asked again.

Holly's gaze pleaded with him.

If he didn't help her, she'd be gone before sundown. A really tempting thought.

If he *did* help her, she might keep looking at him with those eyes that made him want to drown in them.

Idiot, he told himself, even as he held out an empty plate to Jud. "Help yourself. It's breakfast."

Holly smiled.

"From Café Nirvana," Riley added. "It's a special treat."

Jud looked at Holly with a good amount of suspicion, but with Riley holding out an empty plate, and all the steam and good scents rising from the food, he didn't have a prayer in resisting. When the plate was heaped high, Jud dug in with his fork and…choked.

"Yuck!"

"Yuck?" Riley looked at Holly. "I thought you said it was good."

"It *is* good!" she claimed, but she bit her lower lip uncertainly.

Riley whipped around to Jud, who was dumping the food in the trash.

"Those eggs are fake!" he yelled.

"They're low cholesterol," Holly whispered.

"And that sausage!" Jud spit into the trash can. "It wasn't sausage at all!"

"It's turkey meat." Holly winced at the loud, heavy thud they made as they hit the bottom of the can. "It's much healthier."

"It's disgusting," Jud said. "Don't tell me all your meals are going to be this bad."

"I'm thinking of trying other lean dishes, yes. Like meat loaf from low-fat ground turkey."

Riley groaned.

"What's that mean?" she demanded, whirling to him.

"Sounds...lean."

"Exactly!"

"Oh, man." Riley shook his head, grateful he'd already eaten. "You're going to go give us all that newfangled California junk, aren't you?"

"Your cholesterol will thank you. I've got some salads planned—"

"Gee," Riley muttered. "Sounds appetizing."

"I think so."

Jud pulled at his sagging pants. "I want the fat, woman!" He glared at Riley as if this were all his fault, then walked out.

The silence was deafening.

Holly straightened her shoulders, lifted her chin.

Riley sighed, rubbed his hands over his face, then looked at her. "Well, that went well. You were exceptionally charming and sweet."

She crossed her arms over her chest. ''I'm easier to get along with when people agree with me.'' But she looked out the window at the empty parking lot in front of Café Nirvana and chewed on her very red, very shiny and perfectly made-up bottom lip.

A lip he suddenly, irrationally, had the most shocking urge to suck into his mouth.

Where was a cow emergency when he needed one?

4

SLEEP ELUDED Holly that night. No surprise really. She'd set a new record, even for herself. Alienating an entire town in less than forty-eight hours.

She lay wide-awake in the small bedroom of her tiny apartment above the café. The Mendozas had cleared out quickly for their move to Montana, and yes, the thought came with a tad of bitterness.

Okay, more than a tad.

At least they'd left the furniture. The floors were hardwood and bare except for a few southwestern throw rugs. The walls were bare, too, but for such a small place there were a lot of windows.

The better to let the heat in.

Actually, it wasn't that bad, if you didn't count the extremely fat, rude Harry, who'd insisted on coming up with her.

He lay snoring in the kitchen sink.

But other than him, the place was clean and all hers, which made it...almost cozy. Her place in Los Angeles had been rented from a business acquaintance, and so had her place before that. She'd never really had a place of her own, but looking around the very small but oddly homey apartment now, she thought maybe if she could pick her own, it wouldn't be so different than this.

Except for the cat.

It would be nice to be able to call a place her own, but she couldn't do that until she figured out where she wanted to be for the rest of her life.

And where she wanted to be was back in a big city, any big city, where she could lose herself in her work, *normal* work. Where she could be around people like her.

Only the truth was, she'd never been around people like her.

She could tell herself it was the pace of the big city she missed. The movie theaters, the shops... Thai food.

But that was a lie, too.

She didn't miss those things; she didn't miss any of it. She just wanted to belong somewhere. Anywhere.

Damn, now she was right back to where she started, wallowing in self-pity.

She couldn't help it. Everything was wrong. She'd been assured by her parents this would be a short interlude, that the restaurant would sell quickly. That she would be fully staffed. That her duties would be purely managerial.

None of that had happened, which should have made it easy for her to back out. After all, her parents hadn't kept their part of the bargain, why should she?

But the new and improved Holly *wanted* to keep her bargains. She wanted to come through.

She wanted her accomplishments acknowledged.

And to do that, she had to succeed.

At any cost. Which meant if she had to continue to cook and clean and serve until she got it right, if she had to force people back into that café and eat her food so that a prospective buyer would be impressed, that's what she would do. And tough beans to the local population who didn't want to

d, sleep claimed her.

ooking, and how she'd al-
elf today while teaching
m a cookbook. She
he'd been wrong
dreamed about

cooperate. Finally

as cracking a
Checking out   grinning, sexy
atching box

BY THE NEXT MORNING, Holly was ready to dole out lots of tushie kissing and smiles that she didn't especially feel.

The biggest problem, of course, was what to serve for breakfast? The café was low on supplies and she hadn't yet had a chance to get any paperwork going, so she hadn't ordered anything.

She'd have to go get what she needed herself. Determined, she got in her Jeep, unable to help noticing Riley's truck was already in front of the sheriff's station.

So he worked hard, so what? It was no reason to feel a little...*melty* on the inside. She worked hard, too, dammit, and pushing him from her mind, she drove to the one and only grocery store in town.

She loaded five big containers of instant oatmeal—*not* low fat—into her cart, minute added several baskets of color. See? She was thinking lik already.

At the checkout, she was thorou by a midtwenties buxom redhead w hair Holly had ever seen. Though seven in the morning, the woman v big wad of green bubble gum. Holly's cream-colored skirt and r jacket, she sniffed. "Going to be a scorcher today, you know. You'll be sweatin' in those fancy clothes."

Those "fancy" clothes were light and cool, and very chic. Holly knew she looked good; looking good was important to her. It gave her a semblance of being in control. "I'm fine, thank you."

"This it?" Her tone was a one on a friendly scale to ten. "*This* is what you're going to offer at the café for breakfast?"

"Look—" Holly peered at the woman's name tag "Isadora—"

"Dora."

"Dora, then. Could you just check me out here? I'm in a bit of a hurry."

"Why?" She bagged the oatmeal, sniffing disdainfully at the blueberries, as if even she knew that nothing, nothing at all, could decorate instant oatmeal. "You don't have any customers waiting."

"How do you know?"

"My momma's sister's boyfriend's third cousin is the sheriff's receptionist. She can see you through the windows, all by yourself inside the café. Your arrival, and the clearing out of the café, has been the biggest gossip to hit town since

Jimmy Dalton got caught in the bowling alley trying to cheat Lester Arnold.''

"Terrific," Holly muttered.

"And then you went and caught the eye of the sheriff, which really grinds my butt." Dora's long, metallic-blue fingernails clicked loudly on the keys as she punched in the prices. "I've been trying to catch his eye since he came back from college. He's the hottest, sexiest, most amazing man I've ever seen, and he's looking at *you*." She rolled her eyes and blew a huge bubble, popping it noisily. "Go figure, especially since all you've done is give him sass."

"You don't get out much, do you?" Holly took cash out of her purse and slapped it down.

"You're telling me you don't think he's hot?"

"Hot? No." Only a little lie, one of the many she'd told, so she couldn't imagine she was going to hell for this one. "Pesky, yes. Mr. Know-It-All, yes. Insensitive? Oh, definitely. But hot?" Holly laughed. "You can't mean it."

"You're blind, girlfriend." Dora looked disgusted. "Completely blind. That man is a walking, talking fantasy."

Holly thought that just maybe Dora was right, but she'd roll over and die before admitting Riley made her yearn and burn. It'd simply been a while since she'd indulged in any fantasies, much less the real thing, so it was no wonder he set her hormones off. She could handle hormones, and she could handle one Riley McMann. Piece of cake.

What she couldn't handle was everything else.

"I suppose," Dora said, "that you prefer those pudgy, suit-wearing, smart-talking city boys who don't know the back of a horse from their own— Oh, never mind. The sheriff isn't into women like you anyway. He'll look his fill and get over it. There's still hope for me." Dora primped up her already huge hair and sent Holly a nasty grin. "Don't you think?"

"What I think is, you're validating my inherent mistrust of everyone in Little Paradise."

Dora laughed. "Feel free to vacate."

"Gee, this is such a friendly town. Imagine, I thought I'd have trouble making friends."

Dora had the good grace to smile sheepishly at that. "I'm sorry. I'm really not usually so rude to customers."

"Well, aren't I special?"

"It's just that the Nirvana is a town landmark, you know? And honestly, even you have to admit, you've pretty much ruined it all in one day."

The unfairness of that reared up and bit Holly, making being nice back all but impossible. "I didn't ruin it all by myself. You people helped by being as inhospitable and ungiving as possible. I could use some help here.''

Holly couldn't believe that those last words popped out of her mouth. She'd never in her life asked another soul for help. She certainly hadn't meant to start now.

''Really?'' Dora looked intrigued. ''You don't look like a woman who needs help from anyone, you look pretty self-sufficient to me.''

That was quite possibly one of the biggest compliments she'd ever had, not that she was about to admit it. ''I'm capable, thank you very much. But you don't, by any chance, know someone who wants the job of chef or waitress?''

''Working for *you?*''

''Well, yeah.''

Dora feigned disinterest, took Holly's money and gave her change.

Holly thought that was the end of that, until Dora stopped her from leaving. ''How much are you going to pay?'' she asked.

''Can you cook?''

''Better than you.''

''Come prove it.'' Holly knew she didn't sound like a warm, fuzzy boss, but she didn't trust anyone in this town farther than she could frown at them. "Wow me. *Then* we'll talk pay."

Dora sized her up for a long moment. "You're not exactly Miss Merry Sunshine. Are you mean to your employees?"

"Mean? No. Tough? Yes."

"I can handle tough. How about fair?"

"Yes." Or so she hoped. She hadn't gotten a good look at the café's finances yet. Hell, she hadn't done anything yet but sink. But she looked at Dora and willed her to want it, even as she pretended not to care one way or the other. "Makes no difference to me, if you want to bag groceries all your life. But if you're interested in more, in the freedom of cooking what you like when you like it, well then…" With that hopefully enticing speech, Holly grabbed her bag and walked out of the store.

The café was still empty. Just as it'd been since she'd spilled, growled and cooked every single person away.

But she was convinced she could fix this. She could. And she could do it before her parents found out.

She hoped.

Since she was entirely by herself—what else was new?—and she couldn't count on Dora taking the bait, she placed a nice, big, friendly sign in the window, announcing that she needed a chef and a waitress.

Plenty of people stopped to look at the sign, some pointed and smiled, some even laughed, but no one, *no one,* stopped and inquired within.

And the café remained stubbornly empty, despite the fact she'd cooked up the instant oatmeal for breakfast. It'd been easier than she thought, too.

Until it went cold and turned into cement.

Even Harry wouldn't touch it.

Disgusted, Holly went to the front door and checked it, thinking maybe she'd left it locked.

As she opened it, a mangy, ragged mutt walked right in and sat. Half of one ear was gone, his fur was matted and dirty, and yet he walked in like he owned the place.

"Oh, no," she said to him. Her. It. *Whatever.* "I've already inherited a nasty cat. You just take yourself right on back outside, this isn't a charity stop."

The dog cocked his head and panted as if he hadn't had water in five days. Dammit. "Okay, just one little sip of water, then you're outta here. Do you hear me? I've got bigger problems than you."

As if he understood, and smelled a sucker while

he was at it, he lay down and…smiled. She would have sworn he did!

Muttering to herself, Holly went into the kitchen and rustled up a bowl of water. Backing through the double doors, carrying the bowl, she said, "And don't take this wrong, but man, you need a bath."

"Care to scrub my back while I'm in it?"

Oh, perfect. Riley McMann. He was back, and though she hadn't turned around yet, hadn't set her eyes on his tall, leanly muscled body, hadn't looked into his deep-brown, laughing eyes, her knees wobbled anyway.

Self-consciously, she turned to face him, holding the bowl of water and feeling ridiculously stupid.

"You didn't seem like the stray type," he murmured, taking the bowl from her and setting it before the dog.

"I'm not." But she watched the scrawny dog lap at the water gratefully and felt her heart tug.

"Or a people one."

"Why don't you go back to your job?" she suggested. "And while you're at it, rescue me from this dog."

She wanted the dog out because there was something about the way his stomach was practically hollow, the way he seemed so happy to have been allowed to remain inside, with her, that really got to a person.

No. No, she was absolutely *not* sympathizing with this dog simply because they were both loners. "And do it quick before he scares off any more customers," she added.

"Yeah, it's the dog scaring off the customers," Riley said softly, his gaze never leaving hers, the look in it telling Holly he saw so much more than she wanted him to.

"I need to get lunch going."

"For who?"

Good point. "Look, can you take the dog away or what?"

"Why don't you just put out a sign that says, Eat At Nirvana, The Place That Runs Customers Off, And Dogs, Too."

She stared at him, baffled by the complexities of small-town living. "You're telling me that kicking this dog out is going to be bad for my business?"

"Princess, *you're* bad for business. But the dog, he could be good. It could show people you do have a…softer side."

"I don't want to show any softer side."

But he'd given her an idea, and energized, she grabbed another piece of paper and scribbled:

Free Dinner Tomorrow With Your Receipt From Today. Come Try Our New Family-Style Dinner.

She taped the note to the window, right next to the Help Wanted ad. Beaming, she looked at Riley. "With the dynamics of the gossip mill in this town, I'll be full of customers in less than ten minutes. They won't be able to help themselves, they're far too curious—and cheap—to ignore this."

"What's family style?"

"I'll serve one main dish, the same to everyone."

He nodded, looking impressed. "Clever. Now all you need is one little thing."

"What's that?"

"Food. *Good* food."

She was halfway to the kitchen. She'd really intended to ignore him, but something in his tone caught her, something she couldn't ignore. After all, she knew why *she* didn't like *him*. He was too sure of himself, too laid-back, too country, too...utterly, wildly, absolutely *male* for her.

But what she didn't know was... "Why don't you like me?"

Her question surprised both of them. He didn't try to deny it, or offer empty platitudes, which oddly enough only increased her need to know.

"What I feel doesn't matter," he said finally.

It shouldn't, but it did.

"It's not as if you're going to stick around," he added.

Oh, but that cut, and cut deep. Too many people in her life had thought that about her, and okay, yes, maybe up until this point in her life, she'd lived up to that by constantly being on the move, but dammit not this time. Not anymore.

For once, just for once, she wanted someone to believe in her, to encourage her. But it wouldn't be this man, and no way would she let him see how he'd hurt her feelings. "You don't know me," she said quietly.

"I know enough."

And he knew her "type." Or so he thought. Well, too bad; Holly Stone didn't belong to a type. "I'm not leaving until my job here is done, if it's any of your business. The place is going to sell sooner or later, and when it does, I'll go, but not before. I made a promise."

"Do you always follow through with your promises?"

He seemed doubtful, which only stirred her temper all the more. "Why are you here, Sheriff? I didn't call you, you're obviously not here to eat, so tell me. Why do you keep showing up?"

He shook his head, either unwilling or unable to answer.

"Then why don't you do us both a favor and go?" She let out a tight smile. "I've got a meal to cook."

Without waiting to see what he did, she turned, intending to make a great, dramatic exit. Only it was cut short when she tripped over the dog, landing sprawled out on the linoleum floor.

Riley was there in a flash, scooping her up. "You okay?" he demanded.

She blinked up at him. She'd lost a heel. Her hair had slipped from its elegant barrette, and her skirt had risen up, exposing more of herself—and her lingerie—than she'd planned on. But even more important, his arms were around her. In fact, she was practically in his lap. No, wait—she *was* in his lap, and oh my, but he felt big and hard and strong. And warm, very warm. She liked warm.

"Holly?"

Who would have thought he could feel so good? "Holly!"

"I'm fine," she said, forcing her thoughts away from the warm and fuzzy, to the realistic fact that she'd just humiliated herself, again. "Let me up."

As if he didn't believe her, he looked her over. His gaze didn't miss anything, not her rioted hair, her probably smudged makeup, the skirt that had risen so high on her thigh she was still giving him a peekaboo hint at her peach lace panties. She yanked at the hem but not before his jaw clenched and his arms tightened. His eyes darkened.

And time stood still.

"You look...different like this," he said, his voice hoarse.

"Different...how?"

He touched a strand of her hair, then her cheek. His gaze ran slowly over her body, leaving flames licking at her skin everywhere he looked. "Less princesslike," he murmured. "*Way* less princesslike."

Then he was withdrawing his hands from her, standing, backing away, turning toward the door. "Good luck with dinner later," he said gruffly, and he was gone.

Holly was left sitting there, tingling, uncertain as to what had just happened. But then the dog licked her face—*licked her face!*—and she screeched, leaping to her feet. "Yuck! Stop it!"

He sat, panting, and cocked his head at her.

"You have breath like a sewer." She walked to the front door and held it open. "You're outta here, too."

But because he looked so...cute, she softened

her voice. "Go on now, outside with you." Those huge, soulful eyes tore at her, but she lifted her chin and pretended not to notice. "Out."

And just like the sheriff, out he went.

SEVERAL HOURS LATER, Holly was well on her way to having dinner going. She'd run back down to the grocery store—she really needed to get a list going and order properly—and had picked up what she needed. She hoped.

But more thrilling, thanks to her sign, she had customers!

Not many, but there were at least eight people out there, including both Dan, the huge mechanic, and Mindy, the librarian. They were all seated, drinking, waiting for the special of the evening. Now all that was left was for the spaghetti to finish cooking, her sauce to get a bit hotter, and the salad to fully chill.

No one had to know that she'd actually enjoyed making the sauce, though she'd not done anything original, she'd followed the cookbook to the letter. The salad was from a premixed bag, but that had been because she hadn't had time for anything else. She was so nervous she could hardly see straight.

But she was used to hiding her nerves.

Again, she went out front, checking on drink

status, smiling at anyone and everyone who would look at her, and shooing the damn cat off the counter.

Then Mindy pushed up her glasses, stood up and said, "I smell gas."

Across the room, Dan sniffed loudly and nodded. "Yep, definitely gas." He looked at Holly and shook his head grimly. "I should have known you were trying to kill me."

Holly lifted her nose and sniffed…. Oh boy, that was definitely a rotten egg sort of smell, and she couldn't have messed up the spaghetti sauce *that* badly, no way.

Besides, she knew from somewhere that they put that horrible smell into natural gas so you could tell when it was…*leaking!*

She scrambled for the phone, thinking she'd call 911, but Riley was simply right across the street. He'd know what to do. Before she could send someone for him, everyone was screaming and yelling and running for the door.

Two minutes later, Riley came striding in, moving like lightning but looking cool and battle-ready.

And worried as hell until he saw her.

She didn't want to think about that, didn't want

to wonder why he looked so relieved at the sight
of her.

"Out," he said firmly, grabbing her arm. The
image of authority. "We're evacuating until this is
handled."

"But—"

"For once, princess, listen. Until I figure out
what you've done, and make sure your very nice-
looking rear end is safe in here, you'll wait outside
with everyone else."

He thought her rear end was nice.

Oh, and that she was a walking disaster zone.

Just another day in the life of Holly Stone.

5

THE GAS LEAK had been caused by a blown pilot in the stove. Easily fixed, thought Riley.

The panic among Café Nirvana's customers was also easily fixed when Holly offered them drinks on the house.

All Holly's problems—fixed.

But the image of her after a long day of work—hair adorably messy, lipstick eaten off, sleeves shoved up and a spot of sauce on her hip—wouldn't leave Riley's mind.

Not so easily fixed.

What was wrong with him? She was everything he'd never wanted; she was big-city sophistication, she was snooty, manipulating. Stubborn as hell.

And yet he dreamed about her all night; long, haunting, erotic dreams. She wore peach lace, barely there panties, dammit. No wonder he woke up hot, bothered and horny as hell.

At least it was Sunday, his day off.

The physical demands of his ranch chores

ally helped him wind down from a long week. They cleared his mind, and being outdoors, whether he was shoveling horse manure or riding hard and fast over the land, cleared his heart and soul, as well.

By midmorning he'd made some overdue repairs to his barn and had mended some fences on the far north side of his property. He was still hot and bothered, but at least it was from hard work this time, and not the mental images of Holly Stone, wearing nothing but those lace panties and a hungry expression.

And her expression *had* been hungry. Not a physical hunger, but something deeper, something that came uncomfortably close to mirroring his own yearning.

Deciding he needed food to fuel his brain instead of silly, romantic images, he headed toward the house and prayed Maria was still there. He stripped off his dirt-streaked shirt and kicked off his shoes, hoping to get on her good side by not tracking dust into the house. Maybe he could look extra pathetic and squeeze a meal out of her.

He was in luck.

He could hear her in his kitchen, muttering and swearing in Spanish. He could also hear...*Holly?* Wearer of peach panties?

"I just asked you how you made the gravy so creamy, you don't have to act like it's a federal offense not to know," he heard Holly say in that cool, cultured voice.

Maria's voice wasn't so cool. "Why are you here, anyway? The sheriff won't be happy to see you."

"How do you know?" Holly asked. "Actually, it could go either way."

Maria sniffed. "And as for not knowing how to make gravy, it *is* a crime. How could you not have learned to cook? What is wrong with your mother?"

"She's...not exactly the cooking type."

"No? How are you going to catch a man?"

Riley decided now was the time to enter the kitchen, before World War III could break out. He was immediately overcome by the delicious smell of the meal Maria had cooked, by the sight of the two women staring each other down over the steaming stove, and by the fact that he was straining to hear Holly's answer as to how she was going to catch a man.

Neither woman gave him a second glance. Maria, because she never gave him a second glance—unless he was making a mess or not rinsing his plate.

Holly because…who knew.

But she was studiously avoiding his gaze. Interesting, considering *she'd* shown up at *his* house.

"What's going on?" he asked. "Not that I mind finding two women in my kitchen, especially when there's food involved."

"See?" Triumphant, Maria sent Holly a smirk and handed Riley a plate of food. "Ms. Stone was just going to tell me how to catch a man without basic cooking skills."

Holly looked cool as a cucumber, until she happened to glance at him. Then she gave him a double take that had him looking down at himself, checking for toilet paper on his shoe.

He was still shirtless.

For a moment Holly's eyes glazed over. Her mouth opened, then carefully closed. And she purposely turned away from him. "Why would I want to catch a man?" she asked Maria, her voice oddly husky.

"Well, you are *not* going to catch him with your sweet tongue, that is certain," Maria said, not very kindly.

"I'm not going to catch a man at all, thank you very much."

Well, wasn't that interesting? He'd pegged her for a definite need-a-man-in-her-life type.

She looked at him again, quickly, but there was no mistaking the flash of uncertainty in those baby blues.

A distinctively uneasy feeling went through him. That had definitely been vulnerability he'd seen in her expression. But Holly Stone was never vulnerable.

Was she?

And if he'd been wrong about that, what else had he been wrong about?

"You are not interested in marriage?" Maria was scandalized and she stared at Riley in shock when she handed him his plate. "She's not interested in marriage."

"Let's just say marriage isn't interested in me," Holly said, staring down at the bubbling pot on the stove. "Now, can you teach me to make this gravy as good as you, or what?"

The look on Maria's face was priceless. She didn't know whether to hold on to her resentment of the younger woman or be flattered. Watching her torn emotions, enjoying her speechlessness, Riley let out his first grin of the day.

"What's so funny?" Maria demanded.

If she knew, she'd take away his food. "Nothing."

"It is something."

He bit his lip, but the laugh escaped anyway. "I was just wondering if I could learn that trick sometime, the trick of making you silent."

Maria glared at him and reached for the plate she'd just handed him. "You give me that, you should go hungry."

"You said I shouldn't," he said, holding tight to his food. "Remember? You were worried about me, I need my food, you said, I need the nutrition."

"You. You are a snake."

"A hungry snake."

Maria let him keep his food. She looked at Holly. "Okay, maybe if you like my cooking so much, I can teach you," she said gruffly. "My gravy is the best in the world. You can pour it over biscuits. *Handmade* biscuits, not some store bought ones that land like concrete in your stomach."

Holly smiled. Not that fake one, but a real, down-to-earth smile that transformed her into...a human being.

A beautiful one.

One Riley couldn't take his eyes from, even though he wasn't the recipient of that smile. No doubt, she was still screaming "city" with every step she took, but somehow, over the past few days, it had stopped amusing him and started to actually get to him.

Any man would feel that way, he assured himself. She wore a short denim skirt that showed off the longest, greatest set of legs he'd ever seen, and a sun-yellow tank blouse that hugged the nicest, curviest set of—

"Are you going to stare at her all day or are you going to eat?" Maria wanted to know. "Because that dish, it's got to—"

"Soak." Riley cleared his throat and concentrated on his food. "I know."

Holly was looking at him, shock on her face, as if it hadn't occurred to her that he could like the mere sight of her. It was the second time he realized she wasn't quite as confident as she wanted the world to believe. Her eyes were big, and strangely unguarded. Her hands clenched together and that lower lip, the carefully glossed lower lip he'd dreamed about, was being dragged against her teeth.

It reminded him of the day before, when she'd looked so uncharacteristically flustered, so absolutely…adorable. That, he realized, *that* had been when he'd stopped being amused by her looks, and instead, had become intrigued by Holly-the-person. He suspected she hid a lot inside, certainly most of her emotions. His sudden yearning to know what they were, and why she kept them so protected startled him.

So did the simultaneous urge to surge up, grab her, toss her on his table and follow her down. He wanted to kiss that bottom lip, wanted to nibble off every bit of the remaining gloss, then work his way over her jaw to her neck. And when he was done there, he'd work his way down, down, down—

"Your mind is in the gutter," Maria said, shaking her wooden spoon beneath his nose. "Eat."

He was still looking at Holly when he brought another bite up to his lips.

Holly was looking at him, too, she could do little else. For the first time in…well, forever, her thoughts were not her own to control. She couldn't stop looking at him. Dammit, he needed to comb his tousled hair. He needed to shave. He really needed to put on a shirt—it should be illegal to look that good without one. And she couldn't stop wondering exactly what he was thinking…

She needed a lobotomy.

That explained it. Honestly. Because there was no reason to wonder what he was thinking. No reason at all. He meant nothing to her. More important, *she* meant nothing to *him*. In light of that, she gave Maria a shaky grin. "I'll write down the recipe as you give it to me. Soon as I give back—" she dug into her purse "—the sheriff's wallet."

"The sheriff's wallet?"

"My wallet?" Riley asked at the same time as Maria, rising. "How did you get that?"

Maria grabbed Riley's plate and put it in the sink. "Do you need a witness when you arrest her for theft, Sheriff?"

"Uh, no. I can handle it, thanks, Maria. Great food."

"As always."

"As always," he repeated dutifully.

She actually gave him a small smile before turning to Holly. "If you're not in jail, I will come to the café later."

If she was in jail, it'd be for ogling charges. Ogling-the-sheriff charges.

"I will show you some things in that kitchen," Maria added, grabbing her purse and keys. "Things other than low-fat crapola. Though I hear the spaghetti sauce smelled good. Too bad no one got a chance to taste it before you almost blew them all up."

Holly let that go for the more important fact. "You'll come help me?" She could have hugged the ornery, older woman, if she'd been the hugging type. "Thank you!"

Maria nodded her head once, regally, and left her alone with Riley.

Alone. Please don't make an idiot of yourself in front of him this time, she told herself.

It would be harder than she thought. According to what Maria had told her, Riley had been up since before dawn working outside. He didn't look it, didn't look anything but...fabulous.

And utterly, absolutely at home in his own skin, which by the way, was fabulous, too. "About your wallet," she said, forcing her gaze up to meet his. "It must have happened during the gas leak."

"What must have happened?"

"Well, later, in my apartment, I found the dog chewing on something and—"

"Wait." Riley shook his head but took the wallet, which he set on the counter without even looking at it. "Dog? The same one from yesterday?"

"Yes."

"Let me get this straight. You claim you don't like animals. You also claim you don't even particularly like people, and you certainly don't like being out of the big city. And yet here you are, in Little Paradise, running a café where you have to interact with people all day, and you've adopted both a dog and a cat.''

"They adopted me."

"Really?" he murmured, smiling that warm, just-for-her smile. "I don't think so."

"It's true."

"You could lock them out."

"Yes, but— *Yes,*" she whispered. She couldn't tell him she didn't have the heart. It would ruin her tough reputation. She needed that reputation, she used it like a cloak. "About your wallet—"

"You're here to help your parents, right? And yet they appear to—no offense—not be too concerned about you and your needs. You don't have any friends here, and you're out of your element. Some pretty big odds, Holly."

"Look, I don't want to discuss this. I just wanted to give you back your wallet." She tried to turn away, but he gently and very firmly set his hands on her shoulders.

"Know what I think?" he wondered.

"Ask me if I care."

He smiled gently. "I think all your confidence and wisecracking is a front. I think in spite of your bravado, in spite of your best manipulations, everything is starting to slip through your fingers. I think you're learning something about yourself here in the center of exactly nowhere, something that has nothing to do with trying to please your parents."

"I didn't know you were a shrink."

He smiled. "See? That's exactly the fake bravado I'd expect from you. But this isn't the big city, Holly. This is a small town, where people have known each other forever, and they care. They'd care about you, too, if you let them."

"Are you kidding?" She laughed to hide her wistfulness. "I wasn't born and raised here. People will never trust me."

"You're wrong."

She wanted to be; with all her heart she suddenly wanted to be.

"Just let them in," he said, his voice suggesting that he cared, too. "That's all it would take."

She thought he was going to add, *Let me in,* and in that moment, she might have, but she found her inner strength. She leaned on no one but herself, ever. She gestured to his wallet. "Aren't you even going to open it?"

He was disappointed in her change of conversation, and let it show. "No."

"What if I stole your cash?"

"Did you?"

"Well, no." She amused him with that, and she

schooled her features into an even mask of indifference. She was good at it by now, but Riley surprised her by being good at seeing right through her.

He came closer.

She was leaning against the counter and didn't have anywhere to back up to, so as he moved toward her all she could do was lift her chin and stare him down.

It didn't work.

She was used to being as tall or taller than most men, but not this man, so the height intimidation didn't work on him, either.

Still smiling a little, totally at ease, enjoying himself, he tipped his head to the side, so that in spite of her attempting *not* to look right at him, she was.

"You still have the dog," he said gently.

Not a question, but a statement, one that implied he thought all sorts of things. First, that she even *wanted* the damn dog, and second, that maybe she was too soft to get rid of it.

"You really should check your wallet," she said between her teeth. "Because someone might have stolen something from it—a credit card, your license, anything."

"You're in Little Paradise, remember?"

Oh yes, how could she forget one of their most basic differences? He trusted everyone—except for her—and she trusted no one. "You still should check."

"Okay, just for you..." He relented with a smile that was far too innocent for her taste. He reached for it, bringing his torso inches within hers, and oh my, no expensive cologne for this cowboy. He didn't need it. He smelled like the outdoors, like hay, like sweet sunshine and warm, sexy male. If she moved, even a fraction of an inch, she could put her mouth on his bare shoulder. Her knees weakened at the thought.

He opened the wallet, still too close, still giving her that far too guileless smile. "See?" he said, showing her his license. His credit card. His twenty-dollar bill. "Everything of value—" He pulled out not one, but *two* condoms, and pressed them into her palm, "—is still here."

Though she'd never, ever, in a million years admit it, her pulse took off like a shot. Heat flooded her body, pooling in all those erogenous zones she'd ignored for far too long, and all because his long, work-roughened fingers had held up two little packets that would allow him to have protected sex.

That she could imagine him doing just that, with her, was no longer such a shock.

"Mmm, that looks good on you," he murmured.

"What?"

"That unguarded expression. You're not so polished now, Holly Stone, and it's a beautiful look for you."

This was not happening. He was not seducing her with mere words.

But he was, and he dipped his head so that his jaw nearly brushed hers. His eyes were heavy-lidded, sensual, and she had to fist her hands on the counter behind her to keep them from misbehaving.

It was a hard habit to break, not turning on the charm full force to get whatever she wanted, including a man. But she wasn't that woman anymore, hadn't been since the moment she'd pulled into Little Paradise. And no matter how much she wanted him in that moment, she wasn't going to do it. She wasn't going to go after any man, not ever again.

She was going to make a success of herself, she was going to make a success of the café. She was going to learn to run it the way it needed to be run, and in the process, if she was beginning to realize she liked cooking, that she liked the peace and quiet here, that she liked seeing people every day, liked pleasing them with her creations—

She went utterly still and backed up that last thought.

Oh, my God.

She was...*enjoying* herself.

Well, that was allowed, right? She was trying to please her parents, but she could please herself at the same time. And when she was done, she was going to get on with her life.

Any second now.

"I have to go," she whispered, not moving.

"Have to? Or want to?"

Was there a difference? Yes, oh yes, there was. "There's a prospective buyer coming this afternoon. I have to show the café."

He straightened and sent her a smile. "So you can go back home."

Home? She had no idea where that was. "Yes."

"Where is that, Holly? You've never said."

To her absolute shock, her throat tightened. Her eyes burned. "I'll let you know when I figure that out," she said, and bolted.

She was still holding the condoms.

6

THAT NIGHT Holly looked at those condoms for a
very long time. It was no longer the actual condoms she was seeing, but something much, much
more.

Always before, wanting a man had been about
the conquest. She wanted Riley, and yet it had
nothing to do with the conquest. It wasn't even
entirely a physical wanting. It was just a vague,
haunting...*yearning* she couldn't put to words.

Riley represented everything she'd never allowed herself: stability, security, safety. And it was
so far out of her realm to think about them that
she opened up the trash and dropped in the condoms.

They lay there, perfectly good, perfectly wasted.

She wouldn't think about him having to buy
more. That was his problem. She shut the lid of
the trash and turned her back on them.

She paced for a while, trying to clear her mind.

It worked, too, an idea came to her. Granted, she

usually had ideas, but this one was perfect. All she needed was some...help.

At that deflating thought, she sank to her tiny couch in her tinier apartment, stared blankly ahead and laughed at herself.

She'd almost thought there...she'd almost forgotten...that she didn't have a soul in the world she could turn to for help.

She'd always liked it that way before. She'd been pushing people away her entire life, making sure the only person she could count on was herself.

And now, blithely caught up in the moment and her growing affection for this ridiculous little town, and even more ridiculous little café that wasn't hers, she figured she'd just suddenly turn to someone, just like that.

She could turn to Riley.

"I have no idea where *that* thought came from," she said to the big, fat cat who insisted on climbing onto her lap. "I don't need help from anyone, *especially* him."

Harry began to purr. "It's his eyes," she told him. Despite Riley's easygoing, laid-back nature, he saw too much. She didn't trust him, or the way he made her feel. "Ugh. You're heavy, cat."

"Meow," he said with reproach.

Guilt actually swamped her. "I'm sorry, you're right. *Harry*. You're heavy, *Harry*." Then she laughed at herself for being silly. Harry couldn't care less what she called him as long as she fed him. "Why are you here, anyway? And you, too," she said to the dog who lumbered into the room from the bathroom, where he'd been lapping at the toilet water again. "You're disgusting."

He blinked, insulted, and she relented. "Okay, I'm sorry. But surely someone else, *anyone* else, has a bigger pad for you to crash in."

He licked her hand, walked in a tight circle exactly three times before plopping at her feet with a loud grunt.

Her heart tugged. There was no denying it, it tugged hard. Because the dog had chosen *her*?

That's pathetic, she told herself, but she let out a little sigh and leaned back on her couch, totally and completely…content.

It was nice.

Oh man, she'd really lost it if that was the case, if she could feel contented a million miles from nowhere.

Someone knocked at her door, saving her from her own agonizing thoughts. The dog didn't even lift his head.

"You could at least *pretend* to protect me," she

told him, and opened the door. ''Dora,'' she said in surprise to the grocery clerk.

Dora's hair was even bigger today, if possible. It had to have at least an entire bottle of spray in it to keep it that height. She wore tight leggings and an even tighter crop top—white with neon-green polka dots.

Her bubble gum was purple this evening. ''You're in.''

Holly laughed. ''Well…I'm out. Out of my mind, actually. But feel free to leave a message.''

''Is the job still open?'' Without waiting for an answer, Dora pushed her way into the apartment, walked into the postage-stamp-size kitchen and opened the plastic container she carried.

A heavenly scent wafted through the room.

''Homemade lasagna. I brought three different kinds—meat, three-cheese and—'' she shuddered ''—this one is just for you, sweetcakes. Low-fat vegetarian.''

Holly grabbed a fork and took a mouthful of heaven. ''You're hired,'' she said before she'd even swallowed.

''I want big bucks.''

''How big?''

''Bigger than what I'm making.''

''That should be easy enough.''

"I want Mondays off, that's my nail-and-hair day."

"Which I can see is very important to you," Holly said, tongue in cheek.

"I want—" Dora broke off and looked at her in surprise. "You mean it? You want to hire me?"

"Absolutely."

To Holly's horror, Dora's eyes filled with tears. "I'm sorry," she gasped, pulling a tissue out of her cleavage and blowing her nose so loudly it woke up the dog. "Thank you. Thank you so much." Then she rushed to the door.

"Wait—" Holly stood there awkwardly. Tears were a complete bafflement to her. Not her own, which she sometimes shed in the deep, dark of the night, then pretended the next day nothing had ever happened, but someone *else's* tears. Dora's.

"Thank you for believing in me," Dora said softly. "Not many do. I'm not exactly...popular."

"I thought everyone who was born and raised here was popular. It's the outsiders who aren't."

"I've made myself an outsider all my life. I'm pushy, I'm aggressive and I like to gossip. I work at the grocery store because my aunt owns it and it would look bad if she didn't let me. But I've wanted to get my own job for years now, I've just never had the skills."

"You really did cook this lasagna, right?"

Dora blinked in surprise, then laughed through her tears. "Yes. I said I was obnoxious, not a liar. Is the job still mine?"

"Are you going to cry every day?"

"No."

"Then it's yours."

Later when Holly was alone again, she stood surrounded by both dog and cat, marveling at the truth.

She wasn't really alone at all, and she hadn't been since she'd first arrived.

RILEY SPENT the entire next two days dealing with a ring of ranch thieves. The property in question was on the far north quadrant of the county, which meant he spent more time out of town than in it.

He had invaluable help from both the neighboring county sheriff and his own staff, but it was still Wednesday before he was back in his office on a normal schedule.

He pulled up to his building after a morning of chores on his own ranch and took a double take at the Café Nirvana.

The parking lot had cars in it.

Amazed, he crossed the street, envisioning a nice hearty breakfast, something he hadn't had time for since Maria had cooked his last one on Sunday.

Just the thought had his mouth watering.

And his heart pounding.

Because truth was, it wasn't just his stomach he was thinking about. No, it was that odd little quiver in the region above, where his heart lay.

Damn, but he was doing it again. Thinking about a woman he didn't want to be thinking about. Why couldn't it be simple? If he had to start thinking soft, mushy thoughts, why couldn't it be for someone he could *really* fall for, someone who could actually fit into his life?

Not someone like his own mother, someone who would never stick around. He'd had plenty of women in his past, but he'd never felt the earth move or heard fireworks in his head while being with one. He'd never really thought about a particular woman in the permanent sense before, and he wasn't superhappy about doing it now, but he wouldn't shy from it.

He just didn't want it to be Holly.

He opened the door to the café, anticipation thrumming through him in spite of himself.

And found utter chaos.

The stark white walls were halfway painted in a soft pastel color he couldn't have named to save his life. On a ladder, covered in paint, was his deputy sheriff, Jud.

The counter was stripped of its usual disorganization and assortment of salt and pepper shakers, sugar holders and napkins containers. Straddled on top of it, scrubbing for all she was worth was...Dora? The grocery clerk?

Seated in the corner, listing ingredients into a small tape recorder was Maria. *Maria?*

That settled it, he'd stepped into an episode of the *X-Files.*

It got even more curious.

Both the dog and Harry slept on a rug at his feet. Together.

The red booths were all ripped out and upside down on the floor. Replacing the faded red vinyl with new, dark-blue material was Mike, who looked to be in the middle of a sales pitch to Holly about his latest paintings.

"They'll make great wall hangings," he was saying around the two nails sticking out his mouth.

Holly herself didn't look like Holly. Her hair was up, but not in its usual sophisticated style. Instead it'd been shoved into a ponytail holder. Blond strands escaped everywhere, curling around her temples and cheeks. She wore a sleeveless cotton number in can't-miss-me-green and...jeans.

Jeans. He looked twice to be sure, but yep, that was form-fitting, soft-looking denim clinging to her every curve.

When she saw him, she went still. Then she smiled. It knocked his socks right off and for a moment he couldn't remember why he was here.

Then she moved toward him, setting down her clipboard. When she stood before him, separated only by the mat holding the sleeping animals, she clasped her hands together and looked at him.

He wondered if her hands had the same itch to reach for him as his had to reach for her.

"Hey," she said softly.

"Hey back."

"You've been busy."

"Yeah. So have you." He nodded to the animals, both of whom looked as if maybe they'd been washed clean. "You have mascots now?"

Her smile faded. "They're not staying." She looked around her. "Don't you...notice anything different?"

"You're wearing jeans. Nice. Very nice."

"I meant the redecorating."

"I liked it the way it was. Those jeans though, they can stay."

She didn't know what to say to that, he could tell.

"I guess you're not offering breakfast," he added.

"I'm going to reopen on Monday. Newly decorated, with a new style. That family thing I was telling you about. Three meals a day."

"You're...up for that?"

Her smile was a little tight, tenser than before. "I've hired help. This is going to work. It's going to be perfect."

"What do the new owners think of that?"

"There hasn't been an offer on the place yet."

He'd like to think he saw a flicker of relief at that sentence, but he was probably just reading something into nothing. He was sure of it, because Holly was nothing if not utterly forthcoming. If she wanted, for some odd reason, to stay in Little Paradise, she would just say so.

Hell, she'd just buy the place and make the announcement.

But she wasn't going to do any such thing and he needed to remember that.

"I was really hoping for breakfast," he said, rubbing his empty belly.

Her gaze followed the movement. Then as if she were afraid he'd notice her staring at him, she turned away and said quickly, "I have oatmeal in the back. It's not instant this time, honest, I got the recipe from Dora and it's…''

''It's…?''

''Good.'' She smiled as she once again looked at him. ''It's really good.''

He was still digesting the fact that she and Dora—complete opposites—were working together, that Holly had cooked oatmeal, that she was offering him some, when she apparently took his silence for rejection.

As if she didn't know what else to do, she hunkered down and stroked a hand along the dog's back, then Harry's before rising and turning from him.

He just caught her arm before she vanished on him. ''Wait—''

''I have work.''

''Just wait a sec.'' Turning her to face him, he looked into her still-tense face. Lord, what was it about her? Unable to help himself, he stroked a thumb over her jaw.

Her expression wasn't unreadable as it usually was, and he saw her confusion. Then, as if with great effort, she blinked and stepped back, sending a haughty I-don't-care-what-you-think glance over her shoulder at the other people in the room.

He'd never been one to care about what others

thought, either, and he didn't particularly care now. If he wanted to touch her, he would because in truth, they'd been heading toward this since the day she'd stepped out of her Jeep and into Little Paradise. But in deference to her obvious discomfort, he sent everyone a pointed look and suddenly they all became busy again.

"I'd love some oatmeal," he said. "In the kitchen?"

She nodded, and he followed her, enjoying the way her jeans showed off her body in ways her dressier clothes never had.

Mike high-fived him as he passed, looking happier than Riley had ever seen him. They'd gone to school together, until Riley had left for college. Mike had gone into his father's remodeling business, even though everyone knew he wanted to be an artist with all his heart. But painting in a small ranching town with little to no tourism didn't pay the bills, and he had four kids and a wife to support.

"I'm going to put up some of my artwork on the walls," Mike said proudly. "Maybe even sell some."

"Can't wait to see it all. Maybe I'll pick one up for the spot over my mantel."

Mike beamed. "That would be nice." He

stopped to swipe at his brow. "I won't fool myself, I won't be retiring from the building business any time soon, but this is fun, getting to see my work up on walls that aren't even mine. Assuming Holly doesn't accidentally burn the place down next."

Riley had to laugh at that, but he wondered if Holly had any idea how much she'd just given the man. If she cared.

Dora sent Riley a wink and blew a kiss as he passed, and he blew one right back at her. "New job?" he asked. He'd known her forever, too, and knew that beneath all that huge red hair, overdone makeup and major attitude, beat a rare, warm, giving heart.

"Yeah." She laughed, and it wasn't with her usual cynicism, but with genuine delight. "And it's my *own* job this time, not one given to me because of family obligations or pity or because they're afraid I'm going to embarrass them or anything like that." She grinned. "My folks have never really forgiven me for having sex in the frozen section that first year out of high school."

"Maybe because you seduced their best stock boy, and he let all the frozen lobsters thaw."

"Yeah. That was fun. But I paid for that one big-time. Now I'm done ringing up grumpy ranchers. I'm going to cook. For real. Imagine that, being paid to do something you love the most." She let out a wicked smile. "Well, the second-most anyway."

He laughed, enjoying her happiness. Riley knew how much this new job had restored some badly needed self-esteem and confidence to a woman sorely lacking in both, and again he looked at Holly.

She avoided his gaze.

They continued toward the kitchen. As Riley passed Jud, the older man suddenly got busier.

"Slow crime day?" Riley asked lightly.

Jud actually blushed. "She's trying really hard," he said grudgingly, hitching up his slipping pants and looking at Holly. "Just wanted to be neighborly."

"Uh-huh. Neighborly. Was there food involved, Jud?"

Holly smiled, giving him away.

"They offered me lunch, yes, and since—" Jud broke off until Holly disappeared into the kitchen, and he lowered his voice "—and since it's Dora cooking it, not the Low-Fat Queen, and since there's currently no cows on the run, what the hell, right?"

"Sounding a little defensive there."

"Dammit, I'm hungry. Okay?"

"Okay." Riley laughed. "Me, too."

"Nah, you're sweet on her."

"Am not."

"Are, too."

"Jud—"

"Are, too."

Riley walked away from that. In the kitchen, Holly was pulling out a bowl. Which involved her stretching up until her shirt raised high, giving him a nice view of her belly button.

His mouth went dry. "Need some help?"

"No, it's one of the benefits of being tall. I can reach my own stuff." She went up on tiptoe now, and leaned forward another little bit, which had her shirt falling away from her body. She sucked in a breath, as if that would give her another inch, and he saw more creamy skin, the outline of a few ribs, and he found himself wishing she'd stretch more, enough to give him a good shot of breast as well.

That's when he realized it was official.

He was sweet on her, just as Jud had accused him.

7

FORCING HIS EYES CLOSED, Riley stood stock-still, until he heard Holly's voice, which had a smile in it.

"The oatmeal isn't *that* scary," she said. "I promise. Dora helped."

"I'm not afraid of your oatmeal." He took the bowl, which was warm in his fingers.

"What *are* you afraid of?"

That she was standing too close to him, because he could see things in her eyes that made him dizzy. Or maybe those things were in his own eyes and he was just seeing them reflected back at him. "I'm afraid you've been taken over by aliens. You're different."

"Different?" She turned away and tripped over the dog, then bent to pat him on the head.

This was the same woman who only days ago had looked at that mutt as if he were a mite-ridden monster, and yet she was now smiling fondly, as if she'd grown to care for him.

"You ever going to name him?" he asked.

"No," she said, hastily moving away from the dog as if she'd just realized what she'd done. "He's not mine so there's no reason to."

"How do you know he's a *he?*"

Crossing her arms, she went for a haughty look and failed. "He just is."

"How do you know?"

"Because he's cocky and walks with an atti-tude."

"And?"

"And—" she rolled her eyes "—and because I looked, okay?"

He grinned. "Okay. City girl."

"Don't change the subject. How do I look dif-ferent?"

"Different...softer." Yeah, definitely softer. It was a good look for her. "I may be going out on a limb here, princess, but you're looking...*happy.*"

"Don't be silly."

"Why would it be silly to look happy?" He scooped a bite of oatmeal into his mouth and was surprised to find it nearly melted there, it was that good. "You're right, this is fantastic."

"Thank you."

"See? Right there, you said 'thank you' and you

said it with such a sweet, kind voice. Definitely different. Now, tell me why that's silly.''

"Because I don't want to be soft or sweet.'' She let out an unladylike snort and crossed her arms, a definite defensive stance. "I've never been sweet and kind in my life.''

"You're not looking into the right mirror.'' He scooped up another three bites of oatmeal to hide the fact he wanted to take at least three bites out of her. "I can give you examples of your kindness, if you need them.''

"I don't.''

"You're letting Mike hang his artwork. In case you don't know, you now walk on water.''

"His artwork is good. I'm doing myself a favor by putting up something people will want to look at.''

"How about Jud? He wasn't exactly welcoming to you. Don't tell me you turned the other cheek that easily.''

"I needed his help, he wanted good food. We compromised.''

"Uh-huh. And what about Dora?''

She shifted, giving herself away. "What about her?''

"I suppose you hired her away from a job that

was slowly killing her because you actually like loud, slightly tacky, buxom redheads."

"She's not loud." She hesitated. "And it's not up to me to judge her personal taste in clothing."

He laughed. "That was very...tactful."

"I like Dora."

"I like her, too, I just didn't expect you to."

"Why not? She's my—" *Friend,* Holly realized with no little surprise. On the outside, they appeared to be very different, but that was an illusion, for she thought that just maybe she and Dora had far more in common than they'd realized.

For one, neither of them were exactly cherished by their families.

For another, they both seemed to have a problem letting people close enough to form a relationship.

"She's your what, Holly? Your friend?" Riley's eyes shone with something far too close to pride and affection for her tastes. "You've made a friend here in this annoying town, among people you don't like?"

"I never said I didn't like this place. And as for the people...I think that could change."

He smiled, and it was a breath-taker. "So, you do like it here."

She decided to use anger to combat that funny melting sensation in the region of her heart, which was absolutely not going to get involved here. "You know, Sheriff, you have this misconceived notion that I'm this big-city snob. You don't seem to see the real me."

"Don't I?" Both his smile and expression warmed, and he moved closer to her, close enough so she could feel his breath on her cheek, could feel the heat of his body.

She liked it, far too much.

"I see you, Holly," he whispered. "I see the false bravado and confidence. I see beneath it, too, to the woman who thinks she's all alone in everything she does, who doesn't know she already has people who care about her, people who want to help. Not because of what you offer to give them, but because they like you and *want* to help you."

"I sincerely doubt that."

"Why? Why don't you want to believe that you can be liked just for you?"

"Do *you* like me just for me?" The minute the words were out of her mouth, she wished them back. It rated right up there with her most embarrassing moment, next to that time at her last job when she'd pulled out all the stops in catching the man she thought she wanted, only to find out he'd done the same to the woman *he'd* wanted—and that hadn't been her.

Which reminded her, no more men!

"Never mind," she said urgently, trying to back away but suddenly his hands were on her hips, drawing her against him.

"No, you asked, and I'm going to tell you. I want to make sure you hear me, though." His hands slid up her arms, slowly, so slowly, to capture her face, which he gently stroked with his fingers. "Yes, I like you, just for you." He smiled, and it was rueful. "I didn't *want* to like you, I'll give you that. But it's done now, and I won't turn from it."

Panic was new for her. New and unwelcome. *He liked her!* "I think we should stick with your instincts," she said quickly. "We don't want to like each other, so we should—"

He set a finger to her lips, halting her words, and leaned even closer, so their mouths were only a fraction of an inch apart. "Don't say this is stupid," he murmured. "I'm well aware of the stupidity factor."

"So let's get smart!"

He smiled slowly. "Later." And he placed his mouth over hers.

It was what she'd dreamed about every night since she'd come to Little Paradise, whether she wanted to admit it or not. But even in her dream, she hadn't gotten it right.

This was right.

It was also terrifyingly hot, deep, messy and... bone-melting.

Riley didn't just kiss her; no, he had to possess her. Had to make her surrender to it. His hands hauled her closer, his lips claimed hers, and she couldn't hold back her sigh of pleasure because this was even better than her midnight fantasies.

At her little whimper, he groaned and deepened the kiss. Both of them staggered, and she fell back against the counter, Riley right with her, holding her, touching her, kissing and kissing her as if he never intended to let go.

She thought that just might be okay with her. She couldn't get enough, either. Her hands slid up his chest, around his neck, holding his head close to hers in case he decided he didn't want to kiss her anymore.

No chance. His hands held her captive between the hard counter and his even harder body. When she finally had to break off the kiss or suffocate, he simply shifted, dropping openmouthed kisses along her jaw, her neck, nuzzling at her collarbone where the material of her shirt gave away.

She did the same, tasting his skin, tugging on

his earlobe with her teeth, eliciting a deep-throated moan before he cupped her face again, holding her still to kiss her; harder, wetter, deeper than before.

Wrapped around each other as they were, the ringing didn't immediately sink into Holly's consciousness, but eventually they had to stop to breathe again, and that was when she realized she'd totally lost it.

"I have to get that," she murmured, straightening.

He straightened, too, looking hot, bothered and so damn sexy she had to turn away from him to even remember her name.

And she still had trouble.

"Holly," she murmured, placing a hand to her racing heart. "Holly Stone."

Riley let out a shaky laugh. "I didn't expect anything like that."

"But at least you didn't nearly forget your name."

"No, but I forgot everything else." He shoved a hand through his already messed-up hair and stared at her. "That was…amazing."

The phone rang again.

They could only look at each other. Holly actually might have gotten to the phone, but she didn't, couldn't, move.

The machine picked up the call, and after the message had run, Holly's mother's voice filled the room.

"Holly? I heard from the Mendozas, they were upset enough to make a shore-to-ship call! Tell me you haven't really messed up as badly as we've heard. I need to know whether you think you can fix things or if I have to send someone out there. Holly? Is the situation still out of control?"

Holly looked at the machine. "The *situation?*" She had to laugh, with lips that were still wet from the most amazing kiss she'd ever had. She looked at Riley, who's lips were also wet. "Definitely still out of control," she said to herself.

Riley seemed to agree with that assessment as he turned to face the counter, leaning on it with tensed arms as if he needed the extra support.

"Holly?" Her mother's very cultured voice sounded annoyed. "I need you to call me back right away, do you understand? If you're going to do this to me, I need to know immediately so I can save the entire operation—"

Holly whipped up the phone, hoping to stop the words before her mother could further humiliate her in front of Riley. "This is a café, Mother, not one of your patients."

"You're there."

"Yes, and I happen to have things perfectly under control."

"How can you when you're dumping ice water into the laps of big, hungry men? Or hiring the town floozy?"

Riley was looking at her now, and the expression on his face held an interesting and horrifying mixture of pity and compassion. Damn him anyway. Didn't he realize her mother always spoke to her this way? That she'd never had faith in Holly, but that was okay because she didn't deserve it since she'd never done anything to earn that faith? "The water thing was an accident," she muttered.

"How about the gas leak? Killing people is bad for business."

"Yes, I realize that." Holly turned her back to Riley. "Trust me, everything is going to be fine."

"I'm not going to trust you," her mother said, shocked at the very idea. "How can I? You've held more jobs than this entire family put together. You've never in your life remained with one project for more than it took you to lose interest in it."

Well, that hurt.

It shouldn't, Holly reminded herself, not when it was true. But dammit, she was trying to change. "I realize I've never given you a reason to trust me before, but things are different now. I—I really wanted to make you proud of me on this one. I think I still can.''

How embarrassing was this? She was practically begging for her mother's attention.

Even worse, Riley had come close, his big, tall body right behind hers. He cocked his head so his ear was close to hers, next to the receiver. She tried to move away but he slid his hands real soft and gentle around her waist.

She couldn't resist soft and gentle. She'd never felt it before, not like this.

''Holly, this isn't the time to resolve your issues with your family,'' her mother said. ''Just don't make me look bad, I promised the—''

While her mother droned on, Riley switched tactics. He shifted to her other side, to her free ear, and whispered, ''Hang up.''

''I can't,'' she mouthed, pushing him away.

Riley refused to be budged.

''—we're trying to sell that place,'' her mother continued, on a roll. ''It has to look good when potential buyers come through. I should see if I can get your brother or sisters, or someone, out there, I—''

''I can do this,'' Holly said, and dammit, her voice wavered. ''I just need some more time.'' She might have even groveled, because this project had come to mean so much more than she could have ever imagined.

But Riley was right there, listening to every word, watching her with an intensity that made her want to squirm, and she refused to show him her weaknesses.

"I just want you to admit you're in over your head," her mother said.

Over her dead body. "Mother, I—"

Static burst in her ear, only it wasn't the phone. It was Riley, doing a great imitation of a bad connection.

He winked at her and went on making the obnoxious noise.

She grinned back, suddenly feeling…light. "Gotta run, Mother. Bad connection."

"Holly! Don't you dare—"

Riley pushed his finger onto the base, effectively cutting her off.

"Nice timing," she murmured.

"Yeah." He shifted her in his arms, turning her to face him. "Now…where were we?"

"Oh, no, you don't." With an uneasy laugh, she backed out of his arms. On the counter was an open container of flour, salt and the various makings of bread, which she was about to give a shot, compliments of one of Maria's recipes. To keep both her mind and her hands busy, she dipped into the flour and began measuring.

"Why don't you just admit it," he asked quietly. "We seem to have an attraction problem."

"We don't have any such thing."

"Uh-huh." Now he was close again, too close, his body pressed hard against the back of hers, his mouth doing things to her neck that made her eyes cross with lust.

She immediately lost count of how many cups she'd measured and stared stupidly into the bowl.

"Tell me you're not turned on," he said huskily, rocking his hips slowly against her bottom, allowing her to feel the fact that he was exactly that. "Tell me." His hands, oh, those very talented hands, slid from her hips over her ribs and dallied there, outlining each and every one with slow precision.

She ached. "There is a room full of people out front," she managed to reply, just barely stopping herself from melting to the floor in a boneless heap.

"Tell me to stop, and I will." The tips of his fingers stroked the very bottom curve of her breasts now and she nearly moaned out loud.

Tell him to stop? She couldn't even breathe. "I

don't want this,'' she told him, twisting in his arms and flinging hers around him, taking his mouth hard.

"You may not *like* wanting it," he said, tearing away to tell her, "but you do." And then he rejoined the kiss, the all-consuming kiss, until they were both grappling for a better grip, streaking their hands over each other, dying, *dying* for more.

"Ahem."

Holly gasped, then shoved away from Riley to face a broadly grinning Jud.

"Sorry," he said, looking anything but. "I heard some banging around in here and just wanted to make sure everything was okay."

"Everything is okay," Riley said, sounding pressed for air.

"Hmm. Sure?"

"Sure," Riley said tightly. "We've got everything under control."

Jud didn't move. "Can't be too sure, you know."

"Jud."

"Yes, boss?"

"Do you like your job?"

"Very much."

"Good. Get out and you can keep it."

Jud nodded thoughtfully. "Okay, you don't need

to tell me twice. But you might want to wipe those handprints away.''

"What handprints?''

"The ones made of flour that are all over your butt.''

Holly just groaned.

8

By Monday, Holly was ready for business. Really ready this time.

"It'll be great," Dora told her. She was popping her wild-raspberry bubble gum as she prepared for their first family-style dinner. "I've got the lasagna nearly set, you handled the bread—excellently I might add—and we've actually got help out front."

"Assuming we get customers." Holly paced the kitchen in an unusual fit of nerves. "I hope Steve can take the pressure." She was referring to Dora's younger brother, who was going to wait tables in the afternoons after school. "The people here are brutal."

Dora laughed as she stopped in front of the steel refrigerator to check out her reflection. "They are not. They were only brutal to you because you asked for it."

"I did no such thing."

"Oh, really?" Dora smiled, then straightened,

lifted her nose in the air and strutted across the kitchen as if she owned the place. "You didn't walk like this? You didn't maybe, just a little, think you were too good for this backcountry, out-of-the-way little hole-in-the-wall?"

Holly had to laugh at the imitation, which granted, probably wasn't that far off the mark. "If I thought I was too good, you people showed me otherwise in less than thirty seconds."

"No one meant to hurt your feelings. We just have an inherent mistrust of 'them city folk,'" Dora said, drawling out the last two words.

"Well, maybe I deserved to be taken down a peg or two. I guess I thought I was better than this place." It was humbling. "Though I've learned the opposite is true."

Dora dropped the pretense and became Dora again. "Don't you say that. I love having you here. You've given me so much."

"What? A job?" She felt the desperate need to lighten this conversation before she had to face exactly what and how much this place had given *her*.

"Yes, a job. Among other things. Holly...are you going to stay? Maybe even be with Riley?"

Holly forced a laugh. "Any connection between your reality and mine is purely coincidental."

"Uh-huh." Dora smirked. "You're hot for him."

"I thought *you* wanted him."

"Nah, I just said that to be petty."

"I'm going to stay," Holly said. "Until this place sells." And when it did, she'd have to find a new place to go. A new job. New friends.

She didn't want new people in her life. She wanted what she'd started for herself here. She wanted *these* friends, people like Dora. Yes, maybe she wore too much makeup. Maybe her hair was teased into new and dizzy heights and she wore pink spandex that wasn't quite as flattering on her very lush figure as she probably hoped.

But she was smiling at Holly with such affection, such fondness, that she felt tears sting her eyes. To combat that, she imagined herself in one hour, standing at the front door, looking like an idiot as she waited for customers that weren't going to come.

THEY CAME. Riley made sure of it. Due to his influence, and a good amount of called-in favors, the place was comfortably full.

The lasagna was fantastic.

The service was…interesting. Steve did his best, but he was easily flustered, especially when three of his high-school classmates—all girls—came in, sat down at one of his tables and proceeded to giggle every time he walked by.

He dropped a pitcher of ice water, though not in anyone's lap, so that was a bonus. He messed up several bills, giving Jud one for forty-five dollars, and then a family of six one for six dollars.

Both of which were fixed by Holly, who had a smile firmly in place and her best manners on. She was flitting back and forth between the kitchen and helping Steve, lending a hand wherever it was needed.

Her hair was not perfect, she had a smudge of mascara beneath one eye and a red sauce stain across the front of what should have been a simple cotton sundress, but on her nothing was simple.

He shouldn't have kissed her.

He could still taste her, could still feel her body under his hands. No way could he have predicted that amazing, almost explosive chemical reaction between them. He would have thought she'd shove him away.

Dammit, she never did what she was supposed to do.

Without thinking, he headed straight toward her, only to be stopped by a smirking Jud.

"What? You want more flour on your butt?"

"Jud—"

"Yeah, yeah, mind my own business." Jud sat back down and stuffed a huge bite of lasagna into his mouth. Grinning, chewing, he studied an uncomfortable Riley. "Hard to do, boy, when you've got your feelings out for the world to enjoy."

"I don't know what you're talking about."

"Sure you do. You've got it bad. Real bad."

"I do not."

"Oh, you've got it *sooo* bad." His grin spread. "And for a city girl at that."

"Jud—"

"I know. I'll shut up just as soon as I get to my point."

"You have one?"

"Very funny." Jud shoved in another bite and shook his head. "Mmm, that girl really got it right this time."

"Your point," Riley said through his teeth.

"Ah, yes." He wiped his mouth with a napkin. "My point is, I've been worried. I thought you were going to let love pass you by. It disturbed me, because if ever a man was made for having a family around him, it's you, Riley."

"I have family. I have my dad. I have—"

"A woman. I mean a woman. And your own kids."

"Whoa." Riley lifted a hand. "Just stop right there. I'm not even close to thinking about that stuff right now."

"Ah. You're still thinking with your zipper." Jud nodded smugly. "That's okay, too. I figure you deserve that, the rest will come."

"Jud—"

"She's a fine woman," Jud said quietly, nodding to Holly. "I misjudged her, and so did everyone else. Get her to stay, Riley."

"Are you kidding? Soon as she's able, she'll hightail it out of here."

"She likes you."

"No."

"Do I need to remind you about those flour handprints?"

Jud let out a low laugh. "Wants me, maybe. But like? No."

"Son—"

"And even if I'm wrong, it's nothing that won't go away when she's tired of slumming."

"I think you're underestimating the both of you. Get her to stay."

"That's not up to me."

"Sure about that?"

They both looked at Holly, who was smiling a bit nervously at Dan. Dan pointed to his glass of ice water, and must have made a crack about where Holly had spilled it the last time she'd served him, because she blushed.

Blushed. Looking nothing like the sophisticate she had only two weeks ago, Riley couldn't tear his eyes off her. "I've gotta go," he said to Jud, who merely lifted an eyebrow and smiled knowingly.

"Of course you do, son."

RILEY CORNERED HER in the storage room, where she'd gone to get more napkins.

"Riley?" she gasped in surprise when he slammed the door behind them, pressed her back against a shelving unit and slid his hands into her hair.

"What are you doing?"

"This." He took her mouth with his. He had to. And it was no gentle, hey-how-are-you-today kiss. It was a hot, fiery mark of possession, which might have given him pause, if he could think.

"Wait." She tore away after a long, breathless, soul-searching connection. "Wait just a minute."

"No." He leaned in for more, and she gave it, until with a weak laugh, she put a hand to his chest and pushed.

"Riley...I can't think when you do that."

"Thinking isn't required. You look delicious. All messed up and off balance."

Her hands went to her hair. "I'm messed up?"

He laughed at her horrified expression. "Perfectly. Damn, I've got to taste you again."

This time the kiss lasted until they both broke it off, panting. She stared into his eyes, then dropped her gaze to his mouth. She licked her lips, looking dazzled, dazed, and so damn hot he groaned and reached for her once more.

Laughing a little, she pushed at him again. "I have customers!"

"And two employees. Let's go to my place, Holly."

Her eyes widened. "Oh, my God—" She broke off on a moan when he trailed his mouth over her jaw to her ear. "So fast. *Too* fast. I've only known you for a week."

"Two. How long is long enough?"

She bit her lip, her eyes wild with the desire she was attempting to control. "I'm not sure."

"Another month? Another week? Another day? It's not going to make a difference in how I feel, Holly. The only difference will be you could be gone."

"I— Yes," she whispered.

"So, why wait?"

"I'm not leaving yet."

"Do you want me?" His fingers played with the back of her dress, which had a cutout over her spine. When he skimmed over her bare skin he shuddered in delight.

So did she. "Yes. Yes, I want you."

He moved closer, shifted a hard thigh between hers and slipped his fingers beneath the material of her dress.

"You're not playing fair," she said, pressing closer to him.

"Neither are you, looking so wicked in that dress."

She laughed, though she seemed a bit wary now. "It's old, but it's also the only item of clothing I have left that hasn't been stained."

"I told you to stick with that pink apron."

"Riley." Again she looked at his mouth, and her longing was unmistakable. So were her reservations. "I can't. Not with you. I just…can't."

"Why?"

"Because you—you're—" She closed her eyes.

He felt cold suddenly, and forced himself to move back, to separate himself from her. "Yeah." It shouldn't hurt like this, not when he'd known it would happen. "Too small town for you, right?"

He'd opened the door and stepped out when she

put her hand on his arm. "Riley, you don't understand—"

"Believe me, princess, I understand." But he didn't have to like it. "I understand perfectly."

THE DAY TURNED OUT to be an entire waste of makeup.

Yes, the evening at the café could only be considered a success. Maybe they hadn't filled every seat, but they'd satisfied every customer. It was more than Holly could have hoped for.

Businesswise, things were perfect.

Personally, things weren't so perfect.

After Riley had left, she'd been unable to concentrate on anything but the way she felt inside, all humming and throbbing and panicking at the same time.

She'd hurt his feelings. The big, easygoing, laidback sheriff who'd seemed so invincible, and yet she'd hurt him. She'd let him go knowing he thought she felt herself above him instead of the truth—she couldn't allow herself to be with him because he was different from all the other men she'd known.

He alone could hurt her, and yet *she'd* hurt *him.*

She had to go to him and fix things, but there

was only one way to do that, which was to give in to the physical attraction between them.

It was silly, especially since he'd never said he wanted more than sex.

So, what was holding her back? It'd been a long time for her; surely she deserved a little spice.

Right?

Wrong. Because even she, the master of ruining her own happiness, knew that getting a "little spice" with Riley wouldn't end there. Couldn't. Not the way she was beginning to feel about him.

With all that in mind, it was no wonder she took the streets a tad fast. She'd seen all her customers fed and out the door happy.

And now she was headed straight to the grocery store, in need of an entire carton of ice cream all to herself—double-fudge chocolate. It was her most secret, most standard comforter in times of need.

There'd been many such times over the years.

But right now she felt more needy than usual. The store was nearly empty, for which she was thankful. She bought a carton *and* a spoon because there was no way she could wait until she got home to begin pigging out. She was in crisis mode and needed immediate gratification.

A hug might have worked just as well.

The thought came from nowhere and she had to let out a rueful laugh. There was no hug available at the moment, so she'd do with empty calories.

She drove with one hand on the wheel, the other spooning ice cream into her mouth from the open container between her legs. At the red light she had to shove the full spoon into her mouth to downshift, and she was still sucking on it when the light changed.

In her haste to get home and wallow, maybe she stepped on the gas just a bit too hard. So what? The streets were empty.

That's when she saw the flashing lights in her rearview mirror. "Great," she groaned around the spoon. "Great ending to a perfect day."

Pulling over, she shoved another full bite into her mouth and was digging for her license when the knock came at her window.

Looking up, spoon dangling from her mouth, she found...Riley.

He took in the sight of her. She was undoubtedly a total wreck. She could feel him looking at her as she rolled the window down, but because of the dark night she couldn't see his expression.

He couldn't have missed the ice cream, or the fact she was eating all of it, by herself. An entire gallon. Slowly she took the spoon out of her mouth. "At least it's you," she said. "I thought I was getting a ticket."

"You are." He bent his dark head and began writing on his pad.

His stance was aggressive, his posture authoritative, and all thoughts of ice cream vanished, even as it chilled the insides of her legs. "But…"

"You were speeding. You were exhibiting reckless driving with that peel out you did at the light." He peered into the Jeep, his gaze lighting on the ice cream, still resting between her thighs.

Even in the dark, she could see his eyes go hot, hot enough to practically melt the dessert. "You were eating and driving."

"Not illegal," she said.

"It is if you're not paying attention. Step out of the Jeep, please."

"What?"

He didn't wait for her, but opened the door, unbuckled her seat belt and evacuated her without further ado. He pocketed her keys, slung her purse over his shoulder, locked her car and took her by the arm.

"What are you doing?"

"Taking you in."

"What? Riley, stop this—"

His hands were gentle, but so firm she couldn't

break away. He settled her into his patrol car, even hooked up her seat belt. The backs of his fingers brushed against her breasts.

She sucked in a breath as her nipples hardened.

He went utterly still, staring down at her. Then he slammed the door and without another word, walked around and got into the driver's seat.

"This is ridiculous," she said shakily. "Where are we going?"

"I told you. I'm taking you in."

"All I did was rev the engine."

"You were speeding."

"Not exactly a federal offense."

His jaw was tight, he stared straight ahead. He hadn't shaved and no way had his hair seen a comb. His arms were tense, so much so that she could see his every muscle delineated beneath his clothing. "Riley—"

"You really shouldn't talk without your lawyer present."

She stared at him, shocked. *He was really taking her in.*

She was his prisoner.

9

"WHERE ARE WE GOING?" Holly demanded in a voice that gave away nothing.

Riley didn't even look at her, because if he did, he'd have to touch her.

Not yet. "That's on a need-to-know basis."

"And I don't need to know?"

"Not yet."

"You can't do this." Her chin was up, her eyes flashing.

So brave.

And yet Riley felt her nerves shimmering just beneath the surface. It was a tribute to how well he'd come to know her that he felt them at all.

A tribute *and* a curse because he was getting tired of fighting his feelings for her—which meant that what he was about to do was extra idiotic.

It didn't stop him.

"Why can't I do this?" he asked, his voice even.

"Because..." She stopped to fiddle with her top.

A top that had gotten his immediate attention not only because it was snug and spaghetti-strapped, but because the right strap kept slipping down. "Because I need to make sure the restaurant is clean for first thing in the morning. There's someone coming to look at the place."

"A little grease isn't going to sway them."

"I want everything to be perfect."

"So you can get out of here all the faster?"

She was silent. "I'm not in a hurry to leave," she said finally.

"Could have fooled me."

"Harry needs to be let out."

He couldn't help it, he laughed. "Is that the best you've got?"

"He does! And the dog, he'll be wondering what's happened to me."

"The *dog*. Do you think you're ever going to name him, Holly? Or would that be too close to admitting you've come to care about those two animals in the same way you've come to care about this town?"

She opened her mouth, glared at him, then shut it again.

"Speechless? Isn't that a first?" Frustration built in him, both because she wouldn't let him in, and because that's where he wanted to be. He took the next corner a bit tight.

Grabbing the dashboard rather than eat it, she glared at him. "I told you why I couldn't name him before. What if his owner had come and gotten him?"

"Then he'd have two names, and all the love he could ever want."

"Buster," she whispered.

"Why can't you just admit the truth? That you're too chicken? Too chicken to admit he's wormed his way into your heart the same way Harry did. The same way Dora did, and all the others. You're afraid," he said flatly, bluntly, turning away from her pale face. "You're afraid of feeling something for the animals, for the people, for the town. For me."

"Buster," she repeated softly.

"*What?*"

"I named him Buster for the way he's busted into my heart. Like the people around here. Like the town." She paused. "Like you."

He risked a look at her now. "You sound uncertain."

"Not about that. What I'm uncertain about is my future."

"You don't have to be."

"It's…complicated."

"Yeah." He took another turn and the wheels squealed.

"You're speeding." She pointed to his speed-ometer. "I think that makes you a hypocrite. If you'll just stop and let me out, we'll call it even."

"Can't do that."

"Why not?"

"Probably the same reason you can't tell me what's really going on inside your head," he said. "It's called stubbornness. Pride. Ego. Stupidity."

They were on the edge of town now, close to the café, and his office. She bit her lower lip and shifted to face him. "Look, Riley, I should prob-ably tell you…I really can't afford another ticket right now."

"It's not the ticket you should be worried about."

"Yeah, well, actually it is. You see, I sort of already have a few on my record."

"Speeding?"

"Yes."

"Always in a hurry, huh, Holly?"

"It's a character flaw. Anyway, another ticket would be really bad."

"Should have thought about that earlier."

"I wasn't going that fast."

"Princess, you were barely a blur on the highway. You must have been in quite a hurry to have that date with your carton of ice cream."

That got her, he could tell by the mental daggers stabbing into him. He passed the office, but then again, he'd never had any intention of stopping there. No, from the moment he'd seen her whipping through town, he'd known what he wanted tonight.

Her.

Even if it was only for tonight, which is of course all it would be.

She straightened and frowned. "Hey. Where are we going?"

"I told you. In."

She was more than a little pale in the moonlight now. More than a little beautiful. She stirred him in a way no one else ever had, and he only knew one thing to do. "I'm taking you to my house."

"Your— What for?"

"I have this plan. It involves carrying you up to my bed, removing every piece of clothing you have on so that I can touch and kiss and lick my way to heaven."

Her mouth fell open again. Her hand fluttered up to her heart, and above that, at her neck, he could see the wild flutter of her pulse.

"I don't think—"

"Good. Perfect. Go with that." His ranch was right in front of them now, and he parked close to the house. When he came around to the passenger's door, Holly was staring directly in front of her, perfectly still.

He took her hand and pulled her out of the car. They stood there in the dark night, staring at each other.

"You let me think that I was in trouble," she whispered.

"You aren't in trouble, you *are* trouble."

"You can't make me go in against my will."

"Nope. But I can make you *want* to go in."

"No one can do that."

"I can make you want to talk to me, too, tell me your deepest, darkest secrets. Your feelings, your wishes. Your desires, your hopes."

"No." She was looking at him with her tough, beat-this expression, but there, mixed in with the coolness, he saw desire, need, and especially fear—everything he was feeling, too.

He still held her hand, and he reached for the other one. He leaned close to brush his mouth to her cheek. When she turned toward him, it was the most natural thing in the world to kiss her lips.

She sighed, all signs of temper and annoyance

draining away as he tasted her—soft and sweet and so female.

"Riley." Just that, just his name, but it was all he needed. He kissed her again, then again, until she slipped her arms around his neck. At the same time he caught her up against him, and the sheer relief of having her there, pressed to him from chest to thigh, was almost more than he could bear. "You feel good."

"So do you, but I can think so and still not like you."

"Liar." He opened the front door of his house and stood aside, giving her the choice.

She stared inside for a long moment, taking in his big, airy living room. "Now is a fine time to be chivalrous."

"Yes or no, Holly." His entire body clenched in painful anticipation. "Will you come in?"

"To go to bed with you? Or to...talk?"

Trust her to be so forthcoming. She was obviously far more terrified of talking.

Ironic, since that's what he wanted more than anything.

He just waited, and when she let out a loud sigh and stepped over the threshold, he took a huge breath of relief.

"I'm thirsty," she whispered, wrapping her arms around herself.

She was nervous. The realization touched him unbearably, made him feel protective, tender. "Come, then."

In the kitchen she flipped on all the lights, making him smile. "Do you think you're safer from what's between us that way?"

"I'm not afraid of you," she said decisively, but moved to the far side of the kitchen, on the other side of the island, on which there sat a huge chocolate cake.

"Maria," he said. "She left me dessert."

"She left enough for the entire town." She swiped a fingerful of the frosting, then stuck it in her mouth.

At the sucking sound she made, Riley went instantly hard. She could have no idea what she was doing to him. "Holly—"

She did it again, her eyes meeting his.

She knew.

Slowly, very slowly, she did it again, stroked her finger across the topping and then sucked it in. Helplessly, he moved toward her. "You're trying to seduce me so I can't make you talk to me."

"I already told you, no one makes me do anything, and anyway—" she went for another bite "it's your own fault, being so easy. All I'm doing is licking a little chocolate off my finger."

"That's all, huh?" He became intensely determined to bring her to the fevered pitch he was already at, that he'd been at since the first day she'd come to town. With as much slow precision as she'd shown, he slid his finger through the frosting.

Then he looked at her.

She registered the wicked gleam in his eyes and stepped back, hitting up against the counter. "Don't even think about it."

He held up his finger, thickly coated in chocolate. "Oh, I'm thinking about it."

"Riley—"

He merely stepped toward her, effectively trapping her into the corner, and touched her lower lip.

Heat spiraled through her body without warning. Her mouth opened, and before she could think of the wisdom of the action, she sucked his finger into her mouth.

A slow groan escaped him, and he watched her with such intensity she wondered how long she could stand.

"I want you," he whispered. "But not in the way you think. I want to know you, inside and out.

I want to understand you. I want you to open up to me. I want—''

"You don't…want my body?"

"Not before the rest."

She didn't want to talk to him because she knew that would lead—straight to getting hurt. He'd grow to know her, would realize how terribly unsuited she was for both him and Little Paradise, maybe even realize that she wasn't a particularly good person, and then it would be over.

But not before her heart got stomped on.

Yes, she wanted him, maybe even in the way he wanted her, but it wouldn't work, surely he had to see that! All she could give him was her body, not more, please not more.

"Give me the rest, Holly, give me all of you."

"No."

What made him want to know her, anyway? He was her polar opposite. He saw the glass half-full, she saw it half-empty. He saw the good in everyone, she was always expecting the worst.

She couldn't help but wonder what he saw when he looked at *her*. "Let me get this straight," she said. "That kiss? It's going to lead to *nowhere?*"

"Not unless you're going to talk to me."

"About me."

"Yes."

No. It was humiliation that had her scooping up more frosting, with *two* fingers this time, and going at Riley.

He was quick. Catching her wrist, he laughed. "Temper, temper..."

Laughing was his second mistake. Her other hand was free, and she used it, swiping a good amount of the frosting across his jaw. "You made me *want* you, you...you jerk! And then you brought me here, letting me think that we would...that..." She ran out of steam, realizing she'd just admitted she wanted him more than he obviously wanted her.

He stared at her in shock. But he had amazing regrouping capabilities. And unfortunately for her, she'd forgotten his strength. With little to no trouble, he pinned her back in the corner, both hands held captive behind her back with one of his.

Which left his other free.

Not good.

He stuck a finger in the frosting, slowly, letting her suffer, then smiled down at her, his expression pure trouble. "I'm glad you want me," he said huskily, chocolate dripping off his jaw. "I want you, too, but apparently I didn't make that clear enough. I want you, but I want a lot more than a quick roll in the sheets."

She sucked in a breath. "Not me, that's all I want."

"Really?"

Struggling did her no good. Given how he had her arms behind her back, she was at a distinct disadvantage. Not to mention that in this position, her chest was thrust out, slammed up against his.

Her body liked that, too much. She went still.

So did he. Then he brought his finger to the pulse at the base of her neck, stroking it—and the chocolate—down, down, down to where her top began, just above the swell of her breasts.

Against the white cotton material, her nipples thrust out.

At the sight, he made a soft, aching sound. "Then I guess this will have to be enough," he murmured. "For now."

"For forever."

"You're wrong about that," he said, making her nervous, because surely he couldn't read her mind, right? He couldn't know she'd been starting to dream about him, starting to hope and wonder?

"I should just walk home," she said bravely. "But it's dark and dangerous."

"Princess, looking the way you do tonight, you're in far more danger from me than anyone on the street." Then he was back with the chocolate, reminding her that she was his captive. He made another path across the top of one breast, over the soft curve. He made that rough noise again, the one that caused an answering tug from deep within her, a tug that couldn't—wouldn't—be denied.

She leaned forward as much as she could and nibbled at the chocolate still on his jaw. Bending his head, he returned the favor, sucking frosting off her skin, as well. Her hands flexed in his, and she couldn't hold back her shameless whimper for more.

"Good?"

"Just this," she repeated, absolutely breathless. "Just this. No talking, nothing more. Promise."

"I never make promises I can't keep." One of her straps had slipped over her shoulder again. With a nudge from him, the other fell as well, leaving the cotton just skimming across the top of her nearly exposed breasts.

"I shouldn't be here." But she wanted to be, oh, how she wanted to be. She wanted to be in his arms, lost in his touch, in his kisses. She wanted him to make her forget all the impossibilities between them. "Let go of my hands."

"Why? So you can put the rest of the cake in my face?" But he did let her go, and she concentrated on his shirt, pulling it from his jeans, unbuttoning it to expose his broad, smooth chest.

"I've never had fattening sex before," she said, taking another fingerful of frosting and spreading it across him, down his belly. He had the most amazing stomach, she thought, loving how it quivered when she touched him. Then she dropped to her knees and began kissing it off one little nibble at a time.

"Not fattening *sex*," he growled, sucking in a sharp breath when she started on his zipper. "Love. We're making fattening *love*."

"You're determined to make this complicated," she said lightly, gasping when he hauled her to her feet, lifting her so that she sat on the counter.

Her skirt, a gauzy, weightless thing, was easily bunched in his hands and pushed up her thighs, which he opened to step between. "Say it," he demanded. "That you're giving yourself to me because it's right, because it's inevitable, because what we have can't be ignored or shoved into any category so simple as just sex. Say we're doing this because you're giving yourself to me, not because I'm taking, because—"

"Yes," she whispered, giving in to his glittering eyes, to the need tightening his body, to everything. To all of it.

"Yes, what?"

"You're going to make me say it?"

"Oh, yeah." He rocked his hips toward hers and her breath caught. "You've got to say it." His hand stroked up her ribs to her breast. His thumb rasped over her nipple, then again. "I've got to hear it."

"Do you—" Her entire being was centered around what he was doing to her. "Do you always talk so much while you're doing this?"

He let out a low laugh, which turned into a groan when she pressed her breast into his hand. "Just with you apparently. Tell me, Holly, and I promise you, I'll find something better to do with my mouth."

"A promise?"

"One I can most definitely keep."

"Okay." She couldn't help but acquiesce. "We're making love because I can't help it. When I'm with you I lose brain capacity at an alarming speed."

Another low laugh. "Me, too."

It was the most arousing thing, laughing while being intimate. She'd never done both at the same time before.

She liked it.

"More words," he demanded.

"I thought you said you'd find something else to do with your mouth— Oh my," she whispered as he did just that.

"I'll keep my mouth busy, you use yours to talk to me," he urged. "Tell me more."

"Um...okay." That she could speak at all was shocking. Always in the past, being with someone like him had been about power.

What she was doing now, what he was doing to her, had nothing to do with power at all.

Yet another shock for her awakening heart to absorb. "We're making love because I want you," she admitted. "I have to have you."

"Yes." And true to his word, he continued to find better uses for his mouth, starting with her neck, kissing it with the most arousing hot, open-mouthed kisses, eating off the frosting as he went. His hands slipped beneath her, snugging her up to the most impressive erection she'd ever felt.

"You're...big." She wasn't sure whether she was speaking in wonder or fear.

With a laughing groan, Riley set his forehead to hers. "That's sort of the idea."

"How do you know you'll fit?"

"Oh, I'll fit," he assured her, lifting his head to nip at her lower lip.

She lost more brain cells. "Another promise?"

"Two in a row." He moved against her again and they both moaned. "A personal record for me."

"I threw away your condoms."

"I bought more."

"Okay. Good." She bit his neck.

His breathing was uneven and his body was so hard against hers. She set her cheek to his sticky chest. "I don't know what it all means, Riley. I don't know."

"We don't have to know now, it'll come."

He was right. They didn't have to make any decisions right this minute except for where to put their mouths, their fingers, their bodies. It all seemed so necessary, so right; the heat, the desire, the beginning of feelings too terrifying to put into words. She brushed her mouth over his chest, eating more frosting, pushing at his shirt until it fell to the floor.

He tugged on hers. Her breasts popped free, fully exposing her to his gaze. Fueled by the shaky glide of his hands on her, she moved restlessly against him, slipping her hands inside his jeans, releasing him.

Untaming him.

"Riley," she breathed, needing, aching, yearning. "Please."

"Yes. Now." He pushed her skirt above her waist, and skimmed her panties off to cup her, sliding his fingers into her wet heat and softly stroking until she thrust her hips at him helplessly, until she was shuddering, shuddering, falling apart in his hands, hands he slid beneath her to bring her closer to him.

And then he was opening that new condom, filling her, inch by incredible hot inch. In no time he had her so full she thought she might burst, had her at the cliff ready to plunge, but he held her off, to almost beyond what she thought she could bear. Then he bent close, holding her gaze, whispering her name in a voice filled with awe, and she couldn't help it, she couldn't hold back, and she shattered again.

She wasn't alone this time. As she held on for dear life, completely lost in his arms, he lost himself, too, in her.

Frosting dripped off them to the floor.

10

THE NEXT DAY Riley found out about the offer on the café. He got the news through the grapevine, not an unusual occurrence in town since the grapevine often had more news than the local newspaper.

Which ironically enough, came out that very morning with a nice spread on Café Nirvana. The article touted both Holly and her innovative family-style serving, and Dora's wonderful home cooking.

There was a nice picture of the front of the café, and another of the newly decorated interior, with a smiling Dora holding a tin of fresh bread and Holly holding a pitcher of ice water. In the background a group of grinning customers held up their empty water glasses—all except Dan, who was pretending to cower back, covering his lap with his hands.

Riley looked down into Holly's smiling face and

felt the now familiar but no less unnerving feeling of drowning in those eyes, in her smile, her heart.

And after last night, he was sure she felt the same way.

Or pretty sure.

It was late morning now. Due to an altercation between two neighboring ranchers—who were fighting over a downed fence and a misplaced pig, which Riley had had to help capture—he was late getting into town.

Late and filthy.

He had a mountain of paperwork to face, maybe even two mountains. But he could think of little else than last night, when he and Holly had initiated his kitchen in the joys of food fights and making love.

The countertop had been only the beginning, after which they'd moved to his table, then eventually his bed.

Holly hadn't stayed the night. He'd wanted her to, but she'd given him the animal excuse.

They needed to be let out and fed.

He knew better. She was terrified of him and the feelings he evoked.

Well, they were even there, but with that terror came an undeniable warm and fuzzy feeling.

Now there was an offer on the café, from a couple out of Tucson, and his heart, warm and fuzzy only a few hours before, went cold.

Holly was now free to leave.

Forgoing his office, he went straight across the street. It was between lunch and breakfast thankfully, so the place was quiet.

"Hello?" he called, walking past the counter into the empty kitchen, his intentions being to take Holly straight into his arms and kiss her senseless.

Then demand she stay.

No, that wasn't right. Of course that wasn't right. He couldn't, wouldn't, demand anything of her. Ever. She had a life to lead and he would leave her to do that, as she saw fit. Which meant she'd probably go as far from Little Paradise as she could get.

And he couldn't blame her, not simply because they had different hopes and dreams.

The only person in the kitchen was Dora. She had the makings of lunch scattered across the countertop, her forehead wrinkled in concentration as she chewed on her gum with the subtlety of a freight train.

"Hey, Sheriff." She sent him a wink and a grin. "You look hungry. Busy night?"

When he paused at the loaded question, she burst out laughing. "Now that's the same look I got from Holly when I asked her. Sort of embarrassment, satisfaction and bafflement all at once. Imagine that. Wonder what put that look there?''

''Very funny.''

''Yeah.'' She sobered. ''Did you hear? We got an offer on this place. They said all the employees can stay on. All two of us, that is, me and Steve.''

''I'm very happy for you, Dora.''

''But you're not happy for you.''

He tried to look casual and probably failed miserably.

''I know.'' She sighed. ''She's outside.'' She hitched her head toward the back door. ''She's talking to Buster, the dog she doesn't own, while being watched by Harry, the cat that's not hers.''

''Thanks.'' He stepped outside, into the small yard where Marge used to grow herbs.

Holly was hunkered down by an empty bowl, a hose in one hand, her other embedded in Buster's fur.

He was licking her cheek.

''Hey, that's my job,'' Riley said.

Holly didn't move, didn't turn to face him, and that's when he realized she was crying.

Crying.

His stomach somewhere near his shoes, he

stepped off the steps and came around, watching as Buster licked off another tear.

Before he could say a word, there came a ringing, which he realized originated from the cell phone hooked on her belt.

She sniffed, kept her gaze averted, and answered the phone. "Hello? Yes, Mother, I heard about the offer. An inspection this afternoon?…Of course I'll be ready, but I wanted to talk to you…I know, you're busy, but this is really important…It's just that I've come so far with the café, I was hoping you'd come out and see…"

The hose in her hand filled up the empty water bowl. It stared to overfill. Buster played in it.

Riley stood stock-still, anticipation humming through him because it sounded like Holly *didn't* want to rush out of town.

"I know it's not convenient," Holly said. "But it's not like I'm in the Sahara Desert. Yes, I realize you have to get off the phone now, but I just wanted to tell you, I don't think it's the right time to sell. I really want to—"

Riley held his breath, willing her to just get it over with, to put him out of his misery and say she couldn't wait to leave this rinky-dink town. But even as he thought it, his heart ached.

He didn't want her to say it at all. He wanted

the opposite. Somehow, some way, he'd come to realize she was nothing like his mother, was nothing like the woman he'd thought, who could never handle a place like Little Paradise.

Holly could handle it, she *had* handled it.

She belonged here.

"Mother? Hello? Hello? *Dammit!*" Holly yanked the phone from her ear and hit a series of numbers, waiting impatiently.

Riley waited, too. Could she really want to stay?

"Mother," Holly said in relief a moment later. "I just wanted to tell you, the café is in great shape now." She spoke at the speed of light. "I was thinking we could actually sort of keep it in the family… Yes, I know you're not interested in the food business, but— Yes, I also know I've always gotten bored with things in the past and never saw them through, but this is different…Mother, you're not listening very well—"

Riley grabbed the phone from Holly's ear and put on his most polite voice. "Hello, Mrs. Stone. This is Riley McMann, sheriff of Little Paradise."

Holly stared at him in horror. "What are you doing?" she hissed.

"Trust me," he whispered back, but she grabbed at the phone.

"Trust you to ruin my life?" she whispered furiously. "No, thank you."

He merely used his height to his advantage.

Holly gave up and closed her eyes. "My life is over." She meant it. Her mother would not understand that Riley was trying to help her.

Holly hardly understood it herself.

"Yes, ma'am, I do realize you were talking to your daughter," she heard him say. "But I think you should know, Holly has done a marvelous job here. She's changed the serving style and it really works. She got a huge spread in the paper this morning and the café is— No, she's not paying me to say this!" Shocked, he looked over at Holly.

Holly couldn't help it, she laughed coldly. "That's my mother."

"Look, Mrs. Stone, I'm trying to tell you—" His jaw tightened. "Yes, I'm really the sheriff—"

Oh, her mother was in rare form this morning. Now she'd insulted Riley, the only man in Holly's entire life to...to what? To get past her defenses? To make her see herself in a way she'd never seen herself before? To make her want things she had no business wanting, things like a white wedding dress and a picket fence?

Last night had been the most amazing—and terrifying—night of her life. Riley had shown her things she'd never dreamed of. He'd coaxed her in that soft, sexy voice to both say and do things she'd never imagined, and all that *before* the most incredible sexual experience of her life.

His kitchen would never be the same.

She would never be the same.

And now it was over.

Miserable, Holly watched the water from the hose fall into the dog's dish and overflow.

She shouldn't feel so surprised that the café had sold, but she did. She felt as if her world had just slipped out from beneath her feet.

And it made no sense. All along she'd known she would leave here. It'd been simply a temporary phase in her life until she figured out what she really wanted to do.

Only it was occurring to her, this *was* what she wanted to do.

Her timing had always left a lot to be desired.

Riley handed her back the phone, his eyes dark, his mouth grim. "She's gone. She…didn't want to talk right now."

"Right. She probably had something much more important to do than discuss my life."

"I've got to tell you, Holly. I don't think I like your mother very much."

She let out a little laugh. "Don't worry. The feeling is probably mutual."

"You were crying."

"Was not."

"Holly."

Oh, Lord. Her heart was beating fast and it had nothing to do with her phone conversation and everything to do with him. He looked good. He wore faded jeans and his uniform shirt, which stretched across his broad chest. He looked every inch a rough-and-tumble male.

Now he was squatting down before her, trying to see her face, and she couldn't allow that. Couldn't allow him to see her pain. She concentrated on the water flowing from the bowl to the ground, on her silly dog—yes, *her* silly dog—who was attempting to lap at the flow coming from the hose and was instead managing to get himself all wet.

"Look at me," Riley said. "Please?"

"I'm busy." How was she going to walk away from the most wonderful, warm, sexy, gorgeous man on the planet?

She trembled at the thought.

Buster decided he'd had enough water, and with a wiggle that started at his nose and ended at his tail, he shook.

Water flew all over Riley.

Buster panted and smiled, his mission complete.

Riley stroked the dog, then lifted Holly's chin, forcing her to look at him.

"You're wet," she said inanely.

"I'll dry. You wanted your parents to acknowledge what you've done here."

No sense lying. She lifted a negligent shoulder.

"You wanted them to respect it, and you."

"I'm sure that sounds stupid to a man who the entire town loves and respects."

"Oh, Holly." His eyes were fathomless, and filled with things that made her hurt all the more. "Don't you see?" he asked her. "No one can give you love and respect until you give it to yourself."

"Look, I'm...really busy here."

He didn't budge, didn't do anything but look at her with his heart in his gaze, his voice low and unbearably familiar. "Do you, Holly? Do you respect what you've done with your life? Are you happy?"

No. A small part of her had been sure she would screw it all up. That she would make a mess of everything and then move on, just as she always had.

And an even smaller part of her resented him for making her face it.

"I know you're hurting," he said quietly. "I hate it that you are. But can't you just admit that you're upset because you don't want it to be over?"

Dammit, it was enough she was going to have to leave here, the one place in the entire world that had ever felt like home. It was even worse that she was going to have to leave *him*.

But to be forced to admit it? Out loud? Never.

She'd leave with her pride intact, thank you very much. "I'm fine. I did a great job. It'll look good on my résumé." She even smiled at him, though it was so brittle she was certain she would shatter apart if he so much as touched her. "And I especially had a lovely time getting to know you."

His eyes narrowed. "That sounded like a good-bye."

"It was."

"No."

"No?" She managed a laugh. "I'm sorry, but this isn't really up for discussion."

He let out a breath and shook his head. "You're really going to do it to me. God. I didn't think you could, but you are. You're going to walk away. My mother did that, you know. To my father. It's why I treated you so cavalierly when you first came. I took one look at you and pegged you as an uncaring sophisticate, out for a good time. Like her.''

She felt her heart constrict. "Oh, Riley. I'm sorry."

"You're not like her," he said flatly. "Not at all. You're sweet and caring and warm. I know that now. But I don't think *you* know it."

She concentrated on Buster, on how the big, silly oaf was reveling in the growing puddle of water, rolling on his back and frolicking in it as if he were a pup. "I'm trying to make this easier on both of us," she said.

"You're running scared. Again. Things got too close this time, in this place. People got too close. You opened your heart and let it all in, let us all in, and now, because it terrifies you, you're going to use the excuse of the sale to bail out." Disgusted, hurt, he stood up and looked down at her. "I've got news for you, Holly. You can run from here to hell and back, but you'll never be happy."

"My life is fine."

"Sure. As long as you're alone." His eyes were dark and intense. Unreadable. "You're going to find it's not as easy to be alone this time, not after all you experienced here."

Buster stopped playing and licked her hand. She was going to have to leave him, too. Her throat tightened. How had this happened, dammit? How had she tied so many strings on her poor heart in such a short time? "I'll be fine," she repeated.

Riley stared at her for a long moment. "Can you really forget last night?"

Unbidden, the images came to her. Riley holding her, touching her, kissing her as she'd never been kissed before, so that she'd lost herself in passion and joy, in a way she'd never expected to experience.

"Can you?"

"I can try."

Riley closed his eyes. "You can try. Great. Good luck with that." With one last look, his expression filled with haunting sorrow, he turned on his heel and walked away.

Buster sat and looked at her.

"Not my fault," she told the dog. "I warned him I was a bad bet."

The dog whined.

"Well, I did." So why then were her eyes wet again, her chest so tight she could hardly breathe?

Buster shook again, spraying her from head to toe, mingling her tears with garden water.

11

After a brief pity stint, Holly came to her senses. First of all, dammit, *she* was in charge of her own life. Since when did she let anyone dictate it, especially her parents?

So she'd wanted a little acknowledgement from them. She wasn't going to get it, no surprise, but there was no way she was going to just roll over and play dead.

Not when getting even was so much more fun.

She wanted the café. It seemed so ridiculous, but it was the truth. She wanted to stay here forever and work at a café, of all places. She wanted the rangy, laid-back sheriff to love her. She wanted to spend the rest of her life here. It was her heart's choice, and for once, she would go with it.

And Riley.

She couldn't say why the sexiest, most gorgeous man on the planet wanted to be with her. It was the eighth greatest wonder as far as she was concerned.

But she would go with that, too.

She had no idea what she was going to do with a man like that, a man who could see right through her and still, *still,* want to be with her.

Keep him, that's what.

With newfound determination, she stalked across the street, but Riley wasn't in his office. Jud told her he wasn't at the ranch either, but he could be reached by radio.

Great. Radio would have to do.

Jud handed it to her, then sat on the edge of his desk instead of leaving her alone.

"I know how to work it," she said, hoping he'd take the hint and go.

He smiled and crossed his arms, settling in.

"You can...go do whatever it is that you do."

"This is about it," he said.

She sighed and called Riley.

When she heard his deep, husky voice, she had to sit down, she was so nervous. "Hey," she said into the radio. "When are you coming back?"

"Later."

Later. Okaaay. "I...um, have an emergency at the café. I was hoping you could come check it out."

"Break a nail, Princess? Call your beautician."

So distant. So hurt. She bit her lip and thought.

Connived. "No, it's…another gas leak," she said brilliantly.

Jud snickered.

"Call the gas company," Riley said.

Call the gas company. She wanted to stomp up and down and force him to take her seriously. She wanted him to talk to her in that sweet, sexy tone that made her melt. She wanted…to take back all the things she'd said and done to cause his hurt.

But Jud was watching.

"Thanks," she said quietly, and she went back to the café.

Jud swore.

LATER, Holly came up with a new plan, a better plan.

Riley was there now, in his office. She could see his truck.

Perfect.

She entered his office as coolly and calmly as she could with her heart racing as if she'd just run a marathon. "I have something I thought would interest you," she said in a purposely sexy voice.

He pushed up his hat, leaned back in his desk and studied her quietly. "I doubt it."

His distant tone was almost more than she could handle. She thought about the chocolate cake she'd asked Dora to bake, topped with extra, *extra* frosting. "I'll give you a hint," she said. "It's yummy and covered in chocolate frosting, just waiting for you to—"

"Not hungry, thanks." He picked up his phone and started dialing.

"But—"

"I'm really busy right now."

Her own words, echoed back, thrown in her face.

Heart in her shoes, she left him alone.

She went back to the café, where she polished off three huge pieces of the cake all by herself.

THE NEW OWNERS arrived right at the dinner crunch. They wanted an inspection before entering escrow. Holly was a wreck.

"I'm going to mess this up," she whispered to Dora, hiding out in the kitchen.

"You?" Dora laughed. "You never mess anything up, you're too sure of yourself."

"No, you don't understand. I mean I'm going to mess this up so I can stay."

Dora went still. Then her smile spread. "You mean, *you* want to buy the café for yourself?"

"I can't let it go, it means too much to me. *You* mean too much to me. Riley—" she swallowed hard "—Riley means too much to me. Oh, Dora, I've blown everything, all because of stupid pride, and I want to take it back. I want to stay. I want—"

Dora turned and picked up the phone. She dialed seven numbers then thrust the receiver at Holly.

"Who is it?" Holly asked, staring at the phone because she knew, oh Lord, she knew, and she'd never been so scared in her life.

"You're telling the wrong person," Dora said. "Tell him. Tell Riley." She waved the phone beneath Holly's nose. "Hurry, before you lose your nerve."

She'd already lost it!

"Hello?"

It was him, oh God, it was Riley. "Hello," she said as calmly as she could. "I, um…"

"Yes?"

"There's a huge garden snake here in the kitchen," she said quickly. "It's big and mean and it's going to get me. Can you come—"

"I'll call the exterminator for you."

"But—" Holly looked at Dora helplessly.

"Tell him!" her friend hissed.

"Riley?"

"Yes?"

"There's not really a snake here."

"Do tell," he said wryly.

"I didn't have a gas leak, earlier either."

"Big shock."

"I just wanted to tell you something."

"Holly, I think you already said everything you wanted to say." He sounded weary. "You're leaving. It's best just to let it go."

"I can't," she whispered. "Riley, I can't. I was wrong before, so wrong. I thought I could walk away and it'd be no big deal. I thought I could go back, start over and forget about Little Paradise, about you. But I was wrong about that, too!" He was silent and she rushed on. "I'm so sorry I hurt you, I did it because I was too afraid to admit the truth, to tell you how I felt about you, that I love—"

She got a dial tone. She stared at the receiver in shock. He'd hung up on her! And for the first time, a sincere, bone-crunching panic set in.

He wasn't falling for any of her tricks! How was she going to get him back?

"I failed," she whispered to Dora, setting her head down on the counter and closing her eyes. "I pushed him away because of my own stupid fears and pride and I never got to tell him I love him."

"You could tell me now."

"Riley." She whirled around to face him. He was at the back door; hair wild, body tense, chest heaving from his run. His eyes were warm and suspiciously damp.

He cleared his throat. "It occurred to me on my mad dash over here that I haven't been completely fair to you." He came closer, then closer still, so that they were barely an inch apart. "I never told you how I felt about you, either."

"You could tell me now." She was breathless, her heart in her throat.

"Oh yes, tell her now," Dora breathed.

They both looked at the redhead, but she refused to budge. "Oh, let me stay! Please?"

"Dora—"

She lifted up a hand tipped with purple finger-nails. "I'll be quiet, I promise."

Riley looked at Holly, who shrugged.

"She has to stay," Holly said. "Because I can't wait for the amount of time it would take me to wrestle her out of here."

"Exactly." Dora nodded and flexed her muscles. "Besides, I know how to fight. It would take far too long."

"Dora?"

"Yes?" she said sweetly to Holly.

"Don't take this wrong, but if you're going to stay, shut up."

Dora grinned and mimicked zipping her lip. "I'm shutting up."

"Okay." Holly looked at Riley. "Ready."

He smiled. "Good. But I forgot where I was."

Holly smacked him lightly on the arm. "You did not! You're going to tell me about me!"

"Ah, yes." His smile faded and he looked deep into her eyes. "When you first came, I thought I had you pegged. You put on a good show, princess. You played tough and cool to a tee, but it didn't take me long to see right through that to the real you beneath, to the woman who hid behind the veneer to protect her heart. I love that woman." He reached for her hand, entwined their fingers. "You drive me wild, you make me laugh, you make me think, but mostly, you make my heart soar like it's never done before. For all of that, Holly Stone, I love you."

She and Dora both sighed dreamily. "Oh, Riley."

"Now tell me," he demanded.

She smiled through her tears. "And I thought maybe you came back over here for another chocolate frosting round."

"Tell me now," he demanded. "*Then* chocolate."

"Okay." She was shaking. "I love your smile,

your easygoing ways. I love the way you calm me, the way you touch me, how you make me feel every single second of every single day. I love how you want me in your life, even when I'm impossible and restless and—''

''And difficult,'' he added helpfully, and she laughed.

''I've never felt so special, so wanted,'' she said. ''Because of all of that, I love you, Riley Mc-Mann.''

Dora sighed again, her hand on her chest. ''Oh, that's so beautiful. Now don't start kissing,'' she said sharply, slapping a hand between them. ''Or you'll never stop. You've got to get out there and ruin those new people's taste for this place.''

''I nearly forgot!'' Holly looked at Riley in panic. ''They're out there wanting to be served. I've got to hurry!''

''*We've* got to hurry,'' he corrected. ''We're together in this.''

''I want to buy this place for myself,'' she said urgently, grabbing his arms. She had to make him understand how much this meant. ''I want to stay.''

''Forever.''

''Yes,'' she whispered.

"Forever works for me. Especially if you agree to be my wife."

Dora and Holly both gasped. They both started to cry.

Riley grinned. "Is that a yes?"

"Yes," both Holly and Dora said.

"Good." He didn't look too steady, either, but he beamed with happiness. "Now let's go scare off some buyers. Shouldn't be too hard."

"Not with my talent," Holly said, still reeling from the fact he wanted her to be his wife. "Let me start, I've got a knack for this."

ACTUALLY, it was Dora who started off the project nicely by spilling ice water in the lap of the wanna-be buyer.

His wife gasped, stood up and flung her napkin down. "I've never!" she said.

Dora popped her gum, leaned close and winked. "Well, you really should. It's good for the skin."

"Honestly! You're talking to one of your customers that way?"

"Sarcasm is just one of the services we offer."

The woman gaped at Dora until Harry—egged on by Riley—leaped up on their table and sat next to the salt and pepper. With a huge amount of dignity, he lifted his leg over his head and proceeded to clean his…essentials.

And while that had the couple's eyes nearly bugging out of their heads, Holly knew she needed to take more drastic measures. Still, even she couldn't have planned what happened next.

From behind the counter where she was getting the drinks, she heard a drip, drip, dripping. Looking around she saw nothing, but when she walked to the corner for more ice, the floor squished beneath her feet.

She tapped at the loose linoleum in the corner and water gushed in.

A leak! They had a leak!

Perfect!

"Look at this," she said loudly, with probably far too much glee. "We'll need to evacuate right away before the place floods."

"Let me see that." Lap dripping wet from the earlier mishap with Dora's pitcher of water, the potential buyer came behind the counter. He squatted down, peeled back the flooring and frowned. "This is a terrible mess, it's coming from—" He went into the kitchen, following the wetness along one wall to the back door, which he opened.

Holly, Dora and Riley all crowded for space in the doorway to watch.

Holly had accidentally left on the hose, hours ago now. Water was pooling against the building, seeping into the foundation.

Holly bit her lip and looked at Riley, who blew her a kiss. She laughed, then covered the sound with her hand.

"Would you look at that?" Dora asked sympathetically. "You know, I used to be a flooring contractor. That's going to be a mess to fix, trust me."

The man glared at her. "Expensive?"

"Oh, yeah. Astronomical."

Grumbling, he stalked past them, out of the kitchen and into the main room again, where he tripped over Buster.

Buster lifted his nose and howled.

Holly would never know why he reacted that way, but she could have kissed him right on his sloppy wet mouth. Inspired, she wrinkled her nose. "Oh, no."

"Oh, no—what?" the man asked. "What now?"

"I smell rotten eggs."

"Hey, that's lunch cooking," Dora said.

"No." Holly shook her head, trying not to laugh. "It's natural gas. We have another leak, folks."

"*Another* leak?" he squeaked. "As in you've had them before? That wasn't disclosed to us by the Realtor."

"At least the gas company always responds to us immediately," Riley commented. "Especially after the last incident."

"*What?*" The man swiped at his brow. "Oh, no. I think I smell it."

"*Evacuate!*" Dora screeched into the room.

Bless the hearts of the people of Little Paradise. Every one of them, now Holly's friends, leaped up and caused a nice little riot trying to get out of the café.

Holly watched, pride and love brimming from her heart. From behind, Riley slipped his hands around her waist and hugged her close.

"They like me," she whispered.

"They love you. So do I."

"I've finally found my home, haven't I?"

He turned her to face him and kissed her. "Right here in my arms."

CELEBRATE VALENTINE'S DAY WITH HARLEQUIN®'S LATEST TITLE— *Stolen Memories*

Available in trade-size format, this collector's edition contains three full-length novels by *New York Times* bestselling authors Jayne Ann Krentz and Tess Gerritsen, along with national bestselling author Stella Cameron.

TEST OF TIME by Jayne Ann Krentz—
He married for the best reason.... She married for the only reason.... Did they stand a chance at making the only reason the real reason to share a lifetime?

THIEF OF HEARTS by Tess Gerritsen—
Their distrust of each other was only as strong as their desire. And Jordan began to fear that Diana was more than just a thief of hearts.

MOONTIDE by Stella Cameron—
For Andrew, Greer's return is a miracle. It had broken his heart to let her go. Now fate has brought them back together. And he won't lose her again...

Make this Valentine's Day one to remember!

Look for this exciting collector's edition on sale January 2001 at your favorite retail outlet.

HARLEQUIN®
Makes any time special ™

Visit us at www.eHarlequin.com

PHSM

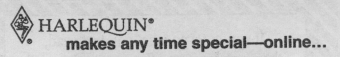

HARLEQUIN®
makes any time special—online...

eHARLEQUIN.com

shop eHarlequin

- ♥ Find all the new Harlequin releases at everyday great discounts.
- ♥ Try before you buy! Read an excerpt from the latest Harlequin novels.
- ♥ Write an online review and share your thoughts with others.

reading room

- ♥ Read our Internet exclusive daily and weekly online serials, or vote in our interactive novel.
- ♥ Talk to other readers about your favorite novels in our Reading Groups.
- ♥ Take our Choose-a-Book quiz to find the series that matches you!

authors' alcove

- ♥ Find out interesting tidbits and details about your favorite authors' lives, interests and writing habits.
- ♥ Ever dreamed of being an author? Enter our Writing Round Robin. The Winning Chapter will be published online! Or review our guidelines for submitting your novel.

HINTB1

Presenting...

HARLEQUIN®

PRESCRIPTION ROMANCE

Get swept away by these warmhearted romances featuring dedicated doctors and nurses.

LOVE IS JUST A HEARTBEAT AWAY!

Available in December at your favorite retail outlet:

SEVENTH DAUGHTER
by Gill Sanderson
A MILLENNIUM MIRACLE
by Josie Metcalfe
BACHELOR CURE
by Marion Lennox
HER PASSION FOR DR. JONES
by Lillian Darcy

Look for more Prescription Romances coming in April 2001.

Tyler Brides

It happened one weekend...

Quinn and Molly Spencer are delighted to accept three bookings for their newly opened B&B, Breakfast Inn Bed, located in America's favorite hometown, Tyler, Wisconsin.

But Gina Santori is anything but thrilled to discover her best friend has tricked her into sharing a room with the man who broke her heart eight years ago....

And Delia Mayhew can hardly believe that she's gotten herself locked in the Breakfast Inn Bed basement with the sexiest man in America.

Then there's Rebecca Salter. She's turned up at the Inn in her wedding gown. Minus her groom.

Come home to Tyler for three delightful novellas by three of your favorite authors: Kristine Rolofson, Heather MacAllister and Jacqueline Diamond.

HARLEQUIN®
Makes any time special ™

Visit us at www.eHarlequin.com

PHTB

Sometimes a little bundle of joy
can cause a whole lot of trouble...

Judy Christenberry
Cathy Gillen Thacker

THE BABY GAME

2 Complete Novels

at the LOW PRICE of $4.99 U.S./$5.99 CAN.!

When wealthy Caroline Adkins woke up at the hospital, she felt like going right back to bed. First she learned she was suffering from amnesia—then she discovered she was pregnant, too! And to make matters worse, three men turned up claiming paternity!

Marrying Abby Kildaire after a whirlwind weekend of passion was the best thing Tad McFarland had ever done. Surely they'd be able to work out the details concerning their marriage, but they never dreamed that the first pesky little detail would be to have to make room for a baby....

Look for THE BABY GAME on sale in December 2000.